Chabnorl's Journal
1

Ceaxtra Awakens
22

Kihakso Awakens
32

Chabnorl Cause The Learning Of Their Powers
57

Gizlae Awakens
65

Awrosk Awakens
82

Water Leads To New Friends
97

Tesirew Awakens
104

Vadixas Awakens
132

The Cold and The Hated
151

Aylnivi Awakens
158

Chabnorl Causes The Remeeting Of Old Friends
169

Aphiqalena Awakens
179

Kaknei Awakens
208

Water Leads To The Hunt For New Items
222

The Battle and The End
238

Chabnorl's Journal
247

Day XX Month 16 Year 1516

He's...
He's gone...
I couldn't protect him...
I didn't know where he was going...
I didn't know he needed supplies...
He didn't tell me but I should have checked...
I'm older...
I should have...
I...
I don't know what to do...
I'm sorry

I'm sorry

I'm sorry

I'M SORRY

I'M SORRY

Rohgren, please forgive me......

Day XX Month 16 Year 1516

How dare they.

How dare they!

I tried to get his body back, to give him a proper burial that...town...refused to give him to me. They said that his body was theirs to do with as they pleased.

They talked to me as if I was stupid, as if I didn't know about the children of the elements. Everyone knows that those are mythical beings, that they can't be real.

If they were...my brother...

No, thinking like that won't help me. If that town thinks I don't know enough then I'll find out more.

They won't provide me with any information but none of the towns work together. There are towns dedicated to each child, each town believing their own was the only real one and that all the others were fakes.

I have already checked Termouron The City of Earth, there are still eight more cities I can look into:

Galssopia, The City of Wind
Harllpool, The City of Water
Willedale, The City of Nature
Mithfield, The City of Lightning
Abeglassco, The City of Light
Blencalgo, The City of Darkness
Whighridge, The City of Ice
Pitydden, The City of Fire

I will get the information I need from them. If they also refuse to give it to me...then I'll take it for myself.

I must find out what I need...and find a way to make Termouron pay

Day XX Month 03 Year 1517

I've been reading all I can about these beings, these "children of the elements". No one has any solid evidence on anything, no proof that they lived, no proof that they died, no proof that they did anything of importance.

And yet, the whole world over believes that they were once alive, some even believe that the version that they have been told about never even died and that they still lived. But there have been no sightings in decades. I've looked over every account and most of them seem to be second-hand or conflicting accounts where no one seemed to get their facts straight.

People fight and argue and look for info like I am and most come up with nothing, just like I have. Each town keeps their information to itself. Only providing it to the civilians of their towns.

I've been making my way through each one, hoping to find a single one that would give information freely. None of the towns that I have visited has yet to but there are still ways that I can get my hands on it. I can always pay someone in town to get it for me.

Day XX Month 03 Year 1517

I've been reading what I can from the townspeople I have bribed. Even so, there still seems to be some information that is missing. Not like it was ripped out from the history books but more like it had never been entered.

They seem to be the most secretive about how they sacrifice the child. Something passed down to each head of the town. I know that the townspeople would have seen this ritual before but they are tight-lipped about it as well, not even the ones willing to take bribes for information will tell me.

What I have been able to find out is how they choose the sacrifice. They can be sorted into five groups:

Termouron - They choose any kid that breaks any law, even stealing some food.

Pitydden - They choose any kid that murders someone.

Harllpool - They choose kids that were important, making it an honor.

Galssopia - They choose a kid born in the first month, believing that will give the child more luck.

Whighridge - They are randomly selected within a set age group.

Mithfield - They randomly select from the population of only children.

Blencalgo - They choose just by what kids they don't want.

Abeglassco - They limit their people to only two kids per household. Any extra are chosen.

Willedale - Is the only one who doesn't choose a child. They claim their child will exit their surrounding forest when the time is right.

I could always go to see the sacrifices but I refuse. I am not like them and will not happily stand by as a child is killed in front of me.

There isn't much information about the children that I can use. I was hoping to gain something as a means to get *revenge. But the only way to do that was to go through what my brother did. I have no hopes that my plan will succeed so I must look for another avenue to gain power to get my revenge.*

Day XX Month 07 Year 1517
   Strange things have been happening, and I don't like what they are indicating.
First Blencalgo followed its name. One moment everything was normal and the next a glob of darkness covered it.
~*~*~*~

They walked along the walls of the pitch black room, groping around in the dark, hoping one of them would give way. "Let me out! What did I do?" They shouted, even though their throat was getting sore. They had been at this for a while, hoping that their banging would find the door they couldn't see. There was no window and there was no light coming from under a door they knew had to be somewhere.

The townspeople had come to the house looking for Kympilej. They refused to move from the door. They looked among the mob to find their mother standing behind it waiting for the mob to finish, checking her nails. Their mother shouted over the mob that either of her sons could be taken. The mob looked amongst themselves before grabbing them and dragging them through town before the mob pushed them into this room. They fell to the floor and heard a door close. They had closed their eyes when they started to fall, but opened them to find complete darkness.

They walked along the wall, keeping a hand there to count how many times they looped the room, trying once more, "Let me out! I'll fix whatever we did wrong!" They slid down the wall, their voice hurting from shouting so much.

They curled up, crying silently, wishing they could leave.

~*~*~*~

   The dome is easy to enter but almost impossible to exit. A man was tethered to the outside before he entered, his goal was to see who he could find from the now covered town.
   No matter what way he walked he could not find the edge of the dome but luckily he was able to be pulled out.

He told of pure darkness. Nothing to see, hear, smell, or feel. As soon as you stepped in it was like the sun was pulled from the sky. The change happened right after he passed the threshold.

As for Abeglassco, it took a few weeks for anyone to realize what had happened to it.
~*~*~*~

She glared at the glass in front of her. She was tied to two poles which kept her still as she watched the sunrise. She turned her head to see the group of people watching. "Let me out of here!" she shouted at them, pulling her left arm as hard as she could. However, the rope didn't break.

She could feel the light climbing up her leg. They were starting to get warm, and she could smell the burning of flesh. She tried to move her legs away from the searing light, but the light covered the whole area between the poles. "Let me out. Let me out now!"

When they didn't move, she struggled even more.

"I will be back!" She shouted more for herself than them, "and when I return, you'll all be dead. I'll kill all of you. None of you will live." She felt the light rising even higher now hitting her stomach. She kept shouting until the light reflected through the glass had covered her completely.

~*~*~*~

There was no trace of it, not a speck or crumb. It was like the whole town had just disappeared, as if it had never existed. Which isn't true as I had gone there before during my search for information.

They had turned me away at the time so I had no sympathy for them. No one was around when whatever happened to either town so no one knows the truth, but that didn't stop the rumors from spreading.

Day XX Month 08 Year 1517

I said I was going to look into other avenues for power, to get my revenge against Termouron.

As I traveled trying to find a new source of power for myself, I still told people that I was looking for information on the Children of the Elements. I figured that if people were informed that I was looking, I would be contacted when some new information was found.

Maybe explorers would find ancient ruins and on the walls, there would be a picture depicting them. Maybe someone would go up into their mother's attic and find a document telling of some great or horrible deed that one of them had done.

That was what I was expecting, if it hadn't all been a lie. And yet, there are reports of sightings. Not of all of them, only two.

The Child of Light and Darkness had been seen wandering together. I should have realized with the strange things that happened to both towns that something was going on.

I wouldn't normally believe that they were children of elements. The few accounts about them I have heard told me that they had magical tattoos located on their bodies. The Child of Darkness was said to have one on his stomach. They had only seen it quickly but claimed it was a butterfly where each wing was a different color.

The people who had seen them seemed to have gotten a better look at The Child of Light, stating that the tattoo was located on her shin. It was also a butterfly. The left wing is lilac and the right wing is black. No one has figured out what it means yet.

The accounts also informed me what happened to her town. The rumors stated that The Child of Light can make people and things disappear with a flash of light. Where they go, no one has found out, but no one seems to have come back either.

Day XX Month 11 Year 1517

With solid proof that children of elements can appear near the towns seem to be ramping up on their desire to make their own. Those who would only do the sacrifice every few months increased their sacrifices to once a month. The only ones that didn't were Termouron and Pitydden who were limited by their own rules.

Though for some reason, Galssopia, who had plenty of kids, seemed to have not added any more sacrifices? Maybe it had to do with how they do their sacrifices? Something was still unknown to me.

It had only been two months since their last big sighting, when The Child of Light randomly went on a crime spree, however The Child of Darkness was nowhere to be seen.

Talking to the people who witnessed these incidents provided more information about the Child of Light.

First, people were able to get a better look and found that the child was a girl, who looked about thirteen years old.

Second, there was actually someone who returned from wherever the flash sent them. The victim said that the area was bright and that he couldn't move but felt like he would fall asleep at any moment. He said that he had tried many times but the brightness of the area never allowed him to. He was only there for about a day and was starting to get hungry when he returned. It is unknown what is the outcome of Abeglassco.

Third, is that the Child of Darkness seems to be able to control her. Three weeks later she attacked an orphanage. The reason it is known is because one of the kids was able to flee the attack and describe running into him. Once she told him who was attacking them he ran off. Soon after the orphans were returned and the two were nowhere to be seen.

Thanks to that orphan, I was able to find out that the Child of Darkness also looks to be thirteen but is a boy.

I am still monitoring the other towns. None have been successful as yet but they are all hopeful that it will work sooner rather than later.

Day XX Month 02 Year 1518
Another town was successful. Harllpool celebrated for a week when their child came back from the lake.
~*~*~*~

He looked along the lake that stood in front of him. He could hear the others singing and chanting his praises. They had a feast and danced from the morning till the sun was starting to set.

His clothes were thick, to absorb more water and keep him warm. His stomach was full and he only needed to head in and everything would be done.

This tradition had been going on for years. He wasn't the first, and he wouldn't be the last. He had always been alone, both parents were lost in an animal attack on the village. Thankfully, the town took care of him as a whole after the incident, taking turns feeding him.

He was old enough and the person who had been picked was his only friend, so he asked the mayor to take their place. The mayor made sure that this was what he truly wanted and that he wasn't coerced into this before he agreed.

And now, here he stood. All that was left was for him to take those final steps. He took a breath and walked forward; glad the water wasn't freezing.

~*~*~*~

The town was still excited, heaping praises on the child. From those that I have talked to, the child doesn't remember anything of his past life. He claimed to have talked to the element itself but I don't know if I actually believe that.

The proof is that the child's looks were completely different and he now had a tattoo on his left side of another butterfly; the left wing is brown while the right wing is red.

This is all secondhand...I could go talk to him. He isn't planning to leave his town...but I can't...I can't look at him. Just knowing what was done to achieve those results...what happened to my brother to try and make a Child of Earth.

These...things... shouldn't exist.

Day XX Month 07 Year 1518
The increase in the number of sacrifices seems to have helped them, or maybe once one is born the rest are to follow. Either way, The Child of Ice has appeared. This time it was a girl again, this one looking like a fifteen-year-old.
~*~*~*~

She looked down into the hole she would enter. She crossed her arms. Even from here, she could tell how cold it was, but that didn't matter. She would be in and out once she had been changed. The others say it wouldn't happen. There were many before who had tried, but none had succeeded.

What made her any different?

But she could tell, she didn't know how, but she could tell that she would be brought back.

She pushed up her sleeves, something they made her wear because it was "tradition". She didn't care about that. The only thing she wondered as she took the plunge was how long it would take for her to be back.

~*~*~*~
She plans to stay in the town to protect it from Pitydden who had been making threats once they got their own child. She has refused to show her tattoo but people had been watching when the sacrifice happened and was sure that there couldn't have been a switch.

Another child, another reminder of what happened to my brother. I don't know what I plan to do….I don't even know what I want to do anymore.

Day XX Month 01 Year 1519
    Tesirew seems to have misplaced their child. They can't really watch what goes on when they sacrifice it seems but there was a sighting of their child in another town. She was a young one, looking only to be about ten years old.
~*~*~*~

    She curled her arms tighter around herself. The rain was cold and the wind didn't help. It was pouring which made it hard to see, her bangs were sticking to her forehead, but she knew where she had to go.
    Every once in a while, lightning would flash and temporarily light the way. This was her third time through the field and she knew it was completely flat. She could do this a little bit more and then she would be fine. All she had left was the last half of her final return trip.
    She could do this. She took another step forward and the sky opened with a flash of light.

~*~*~*~
    It was assumed that she had failed but she was able to disappear in a flash of lightning and a rumble of thunder. No one else with lightning magic has been able to do the same.
    There was also the fact that an older girl had dragged the Child of Lightning away. According to the reports, she looked to be seventeen.
~*~*~*~

    She couldn't move as she felt the dirt start to cover her. Her hands were tied in front of her. She was crying and begging for them to stop, but instead of an answer, only more dirt was piled on her. Some entered her mouth, and she spits it out. That only let more in.
 No one would help her and she couldn't climb out. She felt a heavy layer of dirt covering her body.

She knew this was her last chance and opened her eyes. It was hard to see with the tears, but she could make her out, the one person she always trusted.

"Please...please help me," she reached up to her with both hands.

The person left her view and she cried even harder as dirt continued to enter her mouth and throat as they finally started to cover her head.

~*~*~*~

I'm worried. On my last trip to the tunnel outside Termouron, on the anniversary of his death, there was a crater in the dirt. It hadn't been there last year and I fear that just like Light and Darkness...the Child of Lightning was traveling with the Child of Earth...

If...If she had succeeded where my brother failed...

Day XX Month 06 Year 1519
    Willedale, who claimed that they would wait for their child, seemed to hate the one they received. A girl around the age of sixteen arrived with a butterfly tattoo on her neck, the left wing light green while the right brown.
~*~*~*~

    She adjusted herself slightly on the branch. She was the last one left of the group. Animals had taken out all of the stragglers besides herself.

    She had come here to learn about the unique plants in the area. The group hadn't wanted her originally, but she was slightly proud of herself for proving that she would be fine since she was the only one who hadn't been taken out by the more aggressive animals.

    She pulled some berries out of her pocket, glad that they hadn't been squished during her flight. This would be the only food she had for the night. She would need to save as much of it as she could for tomorrow, just in case she didn't find anything else.

    She placed one in her mouth. It was bitter, but she struggled through it, eating two more after.

    That was when she realized her mistake as the world started to spin around her, and her body started feeling heavy. She tried to put her hand on the branch to stabilize herself, but misjudged the distance, falling off.

    As she fell, her body hit a group of vines that tangled around her. She tried to grab one as she kept falling, but her hand just wouldn't grab it.

~*~*~*~

    They seemed to disagree with the personality she has. There were tales of them trying to kill her, the attempts were futile as she just used her powers to get out of the situation. The fact that they were surrounded by nature and that she was stronger there than anywhere else seemed to aid in her efforts to evade them.

Every month they seem to improve the thing they created to kill her.

Day XX Month 08 Year 1519

The Children of the Elements have been my focus but that is because of the appearance of one of them right after another. Even so, I still looked for a specialized mage that would help me get my revenge against Termouron.

It wasn't the easiest task as most found my reasoning lacking when I asked them to teach me magic. I had to find someone who either agreed with me or wouldn't care what I used it for.

Ironically the only person willing to teach me was a specialist under earth magic.

The power I was taught was to make holes that can swallow anything above them. There is also a secondary ability that allows me to travel through them.

Even though I now have the ability I need to practice with it. That will improve the size of the hole I can make as well as the range of the travel.

There has been an update about the children as well...

Some blacksmiths have made claims that they have made a metal that can seal their powers. Claiming they made a cuff and tested it out on the Child of Water when they stayed in his town. No one was around to see it but people are buying their cuffs hoping to capture them to study.

I....

I haven't decided what I want to do yet regarding that piece of information...

Day XX Month 09 Year 1519

Pitydden finally got its wish. Only a year and two months later and they also now possessed their own child. A girl looking to be the age of ten years old.

~*~*~*~

She struggled against the ties around her hands and feet. They put more wood on the pile as the mayor, Gihmea, talked to the crowd that had gathered. They talked about her punishment and how this was just. How she would be saved if she regretted her crimes.

She would never regret it. He deserved his death. He had been causing her pain while claiming that he loved her for years, some father he turned out to be. And now she had done the same to him, though in a more permanent sense.

She knew this would be painful, they had been sacrificing kids for years and she knew she would die from the fire and not the smoke.

She watched as the guards brought torches to the edge of the pile, that way the fire could come to her.

She turned her head to the sky watching as the stars got covered in smoke. She sighed she had always liked the smell of burning wood too.

~*~*~*~

She seemed to be all ready to fight with the Child of Ice planning to go after her as soon as she woke up. A message was sent from her to the Child of Ice as a challenge, whether she accepts or not has yet to be seen.

The towns have not made any announcements about their battle so I don't know if they care about it or not, or if they will even know the outcome of the battle before one of the kids dies.

Will their battle be one to the death or just a heated competition?

Day XX Month 11 Year 1519

I...I met a Child of the Element...

I think...I assume...it was strange.

I had been walking down the street. She ran into me, I don't know where she was going, I don't even know what was going on.

She bumped into me and the hat she was wearing came off. I helped her up, and when she looked at me, she clenched her head. I don't know why but I moved to hold her up while she cringed. She rubbed at her eyes for a moment, seemed to struggle to say anything then asked for her hat. Once I was sure she could stand, I got it for her. She took the hat and refused to look me in the face.

I was about to ask her if she was okay when she said she was sorry. I asked if she meant bumping into me and she said that wasn't it. When I asked her what for, she said she was sorry I had to go through that. She looked me in the eyes with a sad smile before she was gone in a flash of light and a rumble of thunder.

I...I don't know what she was talking about, but something told me...

She knew about Rohgren...

Day XX Month 13 Year 1519
If my guess is right then the final child has arrived. No one saw the child but Galssopia was found ripped to part by multiple tornadoes.

~*~*~*~

She gulped as she held onto the ropes around her wrist a little tighter. She knew they wouldn't hold when the winds started to pick up, but still, it brought her comfort.

She wished she had been born a little sooner or later, they claimed it was lucky to be born in the first month, but she didn't feel very lucky right now.

She was tied at the bottom of a canyon near the town. It was known for having tornado-strong winds once a year, and that was when they did the ritual.

Usually, they found parts of the body in the river at the end of the canyon. She hoped she would be more intact than the sacrifice from the previous year.

The wind started to blow faster, pushing her slightly.

~*~*~*~

There were a few survivors but none of them saw anything but the tornadoes coming from the entrance of town. It seems any kid that hates their town attacks it with their strongest power. Why some hated their town and others didn't was maybe determined by how they treated the child before they were killed?

Maybe something to look into? That is, if I can find any information about their past lives.

Day XX Month 16 Year 1519

I...It's been three years since Rohgren's death. Three years since I failed him.

I thought I could live with this. I thought that destroying Termouron would be enough...

I saw her today...

The Child of Earth...

I had planned to meet up with an informant in Siverkept when I saw her. I didn't know it was her until she turned to me and I saw a butterfly tattoo peeking out from her tank top. The left wing was dark green and the right was brown.

I couldn't do anything, I could barely breathe.

Why?Why?Why?Why?Why? **Why?WhyWhyWhy?Why WhyWhyWhyWhy?**

Why did she get picked when my brother didn't?

She shouldn't exist....none of them should....

Since that's the case, I'll correct that mistake...

The first thing she realized was that something was calling her and yet not hearing. She felt like her eyes were open and closed at the same time like something was around her but not. She tried to open her mouth, but it wouldn't move. The void she was in felt endlessly dark and light all at once, and she knew nothing.

"You have awoken," the voice came from everywhere and nowhere. She hated this feeling, whatever it was. It felt like something was crushing her but also cradling her softly. "It is wonderful to meet you."

"Who are you?" She talked without a mouth, but whatever it was, heard her.

"You can call me your parent. That would be what you humans would call our relationship."

"Then what are you?"

"I am the wind."

She knew what it was somehow, though not remembering when she had experienced it. Now that she thought about it, she knew a lot but could remember nothing. "What..." that was all she could say, having too many questions to ask.

"You do not need to know," said the voice, as if knowing everything she wanted to say. "I will return you and you will learn everything you want to."

"Return me?" Where had she come from? Where was she going back to?

"Your name is Ceaxtra, and flow like myself to find what you wish to know. It is time for you to wake up."

Ceaxtra sat up with her eyes wide, she felt lost and confused so she just breathed for a moment, trying to collect her thoughts into an order that she could understand. There was a memory far in the past, but everything else was blank. She had knowledge that she didn't know where she had learned it from and then there was her name. She looked around her hoping that her surroundings would remind her of something.

She looked to be at the end of a canyon, the rock walls rising high above her. In front of her, a river seemed to cut it off, running perpendicular to both walls cutting them off suddenly. On the other side of the river was a short field and then a forest. She stood up and took a step forward, but something pulled her back. She looked behind her, and in the distance, she could see what looked like a town. Her heart clenched and she started to walk towards it to figure out why.

She looked up at the walls as she walked, wishing she could reach the top. She felt the wind push up under her and looked down to see her clothes moving with it. She felt the wind for a moment before imagining it building beneath her. She closed her eyes and pushed and felt a rush of air as she opened her eyes. They went wide, as she was suddenly above the walls of the cannon. She reached for the wall and was suddenly pushed towards it. She rolled as she landed and looked around, realizing that she now had a straight path to town.

When she eventually got to the town, it seemed to be in full celebration. She didn't talk to anyone, but as she walked along the streets, she heard the common thread. All the people talked about was a failed ritual. That the child didn't return to them. That they would have to try again.

While wandering the town she saw a poster talking about the Child of Wind. She stopped as her eyes fell onto the words. She remembered her conversation with wind. How she was now its child. She touched the poster lightly. This was about her. They were talking about her. She frowned as people walked by commenting about who they would next choose, some of the younger people joked about who they would kill next.

Ceaxtra realized then what was going on. They killed her, and now she has returned thanks to wind. She turned to the town and saw it for the first time. They killed her, and now they were laughing and joking about who would be the next person to feel what she had felt. She didn't remember the details, but she felt like she could still remember the pain.

She walked along the streets and everyone seemed to feel the same. She knew what she had to do. She got to the entrance to town and turned back towards it. She took a slow breath before imagining what she wanted in her mind. She took a moment, feeling the wind collect around her. Closing her eyes, she pushed towards the town, feeling the power leave her, immediately. The sounds of wooden beams breaking and cries of pain filled her ears. She gave it a moment, and when she opened her eyes, she gave a small smile. There were now three small tornadoes slowly making their way away from her growing bigger and bigger as they moved.

She just stood there for a while watching as the town was ripped apart, leaving nothing but rubble and corpses in their wake. She didn't know how long she watched, but after a while, her vision started to swim and her head hurt. She waved her hand without thinking, and the tornadoes dispersed. When they did, the dizziness was gone though she still had a headache. She looked at the destruction caused by her and gave a small nod, turning from the town and walking away, nothing holding her back this time.

She headed to the edge of the cliff right before the river and gave a small breath. She once again imagined an updraft of air, like the one she had used to get up, the only difference was that this one was a little weaker. She clenched her hands before taking a step off right into the draft, using it to slowly float down to the river bed. She could see it wasn't too deep, so took the chance to walk across it planning to head into the woods across from her old home.

By the time she reached the forest, the sun was starting to go down. She decided to sleep outside of it rather than try to travel through it in the dark. She was starting to get hungry but she knew there was no way for her to get food. All she could do was hope that there was a town in the forest that she could find.

As she lay down, looking up at the sky, she thought about the little that she knew. She knew she was given a second chance at life, but not why. She also didn't have a goal besides learning the answer to her questions. But the reason she was picked was now at the top of that list. She wondered if she would meet Wind again or if that wouldn't happen till she died a second time.

    She was also trying to figure out her powers. While she understood that she now had control over the wind and could do what she wanted with it, she also had a feeling of dread come over her at the thought of doing too much. She did not know how it worked. Would she die again if she used up all her magic, or would she just pass out like a human? Did she still count as a human or was she something completely different now?

    She frowned, annoyed that Wind had given her no information. She looked at the stars as she waited to fall asleep, hoping the stars could give her the answers she felt she needed.

    The next morning, she felt better and worse. Her headache was gone, but the hunger had only grown. Her body ached from sleeping on the hard ground as well. She got up quickly, dusting herself off before looking at the forest once more. It didn't look too dense, but there wasn't a clear path to walk on.

    With no other plan or direction she wanted to go in, she shrugged her shoulders and headed inside.

    It was slow going, having to move carefully so as not to trip and hurt herself. She didn't know what would happen if she was injured and frankly, she didn't want to find out. It took her half a day, but finally, she found a town hidden among the trees. Though once she got to it she saw a clear road leading in and out of the town, so it was only hidden from her.

    When she finally stood on the town's main street, she didn't know what to do. She was hungry but didn't have any money on her. She didn't know if anyone would let her work for food, or even what she could do.

    She must have looked as lost as she felt because a lady with her small child stopped in front of her. She smiled at Ceaxtra, "have you lost your parents?" She looked up at the lady with a small frown.

    If you count Wind's location being unknown, then she had technically, but she also wasn't in desperate need to find it either.

"Actually I'm hungry but have no money." The woman frowned, and Ceaxtra didn't know if she should say more.

"Did you lose it somewhere?" Ceaxtra didn't know for sure, but she nodded nonetheless, seeing that was the easier answer right now.

"Well. I don't have much but you can come to my store and I can give you some food."

"But I don't have money."

"What kind of person would I be if I let a kid go hungry?" Without another word, she turned and started to walk down the street, giving Ceaxtra no choice but to follow her. As they walked down the street, she looked around and for the first time since she had reawakened, she saw her reflection.

She realized that until now she had no idea what she looked like. No memory came to mind when she tried to think about it.

When she looked at her reflection, she could see why the women and poster had used the word child. She looked no older than eight and even if she was, it would be no more than a few days. She wanted to stop in front of a mirror to get a good look at herself but didn't want to lose her chance at food either.

"Here we are," the woman waved to her bakery she turned to Ceaxtra "by the way i'm Nelhona." she said with a smile before opening the door. Ceaxtra ate the loaf of bread that she was given without complaint, though she asked if there was something she could do to make up for it.

Nelhona smiled and gave her the job of cleaning the store, which Ceaxtra was happy to do. It took her some time, but Ceaxtra was quite proud of her work; once she was finished, it was the first memory of her doing something to help another.

Nelhona took the broom back with a smile, "thank you that was a huge help."

"I wanted to pay back for the food."

Nelhona frowned at her, "I haven't seen you around, are you traveling? Alone?"

Ceaxtra decided it would be better to go with a half-truth. Not wanting to burden Nelhona with more information than she needs. "I'm traveling to find my parents. I know they're somewhere I just have to find where..."

Nelhona frowned, repeating her second question, "alone?"

Ceaxtra gave her what she hopes is a reassuring smile "I'm strong." She didn't know if that was really true. But she also didn't know if that was a lie, either.

Nelhona sighed, "I don't like the idea of a child traveling alone but I also can't keep you here." She looked back at her kitchen for a moment before looking back at Ceaxtra. "If you help me clean up the store for closing, you can stay the night."

Ceaxtra smiled, she probably wouldn't get a better offer, and nodded right away, ready to do what the women needed.

It was fun learning what was needed to do to set up a bakery. The women's guest room had a soft bed and a full mirror so she got an opportunity to take a good look at herself. With no memory of what she looked like before, she didn't know if there was any change, though.

The next day Nelhona gave her a few loaves before making Ceaxtra promise to stop by the next time she was in town. Ceaxtra looked both ways at the main road before choosing a random direction.

The path she took seemed to go further into the forest. She spent the day walking and the nights looking up at the stars until she fell asleep. It wasn't comfortable, but she had no choice but to make do. She ate the bread slowly, not knowing when the forest would end.

It was one more day's travel along an empty road before Ceaxtra came to another town. This one seemed bigger than the last. The buildings were taller and some were even made out of stone. The main street had people performing as well. She looked at the few stalls around but couldn't buy anything. What really drew her eyes was the magic users.

She didn't remember if she had ever been taught how to use her wind powers, or even if they were something she had before she had woken up.

But watching them show off their magic made her want to do so as well. She wanted to stay and learn from them, but with no money, and no idea how to gain some, she decided to stay one day memorizing as much as she could to teach herself later.

She didn't stick to just wind magic either, though there were quite a few of them that were showing off. What interested her the most was a magic user who kept making bubbles for kids to play with. She used her appearance to her advantage and was able to get a close look at one of the bubbles, poking it and seeing if she could figure out how it was done by touch alone.

She looked over at the magic user who was talking to some of the other kids. She moved over closer to him and waited until he finished talking and turned to her, "excuse me." she said in a smaller voice.

"Yes?"

"I was wondering what kind of magic user you are. I've never seen it before."

He chuckled, "I'm known as a specialized mage."

"A specialized mage?" she asked, actually intrigued by what he was saying.

He nodded, "unlike most people who have wind magic or fire magic there are also some people who have a power that is unique to them. Mine is this bubble magic," he made a small bubble that she caught in her hands.

"It's really cool," she whispered, looking at the bubble closely. He touched it to make it bigger, then turned to another kid calling to him. She spent a while looking at it before it popped. She smiled at the man before going to look at the others. There were a few others that she got a good look at that she planned to try, but as she was leaving town, bubbles were her main focus.

It was a surprisingly hard technique to copy. While it was easy enough to imagine and form the bubble in her hand as time went on it spun faster and faster, pulling in more air around her. She had to slow it down a few times as it got close to a speed that would cut her hands if she tried to touch it.

Ceaxtra frowned, wanting something that was able to maintain the same speed. She was determined to figure it out as soon as possible. She was so distracted by her training, she didn't notice the people who had surrounded her until they grabbed her arm. Before she could stop them, they started to push up her sleeves, one arm after the other. Once they found the butterfly on her right shoulder, the left-wing black and the right-wing a dark green color, they nodded to each other. "Yep, this is one of them." Ceaxtra blinked, she didn't know she had that or where she had gotten it.

She started to gather wind to blow the men away when something clicked on her wrists and the wind died. She looked down to see the cuffs and frowned. She wanted to ask what they were, but the man that was holding her arm let go of her to talk to his men. Ceaxtra looked at the now distracted men before taking her chance.

Turning back the way she came, she quickly started running before anyone could grab her again. She wasn't fast. She didn't have any memories of being a good runner, but she had to do her best to stay away from them. She noticed that the trees started to thin out to the left and took a chance by diving into them. After she entered the woods, she heard the people behind her stop following.

She saw a clearing in front of her, figuring that would be the location she could stop to breathe. Before she got to it, she gasped as images flashed before her eyes. Of her walking into a clearing and suddenly disappearing. After appearing in a white void which quickly sapped her of all of her energy, her body fell to the ground. She stopped running, not knowing what she saw or what it meant. She frowned, watching the clearing, but also trying to hear if anyone was still following her.

"You should come out," said a cheerful voice.

She bit her lip, looking behind her to see if she was being followed, she took another moment but when she heard no footsteps, she figured she should talk to the voice, "if I come out, I'm going to die."

"I wasn't going to kill you," said the voice.

"I doubt that." She didn't know why those visions happened, but she could tell the images happened because she hadn't stopped running.

"I only meant to capture you."

"Well do it the normal way, not a magical one." She didn't know what that white void was about or why she ended up there, but she figured the voice was probably the cause.

"Alright, I can do that." Ceaxtra saw a girl walk into the clearing. What little of her hair wasn't covered by her hat was pure white. When Ceaxtra didn't move she spoke up again "I know you're nearby, I could just randomly start disappearing parts of the forest if you don't come out."

Ceaxtra sighed before stepping into the clearing. Gizlae smiled at her, "great." She grabbed Ceaxtra's arm and started to walk down a path that was behind her.

Ceaxtra struggled against her, "why are you helping them?"

Gizlae was determined and only held her arm tighter. "Well, it's to find Kihakso."

"Who?"

Gizlae rolled her eyes, "don't act like you don't know who you're targeting. You'll tell them where Kihakso is and then I'll go get him"

"I really do-" Before Ceaxtra could finish, Gizlae pushed her into the man that put the shackles on her.

"Make sure you find out where Kihakso is,"

"Of course," he said with a creepy smile. Ceaxtra frowned, not believing him, but Gizlae seemed to as she smiled and walked away. Ceaxtra watched her for a moment before the man started to drag her away. She was pulled into a wood building that only seemed to have one door and no windows. "Play nice" the man laughed, before throwing her inside and closing the door behind her.

They opened their eyes to nothingness. they felt a presence near their head, though they didn't see anything. "You have done well," it said. They wanted to sit up, but they seemed to not have a body but had one at the same time.

"Done what well?"

"You fought and you never gave up. You also protected your brother."

"I did?" they whispered.

"And now you will be my child."

"I wasn't before?" they felt something touch their cheek, though they still couldn't see anything even though their eyes were open.

"You don't have to worry about before."

"What do you mean?"

"You will learn." They wanted to ask more, but the voice spoke first, "Your name is Kihakso and it is time for you to wake up."

They opened their eyes again and found themselves in a dark room. They tried to sit up and this time it worked. They could only remember their brother and the need to go check on him right away. They stood up to find no window in the room, but the darkness around them felt heavy. They could feel it pushing against the walls, but also the bones and bodies around the room. They frowned, wishing they could do something like burying them, but Kihakso didn't want to delay, they were on a mission.

Kihakso couldn't feel a door with the darkness, so they decided to use the darkness to push the walls away. They took a breath in, and with a slow breath out, They pushed the darkness away. It took a moment before the walls gave way. They blinked at the sudden sunlight but didn't stay around. Not bothering to look if the bodies and bones were still there, they started to walk down the street. They didn't remember where their home was but seemed to know from muscle memory.

They came to a house that was rundown with a broken window. They didn't even think about it before they started to bang on the door.

A woman answered the door with a frown, "what do you want?"

"Where is my brother?"

"I don't know who you are or who he is."

Kihakso frowned, looking down at himself. They were sure that this was their mother. Were they different now? They shook their head, "Kympilej. Where is Kympilej?"

Their mother huffed as she crossed her arms, "that traitor took him. She heard my older son," Kihakso frowned at that. They only had one memory from before and knew that they didn't trust their mother just from what she called them, "was the next sacrifice and decided to take Kympilej and run."

Kihakso glared at her, then looked around, "I see so all the good people have left here." They didn't give her a moment to speak up before taking a step away from her. They concentrated on finding their power, letting it build up inside themselves. They had one wish, to make the town suffer like they had, as those bodies inside the dark room had. In their mind, they imagined a dome to cover the town, one that only they could leave.

They felt inside for the power to achieve what they needed. Raising their hands into the air, darkness shot out of their hands, rising into the air before covering the town in a dome. As it covered the sky, the light was slowly taken away until it was all gone for everyone else. For Kihakso, it just looked like a cloudy day.

They took a moment, watching their mother look around "what's going on?" she shouted.

Kihakso crossed their arms, "what do you mean?"

"You!" she shouted and pointed forward, even if it wasn't at them. "You did something. I know it."

"Well, you watched me do it so I hoped you would be smart enough to realize I did something."

Mother glared at him, "well undo it."

"Make me."

She moved around to try and find them, but they made sure to stay out of her reach. They watched her amused for a moment before turning away from her and leaving her behind. Kihakso walked through the town towards the entrance enjoying the growing confusion they could hear. Once they were out, they looked around, trying to figure out where they wanted to head next, when their eyes were drawn to a cliff across the clearing.

There was a flash that, even so far away, still blinded them. When they opened their eyes to look back at it, the town, that they had only seen a little of, was gone. They looked around for a moment before they noticed that there was a black arrow at their feet pointing in the direction of the cliff. With no other plan on where to go, they shrugged and headed towards the cliff, curious to see what the arrow pointed to.

It took only an hour or so to get to the base of the cliff, looking at the path leading up. They immediately started to head up. Kihakso thought it would take half a day to make it to the cliff they saw, but as they were making their way up the cliff, they bumped into a girl heading the way down.

She glared at them, "who are you?"

As soon as she got into Kihakso's view, the arrow they had been following disappeared. They looked at her closely and could see what looked like a tattoo just under the edge of her skirt on her shin. "The name is Kihakso. Who are you?"

"And what do you want?"

Kihakso frowned, "you didn't answer my question." they said, crossing their arms.

Gizlae copied him, "well how do I know I can trust you?"

Kihakso watched her for a moment. "I think we're the same."

Gizlae stood up straighter, "oh?"

Kihakso looked at where the arrow had been a moment ago. "Did you...were you killed and brought back?"

She watched them for a moment, carefully. "What of it?"

"Did you do something to that town?" they pointed to where the town had been. "Destroy it or make it disappear?"

She looked Kihakso over again; she looked over her shoulder for a moment before answering. "And were you the one that made that dome of darkness?" she pointed, and even from here, the two could still see it.

They looked over at it for a moment before looking back at her and nodding, "We're the same. I was brought back by Darkness."

Gizlae looked him over for a moment before sighing. "I was brought back by Light. My name is Gizlae."

Gizlae held out her hand. Kihakso looked at it for a moment before shaking her hand. They stared at each other, and her frown grew as she looked them over.

"What?"

"When our hands touched..." she looked them up and down, "a bunch of stuff came up?"

"Stuff?"

"Bars, with some weird information," she looked at something over their shoulder, "whatever spell you did last will kill you within a week."

Kihakso looked over their shoulder, though there was nothing there, "How would you know?"

"That's what the info says," she pointed to where she was looking, but they still didn't see anything. They took their hand back and crossed their arms. "Ah, all of the information is gone."

"So, you can only see it when you touch me?"

Gizlae looked at them for a moment before moving closer and touching their shoulder. She shook her head, then moved to touch their neck. Kihakso jumped and moved away from her. "Seems to only work when I touch your skin."

They rubbed their neck, "give a warning next time." Gizlae chuckled lightly. "About what you were talking about, I have a plan for it."

The two were silent, not knowing what else to say. Kihakso watched her for a moment. "Do you...need to do anything?"

She shook her head, "no I already did what I wanted to do." Her smile turned sharp as she looked back at the cliff that she walked down from.

Kihakso nodded, "I need to stay here for a night, preferably near the dome so I can fix it."

Gizlae nodded, "do you want to stick together?" Kihakso looked down at where the arrow had been, then looked around themselves to see if any were behind them. "What are you looking for?"

"Just like you saw bars and info, I saw a black arrow that was pointing towards you," they said as they turned back to her. "I don't see any one more so I assume we are the only ones like us."

"Is that good or bad?"

Kihakso shrugged. "I just woke up a little before you so I haven't decided yet." Gizlae nodded and waved down the cliff. The two headed down and moved back over to the edge of the dome. Gizlae was about to touch it, but Kihakso grabbed her hand, "I wouldn't do that. I don't know if it will suck you in, I know I can leave it but I don't know if others can."

"You made this," she waved at the dome, "and don't know how it works?"

Kihakso frowned, waving at the cliff, "did you know everything about what you did to your town?" Gizlae frowned as she touched her chest before shaking her head. The two were silent, neither of them spoke until well into the night. It was a confused silence, but not an uncomfortable one, both were trying to digesta the little that they knew.

Kihakso watched as Gizlae fell asleep first, but they didn't mind as they turned to the dome, hoping to find out what they had done and how they could fix it. They placed their hands on the wall of the dome and felt the energy slowly pull from themselves into it. They closed their eyes and changed the flow of energy. Instead of pulling it from themselves, it is pulled from the night time, storing it away to use up during the day.

With a small sigh, the pull they didn't even realize was happening disappeared. Taking a moment to breathe and enjoy the stars, they eventually fell asleep. In the morning, Gizlae shook them awake. Kihakso blinked and stretched, "I see you fixed whatever it was that was going to kill you."

"Yes, though I didn't know how it was going to kill me."

Gizlae frowned then moved to touch their hand lightly. She looked them over again. "From what this info says, you would die if you used up all your magical powers," she moved her hand away from them, "I would assume the same applies to me too."

"Then do you have to change whatever you did to your town like I did mine?" They waved at the dome.

Gizlae touched her chest again, "no I don't think so. They feed the place they are in so I don't have to."

Kihakso nodded, "you said you didn't have anything to do?"

"That's correct."

Kihakso looked back at the dome. "I...I need to find my brother."

Gizlae glared, "did he hurt you?"

Kihakso shook his head, "no, I became like this because I wanted to protect him. I want to tell him I'm back and to make sure he knows I'm...well safe."

"Do you know where he is?"

Kihakso shook their head, "he left after I was dragged away. I know he is safe but I have no idea where he is."

Gizlae nodded, "Well then, we should look for the closest town to get money and supplies."

The two of them traveled from place to place for a few months. Since they had no planned direction, the two decided to travel down the coastline. Every town they came to, Kihakso asked around for Kympilej. It wasn't until three months later, at a town where the roads went vertical up a cliff, that they heard anything.

A man working at the inn knew of an older woman that had recently moved to a town on the water's edge south of the cliffs. The woman had been friends with the man's mother, and his mother had talked a lot about the child that now lived with her.

Kihakso didn't know for sure if the kid was their brother, but they couldn't miss this chance. The two planned to split for three weeks. Kihakso wanted to meet their brother on their own in case their reunion went badly.

Gizlae was disappointed but agreed, figuring she would head back up to the wooded towns they had passed a few days ago, wanting to look more into some of the shops they had seen.

"How are we going to meet up again?" Gizlae asked, shifting from one foot to the other.

Kihakso pointed to the ground, "I can follow the arrow. I'll find you in three weeks. I promise."

Gizlae nodded and the two parted ways. It took a day or two for Kihakso to get to Dangrmon. Once there it was easy enough to ask for directions to the house his brother lived in.

Kihakso looked at the door for a long time. They didn't know if their brother would accept them. They took a big breath before taking the leap and knocking on the door. When it opened an older woman was standing there. Kihakso didn't know her. She wasn't in any of the memories that they had. They could only hope she knew Kympilej.

She looked them over before giving them a small smile "how may I help you?"

"I'm looking for Kympilej. I heard he was living here."

Her smile fell, and she gripped the door tighter. "I'm sorry you have heard wrong."

She started to close the door when they put their hand to the door and pushed, trying to keep it open, "Please. If you have any information about where he is I need to know."

"Well, I don't, now if you wou-"

"Please I need to see my brother!"

The woman froze, giving them another look over. "Who are you?" she asked slowly.

They stopped pushing against the door when they were sure she wouldn't close it in their face "I'm Kihakso." She didn't seem to move after that, so they continued "I'm the Child of Darkness."

Gizlae and Kihakso had talked about whether they should tell people this information. The towns they visited seemed to be divided on if the Children of the Elements were good or not. But it didn't matter to Kihakso. This might be the only info that would give them knowledge about their brother's location.

The older woman threw the door open and moved closer to them, "Is it really..." She placed her hands on their shoulders to get a better look at them. "You came back?"

They shifted from foot to foot, "I'm sorry." She frowned at that.

"If we knew each other I don't remember you. I only remember the promise to my brother," they whispered, looking down.

She sighed but smiled, "I'm sad to hear that you've forgotten me but that promise was important so I'll forgive you." She took a step back to get a good look at Kihakso, "well, my name is Letrifda. When I heard what your mother allowed them to do to you, I knew I couldn't leave Kympilej with her. I went to your house the next day to get him out of there."

Kihakso nodded, a small smile appeared on their face, knowing their brother had someone to care for him, "is he..."

Her eyes went wide and she led them into the house, "yes sorry, he's in his room." she led them to the door, "he hasn't been good since..." she trailed off, both of them knowing what she was talking about, "maybe you can help him?" She squeezed their shoulder, then left.

They took a breath before knocking on the door. When they didn't get an answer, they opened it slightly to see their brother sitting on his bed, hugging a pillow to his chest.

"Hi, Kympilej, can I come in?"

Kympilej didn't move or say anything, so Kihakso took that as a yes.

They looked around the room quickly to see a few things had come from their home, but it was still pretty plain. They sat on the bed in front of Kympilej, though he didn't even look at Kihakso.

"I wanted to say sorry," the silence continued "I had made a promise to you and I failed it." They moved a little closer so they could put their hand on Kympilej's knee. That made Kympilej look up at them, "I promised to always stay by you and protect you." Kympilej blinked at them. Though they couldn't remember much, they could make a guess why they broke the promise, "but I had to make a choice...and I chose to keep you safe." Kympilej's eyes went wide and he moved closer to Kihakso.

"Are you...?" Kympilej couldn't finish the sentence, but Kihakso could hear the hopefulness in it.

Kihakso sighed, "I don't know for sure." Kympilej frowned, "I don't remember anything." Kympilej looked about to cry and Kihakso squeezed his knee. "But I remember you, and our promise." They looked Kympilej in the eyes, "I can't promise that I will be the same as I was, but I want to get to know you again. I will do my best to be your older sibling again. Will you let me?"

Kympilej sniffed for a moment before throwing his arms around Kihakso and crying into their shoulder. Kihakso just let him cry while rubbing his back comfortingly.

Kympilej moved to whisper in their ear. "Still they?"

Kihakso smiled as they nodded. "Rules are still the same," they muttered. Kympilej pulled back to look them in the eye with a serious look before nodding his head. Kihakso chuckled before giving him another hug. Kympilej sighed as he got comfortable.

The two stayed there for a long while, neither wanting to move, just enjoying the warmth that they both provided to each other. Eventually, there was a knock on the door and both looked up to see Letrifda holding up a tray with some cups and cookies.

"How are you two?"

Kympilej moved off the bed, and out of the impromptu cuddle, to grab the tray, "this is Kihakso now."

Letrifda chuckled, "I heard when I got the door."

"Oh." Kympilej placed the tray down on the bed between them, "Where did you get the name?"

"That was the name Darkness gave me before I woke up."

Kympilej's eyes went wide. "Did you really meet an element?"

Kihakso nodded, "I couldn't see anything, or move but I talked briefly with it."

Kympilej leaned forward, bouncing in place slightly. "What was it like?"

Kihakso took a cookie from the tray and started to nibble on it, "they were vague. Didn't seem to want to answer anything."

Letrifda moved to sit in a chair next to the bed, smiling at the siblings. "And have you been traveling on your own?"

Kihakso shook their head, "no soon after I woke up, I met someone else like me. Her name is Gizlae, she's the Child of Light."

"And you didn't bring her?" Letrifda said with a frown.

Kihakso shook their head, "I didn't know how this would go. If you didn't want to be near me, I didn't want her here for it."

Kympilej frowned, finishing the cookie he was eating. "Why wouldn't we want to be near you?"

Kihakso looked at Letrifda not wanting to say anything but knowing she knew what they meant. She smiled at them, "well then, tell us about your travels. Anything interesting?" They nodded and started to tell them about his traveling around with Gizlae and the different towns they had seen.

Later that night, after dinner, it was just Kihakso and Letrifda. Kihakso helped her do some cleaning after Kympilej went to bed. The two were silent most of the night until they were almost done when Letrifda spoke up.

"Kihakso?"

They turned towards her "yes?"

"You know how I adopted your brother as my son, right?" they nodded their head, "well...I know you don't know me anymore but I was hoping you would let me adopt you as my child?"

Kihakso watched her for a moment and they could see the hopefulness in her eyes. They thought over what she said before nodding.

"Really?" she asked, her eyes going wide.

"I might not know you now but I know I trusted you in the past." She took a moment thinking over what they said before nodding, "and if there is one person I can believe it's myself," they frowned then, "but I don't plan on living here. I promised to meet up with Gizlae." They looked out the window, "also I wanted to see more of the world to try and relearn about myself."

She placed her hand on their shoulder and they looked at her, "I wouldn't want to force you to stay if you don't want to. Just promise that you'll visit? Kympilej would miss you too much if you didn't."

Kihakso nodded, "of course. I promised to bring Gizlae around next time."

Letrifda smiled, "it will be wonderful to meet her."

Kihakso stayed with the two of them for a week. They wanted to give themselves enough time to find Gizlae, and since the arrow only told them the direction that she was in and not how far away she was, they didn't want to be too late. Kympilej wasn't happy that they were leaving, but Kihakso promised they would be back to visit soon and that they would even bring Gizlae along to visit next time. When that didn't work, the promise of presents made Kympilej pretty much push Kihakso out the door.

The arrow was pointing to the cliffs Kihakso had walked around before. They hoped that meant she had gone into the forest on the other side and not up to them. It took a day or two to walk around the cliffs, but once they got to the forest, they breathed a sigh of relief to see the arrow pointed inwards rather than up.

The forest had a lot of big trees, the roots were big enough that Kihakso had to climb over them to head inside. They knew that there was a town along the edge that might have an easier entrance, but they wanted to get back to Gizlae as soon as possible. It took them a few days to catch up to her, but they weren't expecting the situation they found her in. As they were walking through the nearby town they had heard of this location. When Kihakso had seen the arrow pointing down the trail, they had hoped she was behind it, not in it. Being down the trail had made it cheaper for the person running it.

They had been making good time since they found a trail through all the roots when suddenly a young child ran into their side. This child looked to be the same age as Kympilej and Kihakso couldn't stop themselves from rubbing her back. She looked up at them and then suddenly jumped back from them after realizing she didn't know them. Kihakso could see tears running down her cheeks, "Help us."

"What's going on?"

"I don't know. This lady appeared at the orphanage. And then flashes of light started to happen and my friends started to disappear." There was a bunch of sniffing as she spoke, but they were able to make out what she was saying.

Kihakso's eyes went wide. "You said flashes of light?" the orphan nodded, "Alright. You stay here, I'll deal with her." With that, Kihakso sprinted off at full speed, following the arrow. They hoped since the child was able to run to their location, that the orphanage wasn't too far away.

Eventually, a big building came into view with the door wide open. They could hear shouting inside which made them move a little faster. They went down the hall to enter a big dining room to see Gizlae standing in the middle of it, looking all around. "What do you think you're doing here?" They saw her eyes go wide as she turned towards them.

"Me? I was sent here to remove these thieves."

"Thieves? These are orphans," Kihakso muttered.

Gizlae crossed her arms, "and why should I believe a fake like you?"

Kihakso's eyes went wide before stomping over to her, "a fake? Who would want to fake being me?"

Gizlae glared at them "because..." Gizlae took their hand at that moment and gasped both were silent as she looked them over, Kihakso noticed that she looked at places they had recognized as where the information was located like over their shoulder, before quietly in a whisper she said, "you didn't lie to me."

"Why would I lie to you?"

"Everybody has," Gizlae said, her eyes slowly filling with tears. "First I was told a husband was bad but it was actually the lady who was, then kids told me they needed to get into their house but it was just to steal money. And now..." she started to sniff, "and now a man told me that there were a bunch of thieves that were stealing his employees' money but now you're telling me they aren't." By the end of her story, she was fully crying.

"Have you been on a crime spree?"

"No, I've been trying to help people," she said while wiping her eyes. "But every time I tried, they lied to me."

Kihakso looked over at her for a moment. "But I haven't lied to you."

Gizlae's eyes went wide, "what?"

Kihakso chuckled, "you haven't been paying attention to the days, have you?"

Gizlae blinked at them before slowly counting in her head. She then looked up at them quickly, "it's three weeks since we parted."

Kihakso chuckled, "to the day. I thought I might have been late since I didn't know how far away you were but luck was on my side."

Gizlae was silent for a moment, "why?"

"Why what?"

"Why didn't you lie?"

Kihakso sighed before pulling Gizlae close to hug her. "We've been traveling together long enough to think of you as my friend. I don't have any reason to lie to you."

"Can you promise?" she whispered.

"Promise what?"

"To never lie to me?"

Kihakso was silent for a long moment before pulling her away from her to look her in the eyes. "I promise to never lie to you, I would rather die than do so."

The two were silent for a while before Gizlae nodded and pulled them into another hug. Kihakso hugged her back before sighing, "can you put the kids back?" They didn't know how her snapping worked though he had seen her use it once or twice when they were attacked by bandits. She had never brought those guys back, though, so Kihakso didn't know if it was possible.

"Yeah, I was just going to move them. Even if they were thieves they shouldn't die." She started to snap people back. The kids took a look at the two of them and immediately ran away.

Kihakso watched them leave before pulling Gizlae away from them again. "We need to go. We don't want to be here when anyone comes back."

Gizlae nodded, rubbing her eyes. Kihakso grabbed her hand and started to drag her away from the way they came. The two didn't see a back door so they climbed through a window before getting out of there. The roots were tall and oddly shaped, and since they decided to avoid the trail, traveling became several times more difficult. With the two of them together, Kihakso didn't know where to go, but they both knew that either north or south would lead them to water.

They spent the rest of the day slowly climbing over roots and helping each other when they hit difficult parts. When the night was starting to fall, they managed to make it to the sea's edge. They didn't see mountains so knew they had gone north and now had a relative idea as to where they were. Looking around, the two found a small clearing with a small hill looking over the water. They decided to spend the night there rather than deal with water or trees at night.

It was easy enough to make a fire and the sounds from the forest and the waves made a calming atmosphere. The two were enjoying it when Kihakso broke the silence, " it's...Them"

Gizlae looked up from the fire and Kihasko met her eyes, "my pronouns are they/them"

"Oh," she looked down at the fire for a moment before looking back up at them, "why didn't you mention it before?"

"I didn't care what you perceived me as then."

Gizlae nodded, deciding to change the subject slightly, "are there any others that know?"

Kihakso nodded, "my brother Kympilej and..." The word felt weird to say but wanted to honor her correctly "...my mom, Letrifda. You three are the only ones that know."

Gizlae chuckled, "thank you for adding me to such an exclusive club."

Kihakso smiled, "thanks for being my friend."

It wasn't until after seven months that another arrow popped up. The two discussed if they wanted to go looking for their fellow child or not, but in the end, decided to leave them alone. While it might benefit the other kid, the two had noticed that when they entered a town, people would start to watch them more closely. They didn't know if that was because of what Gizlae did before or if it was because they were noticeable. Either way, they didn't want to bother the new kid but kept an eye out if they heard of any plans to hurt them.

Over the next two years, their relationship changed, and the two started to date with the help of Kympilej. Along with that, more and more arrows started to show up. Even with Gizlae by their side, the ground was still covered in black arrows. Sometimes, depending on where the two were, the floor was covered in darkness.

The two had gotten into the habit of counting the arrows once a week. Kihakso would count them while holding Gizlae's hand, tapping on it as they counted to keep her informed while not informing others that they were counting anything.

When the number of other children hit five, the two noticed that men were waiting for them in almost every town. They had these weird cuffs that seemed to be made of a strange metal that could cut off their connections to their elements somehow. They found out that if the metal wasn't made for them, then it wouldn't work so they were able to get out of them the few times they were caught together.

The first time the two kissed was the first time they dealt with the cuffs. They had been walking when Gizlae said she had a surprise she wanted to buy for Kihakso. She led them to a store entrance telling them to wait there and entered it herself.

She was in there for a while, but Kihakso didn't mind. They assumed that Gizlae was taking a while to pick up whatever it was or that the store was busy.

When one of the arrows rapidly changed from somewhere behind them to in front of them, they frowned, an arrow only moved that rapidly if they were close. Kihakso's eyes narrowed, and they turned to the store. They ripped the door open to find the place empty but disheveled as if a struggle had occurred.

Kihakso immediately turned around. There were a few arrows in front of them, but they would figure out which ones was Gizlae's and would find her.

Kihakso ran out the door, not caring if it was suspicious or if they were blamed for the damage, and once they found Gizlae, they were out of here. Kihakso watched the arrows carefully, looking for any rapid changes. When one shot to the left they ran back, taking the first right they could. But when they passed the first building, the arrow shot backward.

They quickly did a lap around the building to see if the arrow would keep pointing to it. They could tell from the outside that it was a residential building, and when they got closer, the arrow pointed down, telling them she was in a basement.

They moved away from the house. They would probably get caught if they went in now so they had to wait for the night. But they watched the arrow carefully to make sure it didn't move.

When night fell, Kihakso moved from where they were sitting. They had picked a spot that could watch the arrow but also blend into the shadows so they weren't seen. Throughout the day they had seen people enter and leave, but no one stayed for long. That didn't mean people weren't guarding Gizlae, though, so they had to be careful.

They moved to the window, they saw it was locked but could see a small crack where the lock was so they used that to their advantage. They formed a flat plain of darkness and slid it under the window to catch any glass that fell. They then collected darkness into their hands and slammed it into the window, making it grab any glass it could. Once the glass was out of the way, they climbed through the window, listening for any sounds. They didn't know where the basement was, but they sent out tendrils of darkness to slide under any door to find the stairs. Once they did, they dismissed all the unneeded ones and moved quickly to the door. Making a platform of darkness above the floor so they wouldn't make any sound.

They were relieved to find that the door was unlocked and slipped inside, keeping the platform going down the stairs to prevent any squeaks from giving away their intrusion.

Once they were on the ground, they looked around to see Gizlae huddled in a corner.

"Gizlae," they said, moving over to her. She sat up quickly, looking around till her eyes adjusted and she could see them

"Kihakso," as soon as Kihakso got close, she threw her arms around their neck and cried into their shoulder. "I was so scared." She was shaking.

Kihakso held her tightly, rubbing her back. "It's okay, it's night time so nothing will hurt you. I'm here, I will keep you safe."

"I...I went into the store...and then they attacked...and then..." she broke down, crying again, this time curling into their chest seeking comfort.

Kihakso didn't want to stay longer, not knowing when someone would come for her, but they didn't want to rush either.

After a moment she was able to speak, moving her arms from around his neck to show him the cuffs on her wrist. "They put these on me...and...I couldn't snap them away, or bring any back...it was like..." she touched her chest, where she usually felt her area.

"It was locked from me." She curled in on herself and they wrapped their arms around her. "Then once they brought me here...I tried to...use the light to find you...but it didn't work...and... I... I...I felt so scared and alone." She started to cry again and they pulled her into their shoulder again.

"Shhh, shhh it's okay Gizlae." They kissed her on the top of her head, "even if you are taken from me." They moved to hold her chin so they could look her in the eyes "I will always find you." They kissed her forehead, "you will only be rid of me when you want. Okay?"

She sniffed, "and if I never want you gone?" she whispered.

"Then I guess we'll be together for a while then," they whispered before pulling her into a soft kiss. When they parted she had a small smile on her face. She then laid her head on their shoulder. Kihakso sighed before lifting her and moving up the stairs.

They looked down to see that Gizlae had fallen asleep and knew they wouldn't get out the window without waking her. They looked over to the front, shrugged going out the front door.

They made their way to the inn they were staying at and placed her on the bed, working slowly to remove the cuffs so that Gizlae wouldn't have to feel that way when she woke up, hopefully. They slowly picked the lock of the cuffs looking up every once in a while to make sure she was just sleeping.

They had to start going solo into town for supplies because people were looking for them as a pair. That worked well for about four months. By that point, the number of arrows had increased to seven. Whoever was going after them seems to have planned or known where the two were traveling.

One day, Gizlae headed to town to get them new supplies while Kihakso set up their camp. After they set up a fire, they were attacked. Before they could even tell what was going on, the men attacking had clicked a cuff onto their wrists. They frowned when their connections to the shadows were cut off and their planned attacks fizzled out. They tried to pull away, but another man grabbed their other arm and the two lifted them with only a little effort. Kihakso wasn't short, but these men were still taller and stronger.

The men brought them to another camp that Kihakso hadn't known about. Once they were brought to the camp, the men tied their hands even though they already had the cuffs on, this was to ensure that they couldn't get away. After that, they threw them into a dark room. Kihakso felt that was more insulting as they could feel the darkness but couldn't do anything with it.

They did their best to try not to shake as something seemed to tighten in their chest. Though they didn't remember what happened to them, Kihakso remembered what the room they woke up in was like and assumed it was a fear that had left a mark on them due to what they went through, even without the memory.

They just had to wait for Gizlae to get them. They hoped it wouldn't be too long, maybe a day or two. The only other thing they could do was watch the arrows move around them, they were surprised that the arrows were still around but thought since they didn't control it that it couldn't be stopped.

They didn't know how long had passed, but eventually, they noticed one pointing right at the door. They wondered if Gizlae had finally come to save them. Then suddenly the door was thrown open and someone was thrown in. They blinked as the arrow disappeared as she came into their view.

"Ah, they caught another one of us." They muttered. If the arrow hadn't told them she was A Child of the Elements, then the shown tattoo on her shoulder was another clue.

She looked up and looked around the room before noticing them. They knew that in this type of room they were hard to find.

"What?" they didn't say anything just looking at the shown tattoo. She quickly pushed her sleeve down.

"Well, that answers that." They muttered before sitting up a little straighter, managing to hide themselves even more into the shadows, without meaning to. "I'm Kihakso."

"Oh, you're who she's looking for."

Kihakso blinked. They hadn't met this person before "Who?"

"Didn't catch her name. She had all white hair?"

"Ah Gizlae. You met her?"

"Yeah, she's working with the gang."

Kihakso frowned, "what?"

Ceaxtra shrugged, "Yeah she said they would get me to talk about where you were, and then she would go save you."

Kihakso sighed, "they tricked her." They shook their head, "I was hoping she would be saving me. Seems like I need to get out of here by myself then I guess." They had wondered why she hadn't gotten to them yet. It would make sense if the bandits or whatever they were had talked to her. Kihakso wondered how whoever was hunting them down had found out how gullible she was. They had tried their best to keep that information hidden. They shifted slightly, "if I could only get these cuffs off."

"What are they?"

Kihakso blinked at her. Had she not dealt with them before? "Metal made to block our powers. Each metal is made for each of us so yours wouldn't work on me but they figured out which one I was."

"Did they use your tattoo to figure you out?"

Kihakso shook their head, "someone has been hunting us down, Gizlae isn't subtle a lot of the time." They sighed, "if only I could reach the lock. Then I could pick it off."

Ceaxtra frowned, "do you think you could pick mine off? Then I can cut yours off?"

Kihakso nodded and the two shifted closer. It took longer than Kihakso would have liked, but eventually, they did it. Ceaxtra cut off theirs without cutting them, even if she couldn't see well.

Ceaxtra looked around, rubbing her wrist, "how are we going to get out though? I might be able to cut the door but I don't know what will happen after that," she said with a frown.

Kihakso smirked, "they put us in the worst cell." They took a breath and felt the darkness around them. They poured their magic into the darkness allowing it to build up. They slammed the floor and the darkness pulled away from Kihakso, pressing against the walls and ceiling until they ripped apart. They wiped their hands as the two stood up. "That takes care of that." The two looked up as people started to rush over. Kihakso looked around before their eyes landed on Gizlae, who joined the growing mass of people last.

Her eyes went wide, "Kihakso?"

The boss was smarter than Kihakso would normally give them credit for, "That's a fake."

Gizlae glared at them, "it is?"

Ceaxtra opened her mouth to say something, but Kihakso beat her to it. "Gizlae," they held their hand out to her. They didn't move, waiting for her to take it. This was something they could wait for as long as she needed to confirm. Ceaxtra looked around at the men glaring at them but they seemed to be waiting for Gizlae to make a move.

Gizlae watched them for a moment before moving over to them. When she was standing in front of them, she watched their hand for a moment before slowly taking it. They could see as she looked them over her eyes, landing on regular locations.

Eventually, she looked them in the eyes, frowning and holding their hand a little tighter. "Kihakso? where have you been?"

Kihakso smirked before pointing to the boss, "they captured me."

She turned to glare at the boss, never letting go of their hand, "They what!"

"He's lying," the boss shouts.

That made her stand up straighter, "Kihakso would never lie to me."

"You don't know that!"

Kihakso chuckled, already knowing her answer. "I know!" and with that, she snapped. With a flash, the man was gone. She kept snapping, and with each flash that happened, another man was gone. Once they were all gone, Gizlae sighed.

Kihakso looked over at her slowly, "Feel any better?"

"No," she muttered, turning to them. They watched as she looked over them again, making sure she was right about what she saw.

"Do I want to know?" Ceaxtra muttered. Kihakso shrugged, and Gizlae seemed to ignore her for a moment.

"I'm sorry but they said you had been captured by someone else but..."

They shrugged "really I should have expected that. Thankfully you also caught her which helped me to get out of the cuffs." They waved to Ceaxtra, and Gizlae turned to smile at her.

"Thank you for helping Kihakso. Sorry I was mean to you."

"You weren't really," Ceaxtra said with a shrug. She looked around, "why did they go after you two anyways?"

"They were after you as well," Kihakso muttered. Gizlae looked back at Kihakso with wide eyes. "They were probably paid to go after children of the elements. Someone wants to hunt us down."

Ceaxtra took an awkward step back, "Children of the Elements?"

Gizlae smiled, "it's what we're known as. Did you never hear someone mention them being a thing? It's for any kid sacrificed to an element and was brought back by it."

"I'm not-" as Kihakso raised an eyebrow, she crossed her arms, "and what makes you think I am one?"

"Besides the bands, they put on you to block your powers in the cell?"

"That worked just because I have wind magic."

Gizlae shook her head, "no those only work on us. Something about how they were made it seems."

"And the tattoo that I saw on your arm?" Kihakso shrugged "you had an arrow before but now you don't."

"An arrow?"

Gizlae nodded, "Kihakso can see the direction of other Children of the Elements. When Kihakso sees the person, the arrow goes away."

"Doesn't that get annoying?"

Kihakso sighed, "it used to be not too bad when it was just the two of us," they said as they waved to Gizlae with their free hand. "Now though, there's a lot more of us so it's a bit more annoying."

Ceaxtra turns to look at them, "What do you mean?"

Kihakso looked around, starting to count the arrows around them, tapping Gizlae's hand as they went. After a moment they spoke up again, "there are six others besides us three. That's a lot."

"This group was probably paid by the guy that has been chasing us down," Gizlae said with a sigh.

"What?" said Ceaxtra.

"Oh yeah, that guy." Kihakso muttered, "we would probably have a better chance against him as a group."

"What guy? Why?" The two seemed to ignore her as Gizlae turned to Kihakso.

"Then should we be going and finding everyone rather than randomly traveling?"

"Randomly traveling has been nice," they muttered.

Gizlae smiled, "it is but we should think of the group rather than just us."

Kihakso sighed, "you're right." They turned back to Ceaxtra, "so we-

"You didn't answer my question."

The two blinked at her before Gizlae smiled at her, "I'm sorry we're not use to spending time with others, what did you ask?"

Ceaxtra huffed, "What guy is chasing you?"

Gizlae shook her head, "no we believe he is hunting down everyone, though we didn't have proof of that till they targeted you as well."

Ceaxtra frowned, "Why? Why is he after us?"

"We haven't figured that out yet" Gizlae gasped "oh we never introduced ourselves. I'm Gizlae and I was brought back by Light."

Kihakso sighed, "probably obvious but I'm Kihakso and I was brought back by Darkness."

The two just watched Ceaxtra for a moment, who sighed, "I'm Ceaxtra brought back by wind."

Gizlae smiled, "oh yes your town was close by here wasn't it?"

"It was but it won't be there if you go now." Ceaxtra said as she watched them. shrugged and took a step back, "well this has been fun?"

"Has it?" Kihakso muttered.

Ceaxtra frowned at Gizlae, "no. But I should be going. I had plans so..."

"You do?" Kihakso asked, looking around them, "you probably missed those plans since those guys kidnapped you."

"You aren't going to stay with us?" Gizlae frowned.

"Why would I? Just because you claim someone is after us?"

Kihakso frowned, "you were just kidnapped because you were one of us."

Ceaxtra shifted, "it could have been fake. What if you set it up?"

Gizlae frowned, "it wasn't fake."

Ceaxtra rolled her eyes, "sure."

"But-"

Gizlae was stopped by Kihakso, grabbing her hand again. "It's fine she can go where she wants."

Ceaxtra looked between the two, "Can I really?"

Kihakso shrugged, "Yep, just means we'll follow along for now."

Gizlae turned to them, "but you-"

"I can handle with two arrows gone. They are annoying, not headache-inducing."

Ceaxtra watched the two. Gizlae looked Kihakso over before she sighed and looked over to Ceaxtra, "I don't like this but..." she smiled "lead the way."

Ceaxtra glared at them, "I don't need your permission." She turned away from them and took a step forward before looking around. She stood there for a moment before turning back to the two. "How do we get out of here?"

Gizlae chuckled and waved behind her and Kihakso, "the main road is that way. We're probably two days away from the nearest town though."

Ceaxtra sighed, "then I guess you can lead the way." Gizlae smiled and turned from them. She pulled Kihakso along with her, but they didn't seem to mind. Ceaxtra followed behind them and watched the two. Letting them talk and ignore her presence.

Chabnorl Cause The Learning Of Their Powers

The three of them walked along the street of Nessvarry, Ceaxtra being the one at the front while Gizlae and Kihakso followed behind. Ceaxtra looked around, her eyes filled with amazement which made Gizlae chuckle, "how long has it been since you woke up?"

Ceaxtra looked at her "this morning?"

Gizlae chuckled again "no I mean..."

"She's wondering how long it's been since you were brought back to life," said Kihakso after moving closer to speak quieter.

That also confused Ceaxtra, "can't you tell? Don't you see arrows for all of us?"

Kihakso sighed, "Sure, but they're all black. Also, there's no indication as to which one goes to who, and when I turn and move around so do they. I can't keep straight which is for who."

Ceaxtra watched for a moment longer before she sighed, "I've only been...awake? Is that what you call it?"

Gizlae nodded, "since that is what the element told us when we opened our eyes."

Ceaxtra remembered that and nodded her head looking forward again, "Then I've been awake for about a week or so now."

Gizlae gasped, "oh, you're a baby."

Ceaxtra glared at her, "I am not."

Kihakso nodded, slowing down to let Gizlae catch up to them. "You are to us."

"And how old are you two?"

"Two years, we woke up at the same time pretty much," Gizlae said laughing to herself.

"I'm older though," Kihakso smirked at her.

Gizlae sighed, "you always claim that."

"I saw your attack on your town. Mine was already there when your's happened."

Gizlae rolled her eyes and crossed her arms. "That doesn't mean anything. It took me longer to attack them. Needed more time to wake up."

Kihakso looked towards Ceaxtra just in time to see her duck down an alleyway. They sighed as they grabbed Gizlae's hand to pull her along. Once they got to the mouth of the alley, they shouted into it, "Did you really think you could get away that easily?" They ran in, still dragging Gizlae behind them when her hand was ripped from theirs and she gasped. They turned to see that a man had clipped a cuff around her wrist.

"We can't be having you snap us away," Chabnorl said with a chuckle.

Kihakso glared at him. "Who are you?"

"I've been the one trying to hunt you all down. My name is Chabnorl," he pulled Gizlae closer to him with the chain attached to her wrist.

"Since my hired help is failing, I decided to do it myself."

Kihakso glared at him, "Ceaxtra you better not have been working with him," they muttered but Chabnorl still heard him.

He chuckled, "do you think I would actually work with any of you." He walked past Kihakso farther into the alleyway dragging Gizlae along as he did so. Kihakso tried to reach for her but Chabnorl pulled her away before they could. Chabnorl then took a right turn dragging Gizlae around the corner. She tried to reach out for Kihakso before she was pulled around the corner.

Kihakso looked back at the entrance before sighing and rushing after them. When they turned the corner, they found Gizlae still pulling against the chain and Ceaxtra, who was also struggling with a cuff on her wrist while trying to struggle out of the grip of the person that was holding her.

Kihakso looked around to make sure there wasn't another person to grab them as well. "What, worried I'll have someone to grab you too?"

"You grabbed them."

"I needed to make sure I got the stronger ones first."

"Stronger?"

Chabnorl nodded, "of course," he waved at Gizlae, "She can snap anyone away and it's the daytime which is when she's strongest." He then waved to Ceaxtra. "And this is a closed off area where a little wind could cause a lot of problems." He then waved at Kihakso. "But you, what can you do?"

Kihakso chuckled, "so you learned about Gizlae but nothing about me, huh?" Chabnorl watched them, "I admit I let her use her powers first."

"Don't make it sound like I had to get your permission," Gizlae shouted at them.

"Now isn't the time to fight between you two," Ceaxtra said trying to kick the guy holding her.

Kihakso shook their head ignoring the two girls. "My power isn't night, it's darkness." They reached into the shadow right next to them. Their hand grabbed something and threw it out.

A spike of darkness flew through the air cutting through the chain holding Gizlea. She moved back over to their side. While she was moving, Kihakso threw another spike. This second one went through the man's arm that was holding Ceaxtra. Once it hit his arm, it dispersed into nothing. She couldn't get around Chabnorl, so she decided to just hold her hands up, ready to attack whoever came at her.

"So now, what are you going to do?" Kihakso said, crossing their arms.

Chabnorl turned to the guy who was still bleeding from the arm. "You get extra if you can take care of them now." A hole then appeared below him. Once he was fully in the hole it disappeared. The guy looked between the three, back at his arm, then shook his head running and took off past Gizlae and Kihakso, blood trailing behind him.

The three waited for a moment before Ceaxtra sighed, walking over to the other two. Kihakso used a spike to remove the cuff from each of them. Gizlae smiled at them, "you did so well."

They raised an eyebrow at her. "Just because I let you take care of all the people attacking us doesn't mean I can't handle the fights on my own."

"Then why am I taking care of everyone then?" she said, looking annoyed but still grabbing their hand, looking over their information quickly. Kihakso rolled their eyes before looking at Ceaxtra. "when did you say you woke up?"

"A week or two ago."

"And besides the two times you've been with us, have you fought anyone?" Ceaxtra shook her head and Kihakso sighed, "we need to fix that," they muttered.

"you have used your powers before, right?" Gizlae asked, pulling the two out of the alleyway.

"I mean...I used it to take out Galssopia. But other than that, no."

"We'll have to figure out what you can do then." Gizlae said, skipping slightly.

"Gizlae, this is serious."

"That doesn't mean it can't be fun."

"What would you even do to figure that out?" Ceaxtra asked.

"Practice fight," Kihakso muttered.

Gizlae hit them on the shoulder "that isn't fun."

"When has practice ever been fun?" they muttered.

Gizlae smiled, "We used to practice with hide and seek."

"How did you do that?"

Gizlae turned to Ceaxtra, "It was to practice our bigger spells. I can feel what the light touches when I concentrate and Kihakso can use the shadows to hide by blending in with them."

Ceaxtra looked at Kihakso and they sighed. "I can make it so that I am just a shadow, you can't touch me or see me, but I'm still there. I have to be very still as movement gives me away."

Gizlae nodded. "So we would play hide and seek where Kihakso would run to a group of shadows and I would try to see if I could spot which one he was hiding in. My light sense could tell if Kihakso moved even if I wasn't looking at the right one."

"Do you use those abilities often?"

Kihakso shrugged, "we haven't needed to but it is better to have them practiced than not."

"I used it to find you when you were running away."

Ceaxtra sighed, "Alright we can practice."

Kihakso nodded, "We'll do so after we set up camp."

"I'll try to think of a fun idea by then." Gizlae smiled, pulling them a little faster.

"We don't have to rush," said Ceaxtra trying to drag her feet but Gizlae was older and bigger than her.

Kihakso sighed but didn't fight her at all. "We need to get to the edge of town. It's your turn to set up camp while I get supplies."

Gizlae gasped and turned to them, "Oh, we should split up here then." She turned to smile at Kihakso, "meet up before nightfall?"

Kihakso shrugged, "I'll be able to see either way but I'll do my best." Before Ceaxtra could say anything else, Gizlae started pulling her again towards the edge of town. She tried to look around as they went but Gizlae seemed to be too excited to let her give her any time to look around.

Once they got out of town they walked for a little longer before Gizlae stopped and nodded, "This should be a good spot." The two spent some time setting up a firepit, with Ceaxtra keeping watch the entire time.

Eventually, Gizlae turned to Ceaxtra "well now that camp's been taken care of," Gizlae sat down, patting the ground next to her.

Ceaxtra sighed and sat down, "you were serious about the training thing huh?"

Gizlae nodded, "yes, though I'm not much for attacking as you heard, I think I have something I can teach you."

"Yeah, you don't really need it because your snapping causes death."

Gizlae frowned, "It isn't death. It's... something else."

Ceaxtra frowned as memories of her dying in a white area came back to her. She shook her head and leaned closer, "what do you mean?"

"It's more like I'm moving them..." Gizlae said as she touched the center of her chest with both hands "...to a place."

"A place?"

"Yes...I can feel it...like a hole that can be filled."

"Does it have a limit?"

Gizlae nodded, "I haven't reached it before but I believe so. Though if I remove things from it, I can put in an equal amount back in." The two were silent afterward, both lost in thought. Gizlae concentrated on the place and the people she had stored away so far, Ceaxtra wondering whether she should tell her about the flashes she had when they first met.

Gizlae shook her head and placed her hands in her lap "that isn't what I wanted to teach you about." Ceaxtra focused on her every word "as I said, I don't do much attacking. So, Kihakso will have to teach you about that but," she smiled brightly at Ceaxtra "I do think I can teach you my hunting power."

"hunting power?"

Gizlae nodded, "the one I told you I worked on through hide and seek? The ability to gain information through the sunlight."

"I don't have a connection to that."

Gizlae laughed, "that's true. But you might be able to work with wind whether created by you or the natural kind."

"how would this be useful?"

Gizlae thought for a moment, "Well, say you're hiding and need to check if any enemies are around you. You can do this by throwing out the wind instead of looking around. It would be safer. You could also use this in total darkness or if you are blindfolded."

Ceaxtra slowly nodded, "alright I can see some reasons." she shifted to get comfortable, "So, what do I do?"

"Well, first I need to ask how do you use your energy?"

"Usually I just imagine what I want the wind to do and then flex outward and it does it."

"I see, how do we bridge our two ways." Gizlae muttered to herself.

"Are they that different?"

"A little. Yours is all about concentration while mine is letting my mind wander enough to grab outside information."

"And how did you do it? The first time you started to work on this."

Gizlae sighed "Kihasko but-"

"Since you mentioned me, I assume you got in trouble?" They said, entering the clearing.

Gizlae chuckled, "No! I was just teaching her to gain information from the wind and she asked how I was able to let my mind wander enough."

Kihakso frowned, "If she is starting training, she should start with attacking. It would keep her safer if we aren't around."

"Information from the wind would keep her safe," Gizlae said, crossing her arms.

"I said safer."

Gizlae opened her mouth to argue but Ceaxtra interrupted her, "can I just be taught something, so that we don't have to go through what we went through earlier again?"

Gizlae sighed but waved at Kihakso to continue, she realized her method would take longer to teach.

Kihakso nodded "I heard a bit as I was walking up. You said you need to visualize the act when you use your powers?"

Ceaxtra nodded "Do you have any connection to the wind in general?"

"If I concentrate."

Kihakso nodded, "So, you saw how I fought when I took out those two. I use what is already there and make it work for me."

"Like when you made those spikes?"

They nodded again, "it uses less energy since you only need to create the extra you need rather than all of it from scratch." They moved over to one of the shadows, where they grabbed a part of it and pulled it out, holding a bit of shadow in their hand. "You need to focus your energy into what you're working with rather than the whole thing." They then took a part of the shadow and molded it into a spike. "The more energy you put into the shape the harder it is to control but using your hand helps."

They then plunged the spike into the ground and let the shadow just stick up for a moment, "if you are doing this method, you need to make sure you can focus on it even when you aren't touching it." The three watched as the shadow dissolved leaving an empty hole behind.

Ceaxtra looked at the hole for a moment, "it's useful information but not something I think I can use."

Kihakso frowned, "why not?"

"Wind is around at times but it is not as prevalent as shadows," Ceaxtra said with a shrug.

Gizlae chuckled, "it seems both of us aren't very helpful."

Kihakso huffed, "Gizlae." Which only made her laugh harder.

Ceaxtra watched the two, "you two have known each other for a while, huh?"

Gizlae nodded, "As I said, we have known each other for more than two years. We pretty much spend every day together."

"Not every day." Kihakso said with a smirk, "you still had your crime spree that happened while we were apart." Both girls gasped, Gizlae in betrayal and Ceaxtra in amusement.

"A crime spree?" Ceaxtra said with a laugh.

"No, don't talk about that Kihakso."

Kihakso smirked while sitting next to Gizlae. The two went back and forth, telling embarrassing stories about each other to the amusement of Ceaxtra.

It was the next morning when both of them got a surprise, "so where are we going next?" Ceaxtra asked.

Gizlae's eyes went wide, "you want to travel with us?"

"Well, it's safer to travel together, and..." she looked away for a moment. "It's not like I really know how to defend myself."

"You didn't believe us before. What changed your mind?" Gizlae asked with a smile.

Ceaxtra pointed back to the town that they had just left. "We were attacked just yesterday and were finally able to meet the guy that wants to kill us. Hard to ignore it after that."

Kihakso chuckled while Gizlae frowned before turning away from town, "well..." they said, opening their arms out in front of them, "All the arrows are that way, so going in that direction would be a good start."

"Looks like you're back to leading Kihakso," Gizlae said, standing up and brushing herself off. Kihakso nodded their head and picked a random arrow to start heading towards.

She felt weightlessness, it was as if she was floating through nothing. She couldn't tell if her eyes were open or not, either way, it was bright with nothing else. "You are the one."

"The one?"

"Your passion, your drive, that is what I have been looking for. All the others were weak and whiny."

"I don't understand," she said as she tried to move, tried to look around but she couldn't.

"You are my child now. I have chosen you." she felt pressure on her chest, "Never give up, use that passion to do all that you have ever wanted. Your name is Gizlae. It is time for you to wake up."

She was about to say something when suddenly the pressure was gone and she opened her eyes to see the clear skies. There was only one thing she remembered, a promise she needed to complete. She stood up to see that she was standing on the same cliff where she had made her promise. She turned around, saw the town behind her, and glared at it. She closed her eyes, trying to figure out how to deal with them all. A thought came to mind and she smiled before heading towards the town. Once she got to the edge, she looked over it for a moment before taking a big breath and clapping her hands. Once she did, a flash of light covered the entire town in front of her. It hurt her eyes but she couldn't look away. Once the light faded the town in front of her was gone. She could feel that they had been teleported somewhere, a place inside her that allowed her to pull from it.

She went back to the cliff to take a breath. She wanted to test one more thing. She moved just to the edge of the cliff, her toes over the edge. She reached into that place inside her and looked around it. Finding the person that she was looking for. She took a breath again pulling the person out in front of her. She watched as there was a flash and when it died down, the guy who had tied her up was standing in midair. She smiled and waved at him before gravity took effect. His screams as he fell soothed some of the anger she held from the last moments of her last life.

With that taken care of, she looked around and noticed the black dome over the planes that she didn't recall from her scant memories. She nodded as she turned, planning to at least see where it came from. As she was working her way down the cliff, she bumped into a boy who had been heading up the cliff.

Through the conversation, she met Kihakso and learned that when she touched the skin of someone like her, there was information that covered them. Health bars and numbers that informed her of their status.

For three months, the two of them traveled together, going from town to town. She was pleasantly surprised by the beach, having no memories of it before. The first day they stepped on the beach, Gizlae ran to the water stopping right before she touched the waves.

"If you want to go into the water you should take off your shoes," Kihakso shouted, staying farther away.

Gizlae nodded her head and started to do that, "Will you be joining?"

"I wasn't planning to."

Gizlae frowned and turned to them, "really?"

The two stared at each other before Kahakso sighed, "alright."

Gizlae cheered, throwing her shoes up into the air. She moved closer to the water while Kihakso collected her shoes and put their own next to hers. They went over to where Gizlae was still standing in front of the water, just watching it.

"Weren't you going in?"

"I...I..."

Kihakso watched her for a moment longer, "do you want help?" They said, holding out their hand to her.

Gizlae looked at it for a moment before giving a small smile and taking their hand. She took a small step and gasped as the waves brushed her legs and covered her feet. She looked to see that Kihakso hadn't moved, so she pulled them forward. She pulled them a little too hard, causing Kihakso to stumble and fall into the ocean.

Kihakso spat out water as Gizlae laughed at them. They glared up at her, "Oh, you think that's funny?" They muttered before lifting their other arm to grab her arm and pull her into the water.

She pushed her bangs out of her face and Kihakso chuckled at her. "Actually, you do look funny with that look on your face."

Gizlae glared at them before splashing water on them. That started a splash fight between the two before they were both caught off guard by a wave that crashed over their heads. After coughing out the water they had accidentally breathed in, they moved back to the beach. The two spent the rest of the day there just enjoying the sound of the waves before moving on to the town they could see down the beach line.

When they heard information about Kihakso's brother the two parted ways for three weeks. Gizlae didn't know what she wanted to do. She didn't have any plans but was willing to give Kihakso the space they needed to get to know their brother again.

After three days of travel, she made it back to the town that was in front of the forest. It was a pretty-looking place with buildings interspersed between the trees that were spaced out slightly more than the forest.

She had been here for two days and was still trying to figure out some way for her to earn money. It was later in the day, when no one was around, that a lady in tears ran into her arms.

Gizlae was surprised but tried to console the person. "Are you okay?"

The lady shook her head, "No one will help me. I feel so...so trapped."

Gizlae frowned, "How can I help?" she asked

The lady gasped and grabbed her arms, "Could you...could you make my husband disappear?"

Gizlae blinked at her, "disappeared?"

"Gone, away, gotten rid of. I don't know how long I can survive with him around."

Gizlae watched her cry and shake for a long moment before slowly nodding. "Okay, who is your husband?"

Gizlae didn't want the lady to suffer anymore, so she planned quickly to make the husband disappear. She found out who he was as the lady was more than willing to show her where he worked, which was at an art store that he owned. She waited until he closed up shop before she snapped her fingers and made him disappear in a flash of light.

The next day she went around till she found the lady. "I did it. He's gone."

The lady gasped, "You did? That was quick. I didn't hear anything about it."

Gizlae smiled, "I took care of it in a quiet way. That way, it wouldn't affect you."

The laugh she was expecting was a happy one or even one full of relief. What she got was a cruel laugh, "Thanks to you I'm finally rid of that annoyance."

Gizlae's eyes went wide, "What?"

The lady clapped her on the shoulder. "I knew going with a traveler was the best idea." Gizlae's mouth opened and closed but nothing came out, "You worked faster than I thought, though. Makes it easier for me either way."

"He...he wasn't a bad husband?" Gizlae whispered.

The lady chuckled, "Not unless you consider hounding me for money for our kids makes him bad." Gizlae's eyes went wide. "Next time you're in town, look me up. I might have another husband for you to deal with." With that, the lady turned and waved.

Gizlae just stood there staring at the spot she had been in for a long time. She didn't know how long she was there but eventually, she noticed that it was getting dark so she headed towards the inn she was staying in.

As she walked along the main street, a sheet of paper was thrust under her face while a voice said. "Have you seen him?"

She looked up to see a girl standing in front of her, the girl looked no older than she did.

"What?"

She took the paper as the girl said, "My dad, he went missing yesterday. Have you seen him?"

Gizlae frowned at the picture of a smiling man she recognized immediately. "He's...he's your father?"

"Yeah, it's just been him, my sister, and I for years. He normally always comes home for dinner. But he didn't come last night and still wasn't home in the morning."

Gizlae immediately started to cry, "I'm so sorry. I...I...I..."

The girl glared at her, "You're sorry?" she looked at how tightly Gizlae was gripping the paper. "What did you do!" the girl said with venom in her voice.

Gizlae's head snapped up, her eyes wide open. "No...I was told..." She shook her head, "no...I can fix this," with that, she snapped her fingers and in a flash the girl's father was standing next to them.

He blinked at the two before the girl tackled him in a hug, "What's going on?"

"You were missing all night," she said as she held him tighter, not caring about the papers all over the ground, "what do you remember?"

He frowned "I remember closing the shop...and then...a flash...and..." he squinted his eyes trying to concentrate, "then a white place...everything seemed to blur there...then after some time I was back with you."

"I'm sorry." Gizlae said, drawing odd looks from both of them. "I was told you were a bad husband, that your wife wouldn't survive if you were still around."

The father frowned and opened his mouth to say something but Gizlae didn't let him. She didn't want to hear about her failure. "I'm so sorry!" she shouted before running away. Leaving both them and the town behind, heading farther into the forest. She had paid for the night at the inn but she didn't care. She just needed to get away.

It took her two days to get to the next town. By then, she was hungry and the silence of the forest had given her too much time to think, so she needed to enter it to get away from her thoughts. She avoided anyone who was walking by themselves, not wanting a repeat of what happened last time. Another day and she passed a group of kids standing around the back door. One of them had his head pressed against the door. She watched them for a while and the kid sighed multiple times. She looked the group over for a moment before walking over to them. "Do you need help?"

The kids looked up at her, "we...do but i don't know if you can."

"Well...what do you need to do?"

The kid that was leaning on the door turned to her. "I locked myself out of the house and none of us can get the door open."

Gizlae looked at the building, "Why don't you go to the other side?"

The kid shook his head, "that's not how the building is set up. There isn't any connection from the front side to this side."

Gizlae looked over at the other kids, who all nodded to themselves. She looked at the door again then sighed, "if you move from the door I can take care of it."

The kid's eyes went wide. "You can unlock it?"

Gizlae shook her head, "No but I can move it for a moment. You can then walk in and I can put it back. After that, you can unlock it and let your friends in." She waved to the rest of the group.

The leader looked to the others who all nodded their heads, he then turned back to Gizlae.

"Sure," he said and moved away.

Gizlae nodded and stepped forward, snapping the door away in a flash of light. The kids looked at the now empty door frame.

"Okay you can go in," Gizlae said, turning to the leader but once she finished saying that, all the kids charged in at once. She just stared at the door frame while she heard noises and shouting from the other side. After a moment most of the kids ran out of the room carrying something. The last one out was the leader, who held two bags.

He smiled at her, "I didn't think you would be that helpful. Here's for your trouble," he handed her the smaller bag. She looked inside and saw a pile of money. She dropped it and looked up, only to find that the leader was now gone. She looked between the empty door and the bag. She could feel the tears building up as she looked between the two. Eventually, she picked up the bag and headed towards the exit of the town. She didn't know if she would be able to use the money but at least now she had it.

She walked until she was too tired and then just curled up on the ground. She didn't know if she actually slept or not but eventually she opened her eyes to see that the sun was now high in the sky.

She spent another day walking and didn't bother to pay attention to where she was going, or how long she was walking. She again just curled up on the ground to sleep. On the third day she bumped into someone who looked over her.

"Are you okay?" the man said.

Gizlae shook her head just watching him.

"Do you need a job?"

Gizlae watched him but didn't say anything still.

"Can I take that as a yes?"

She still said nothing, but she moved closer to him. He watched her for a moment before walking away. She followed him until she was led to a big mansion and then up into an office on the second floor.

The man sitting behind the desk looked up at the man that led Gizlae to the office. "What is it?"

"This girl looks like she needs a job." He waved to her and the leaves and sticks in her hair and the dirt on her clothes.

The man behind the desk nodded at her, "Are you able to get rid of some annoyances for me?"

"What kind?" Gizlae asked, talking for the first time in days.

"I have a group of kids that keep stealing my employees' stuff. I need them to be stopped."

Gizlae blinked for a moment looking between the two men. "So, I just have to make them move?"

The men looked at each other then shrugged their shoulders.

"That would work."

Gizlae nodded slowly, "I can do it," she whispered, This would be able to help make up for what she did a few days ago. They let her have a room to clean herself up which she graciously accepted. She took an extra day which they allowed because she claimed that she was too weak to do it. She tried to look around to learn anything about her employer but even asking his other staff members just gave her the same answers that he did.

They told her the location on the third day and she headed out immediately. She took four days to get to the place and another two days to scout the place to see if she could find anything about it. All she could tell was that there weren't any adults living in the building. That the older kids took care of the younger ones and that they brought money back once a day, usually a small amount around night time. Seeing all she needed, she planned to attack them the next day.

When the day finally came, she waited till the older kids left before moving towards the back of the building. She quickly entered the house, snapping away anyone that she saw. She heard the front door slam open but she ignored it as she had the other kids to worry about. She heard someone running towards her but she was focused on her job and knew she could take anyone here.

That was when she saw Kihakso, she hadn't thought it was really them at first. But as soon as they grabbed her hand the relief she felt from being told the truth was huge. The hugs and promise Kihakso gave her, were a comfort she didn't know she needed. The climbing over the roots and the waves they spent the night at was calming. Learning that Kihasko trusted her with such personal information because they thought of her as a friend had increased her trust in them. Even so she was still constantly looking over her shoulder until they had left the woods. They went more inland. After that Kihakso kept an eye on her, not letting her accept deals herself. Which she was fine with.

A month later Kihakso finally brought her to meet their younger brother Kympilej and Letrifda. The two were standing on the doorstep, Kihakso wanted to knock but Gizlae kept stopping them "Wait, I'm not ready," she kept whispering.

Kihakso chuckled, "It's my family that you're meeting. Why are you more nervous than I am?"

"I just want them to like me..." she whined, "and if you knock before I'm ready I-" but before she could finish what she was about to say a shout interrupted her.

"Kihakso, you're back!" the two turned to see Kympilej running up the street at them. Kihakso smiled at Gizlae before pulling their arm free to properly give their brother a hug.

"I said I would be."

Kympilej pouted up at him, "but it's been so long."

"It's only been a month."

Their brother sighed, "I can forgive you since you brought gifts."

"Who said I did?"

Kympilej's frown got bigger, "you said you would."

Gizlae chuckled before poking Kihakso in the shoulder, "you shouldn't go back on a promise, you know."

That made Kympilej look over at her. "Who are you?"

Kihakso waved at her, "this is my traveling companion that I told you about, her name is Gizlae," he then turned to her, "and this is my little brother, Kympilej"

She smiled at him and kneeled down to his height, "you know, since they didn't bring you any gifts, you could get back at them by telling me embarrassing stories about their past."

Kympilej looked between the two for a moment before smiling at her, "I can do that. I got a few, and what I don't remember, mama certainly does."

Kihakso covered their eyes, "Don't think about it, I got you both a gift. I just wanted to give them at the same time." Gizlae held up her hand for a high five which Kympilej happily finished.

The two were then let in and Gizlae had a wonderful time talking with the both of them. It was nice to see that even if Kihakso didn't have memories of their past life that they still had a happy connection to it.

They couldn't stay in that town forever though, so the two left to travel again after a week. They went back to check up on Kihakso family every now and again just to spend time with them. On one of their visits, Gizlae and Kihakso arrived when Kympilej and Letrifda weren't home. Kihakso moved to do some cleaning while Gizlae walked around the house looking at the gifts they had brought back from each trip. They had some cute cups for their gift this time that Gizlae was excited to show them.

By the time Kihakso was done with the dishes, the front door was opening. Kihakso moved to grab the bag Letrifda was holding. "Oh Kihakso , Gizlae I didn't realize you had arrived."

"We let ourselves in," Kihakso muttered.

Letrifda smiled, "you always can."

When Kympilej saw them, he rushed forward and hugged Gizlae. "You two are back."

She smiled down at him, "we are."

He looked up at her, "is it true you and Kihakso are dating?" Gizlae blushed and Kihakso almost dropped the bag they were moving to the table. "That's what mom said, she said it was obvious."

"This is the last time I share gossip with you," Letrifda muttered, shaking her head.

Gizlae, still blushing, looked over to Kihakso, who was still facing away from her. She then looked down at Kympilej, "that's...that's something we haven't talked about yet?" She looked up briefly to see Kihakso staring at her with wide eyes and a slight smile.

Letrifda looked between the two, "kympilej help me to put stuff away and then we can start on dinner, alright? These two are probably hungry." She moved to the kitchen, giving Kihakso a little push to move him closer to Gizlae.

"Okay!" He quickly ran to hug Kihakso before following Letrifda into the kitchen.

"Um..." Gizlae said, still blushing, looking anywhere but at Kihakso .

"You didn't tell him no."

"I...what?" Gizlae said, looking into their eyes.

"You didn't tell him that we aren't in a relationship."

"Well...I mean...you see..."

"Does that mean...you would like to?"

Gizlae couldn't look away from their eyes "I..." she wanted to ask them but knew they would want an answer first. She gulped before nodding, "I don't know how strong these feelings are, or how long they will last, but I would like to try," she whispered the last line but seeing as Kihakso had moved closer as she spoke, she knew they had heard her.

Kihakso slowly wrapped their arms around her and pulled her into a hug, giving her every opportunity to pull away.

"I want to give it a chance as well," they also whispered.

Gizlae nodded into their shoulder, wrapping her arms around them as well. They stayed there for a few minutes before joining the other two in the kitchen. No one commented on the blush on their cheeks.

A year later, the two noticed that they were starting to get hunted down whenever they went into a town, which made them more reluctant to go back to Dangrmon in fear that whoever was after them would find out about Kympilej and Letrifda.

The hunters seemed to be after a group of two, so they started going into town one at a time. It was her turn to get supplies but when she got to the planned location for their campsite, a fire was set up but Kihakso was nowhere to be seen.

She waited by the fire for a bit wondering if Kihakso had gone off somewhere and was going to come back. Once the sun went down, she lit the fire but Kihakso's disappearance worried her. She stood up, deciding to look for them herself. She concentrated on her clenched hand for a moment and then opened it to allow a small ball of light to form. With that, she started to walk around using the light from the small fire as a beacon to make sure she didn't go too far or get lost.

As she walked along the dimly lit surroundings she eventually ran into a group of men, "oh..." she took a step back from them as a man that looked to be the leader looked her over.

He frowned.

"Hey kid, are you lost?" One of them tried to speak up but the leader hit him before looking over at Gizlae again.

"Oh no...I'm fine."

"You're out at night in the middle of the woods. Most wouldn't call that fine," said the leader.

Gizlae took another step back, "I...I'm looking for my friend who I was supposed to meet."

The leader frowned. "That isn't good. What does he look like? We've been traveling between the towns today, so we might have seen your friend."

Gizlae took a small step closer, "Kihakso is my age, and has black hair."

The leader nodded his head, "oh yeah, we saw him getting taken away earlier today. We didn't know if that was his parents, so we didn't get involved."

Gizlae's eyes went wide, "someone took Kihasko?"

The leader nodded his head, "I don't know who took him but I could recognize them if I saw them."

Gizlae bit her lip. "Oh no, what if someone hurt them?" she whispered quietly enough so that the leader didn't hear.

The leader frowned, "You should camp with us. It might be easier to find him with more help."

Gizlae looked back at her fire, she had the supplies so she wasn't worried about camping alone but they had seen who took

Kihakso and would be able to identify them for her. She stood up straight, her mind already made up. She had to save Kihakso.

She nodded at the leader and he smiled, "wonderful we're living over this way." She followed them to a clearing filled with a mix of wooden buildings and tents.

"What do you all do?" she asked, looking around.

The men looked between each other before the leader spoke up, "We're traders. This is our main location since it is in the middle of a few towns. We trade among them."

Gizlae thought of the town she had got supplies from and the fact that there were also a few others close by, so she nodded her head. They eventually brought her to a room and she sighed as she lay on the bed. She was too worried about Kihakso to sleep that night.

The next few days found her just milling around the place. They had told her a few buildings she couldn't go into because their stock was in there and she accepted that.

It was rather slow progress, with a few men leaving each morning and coming back later in the day. The leader told her that he had them keeping an eye out for her friend and the kidnappers.

It was on her third day there that she got some info about Kihakso's kidnapper.

She was just spending time in the center of their little hideaway when one of the men that left in the morning came running up to the camp.

"Boss, we got one but she ran away"

"Who?" the leader asked but the minion looked at Gizlae then back at the leader. He nodded before turning to Gizlae "I'm sorry."

Gizlae blinked at him, "for what?"

"It seems we were almost able to catch one of the people who kidnapped your friend but they got away from us."

Gizlae gasped, "are they still nearby?"

The leader looked at the minion who nodded, "yeah she just ran from us. Some of the other men were following her but she ducked into the forest and we lost her."

"I'll go get her," Gizlae stated and before any of them could say anything, she took off the way the man came from. As she ran, she took a breath. This wasn't a power she used very often but she needed to find this girl. She let herself take in the light and everything it touched. She could feel the trees, of which there were obviously a lot of, but she could also feel something moving between them. Going in and out of the light that broke through the branches.

Gizlae stopped for a moment, trying to tell where the girl was going and when she saw that she was about to enter the clearing in front of her, Gizlae dropped the sense and moved to it. Waiting for when she could snap the girl away.

Gizlae waited for a few moments, and considered bringing up the senses again to see if the girl had moved a different way when she heard the snap of a branch. She waited for anyone to enter and when nothing happened, she called out, "You should come out."

"If I come out, I'm going to die," a weak voice replied. Gizlae's eyes went wide. She had only planned to snap to move her quickly. She needed answers, she did not want this girl dead.

"I wasn't going to kill you," she muttered but the girl must have heard her as she replied.

"I doubt that."

"I was only meant to capture you," Gizlae said with a sigh.

"Well, do it the normal way, not a magical one."

Gizlae nodded her head, "Alright I can do that," she stepped more into the clearing, looking around for her to enter. When she didn't, Gizlae called out again "I know you're nearby, I could just randomly start disappearing parts of the forest." Several moments passed before she heard a sigh and a girl walked into the clearing. Gizlae smiled at her, "great." She grabbed Ceaxtra's arm and started to walk down a path that led back to the hideout. She handed off Ceaxtra to the trader's men and headed to her borrowed room. It was only an hour later when she heard a crunching sound.

She ran to it, only to see Kihakso in the remains of one of the buildings she wasn't supposed to enter. The reunion with them was easy, with them offering their hand to her. After she got rid of all those liars, she had fun getting to know Ceaxtra.

The fight with Chabnorl was a surprise. And just to make sure they were safe, they left the town right away. The night had been fun sharing stories about Kihakso, even if they included her in the stories. They traveled for a day to make sure they were far enough away from Chabnorl.

Once they found a new town to camp out of, they decided to split up. Two of them went to town to get supplies while one stayed to make a camp. Ceaxtra was not as known as them it seemed, probably because she was so young. Since that was the case, she would go to town with one of them since it reduced suspicion. Gizlae was left to set up camp and found a clearing near a lake. She started to set up a fire pit when movement caught her eye. She looked up to see a group of men carrying a young boy that was tied up closer and closer to the lake. Her eyes went wide as she watched them throw the boy into the lake before turning away and leaving him.

She watched him struggle to keep himself up and she moved closer to try and see if she could help him. As she was moving closer, Kihakso and Ceaxtra arrived with the supplies. "Gizlae?" Kihakso shouted as they noticed her watching the lake.

Just as they shouted at her, the boy's head went under the water.

"Oh no!" Gizlae shouted, covering her mouth.

The other two moved closer to her and Kihakso put their hand on her shoulder. "You okay? What's going on?"

"Some men dropped a kid into the lake," she said, pointing to where the kid went under. "We need to go save him. He was tied up," she looked between the two before focusing on Ceaxtra, "please, we need to get down to him."

Ceaxtra looked between Gizlae and the lake before sighing, "let's see what I can do." Gizlae watched as Ceaxtra closed her eyes and everything was silent for a moment before the three of them were suddenly picked up by a wave of wind.

When they entered the water, there was a dome of air around them that kept them dry and made sure they didn't drown. Ceaxtra looked around the dome, "it's a good thing I practiced that bubble spell." She then looked at the other two, "I wouldn't touch the walls just in case this bigger version has the same flaw as the smaller version." It took a minute to find him as he had sunk down to the bottom of the lake.

"Oh no!" Gizlae whispered as she saw that the body was just lying there, "we should at least pick up his body. Maybe someone in town knows him."

Ceaxtra nodded her head and moved them closer to the body. When the air bubble was about to touch him the boy's eyes popped open and he stared right at them.

He awoke, his lungs didn't hurt but when he tried to breath in he couldn't. It still felt like he was floating but the feeling of wetness was gone.

"Such a sweet child."

He tried to open his mouth to speak but something pressed against his mouth. "Giving up yourself when your friend was supposed to." His eyes were open but yet there didn't seem to be anything around him, he certainly couldn't see the thing that covered his mouth. "You will be given another chance, and this time it will be twice as good as the first time. Your name is Awrosk. It is time for you to wake up."

He really didn't know what the person was saying but with what felt like a blink of the eye, he woke up surrounded by darkness with a pinpoint of light from the sun breaking through the water. He gasped and unlike last time this led to breath rather than choking.

He laid there for a moment enjoying the silence before trying to sit up. But his clothes were heavy due to the water they had absorbed so he had to take breaks as he walked to the edge. The weight was too much for him to swim.

He jumped when there were cheers as his head broke the surface. The lake he woke up in was surrounded by people. He struggled to get out of the water as someone ran forward to help him out. "You did it!" his friend, Alpfeno whispered, throwing Awrosk's arm over his shoulder, seemingly not caring if he got wet or not. "We had assumed when unlike every year, the water condensed a bit only a little while ago."

Awrosk gave him a smirk, "told you I would be able to become one unlike you."

Alpfeno rolled his eyes, "you still shouldn't have gone and asked my dad behind my back."

Awrosk was silent for a moment, "Did I? Sorry I don't remember."

Alpfeno's eyes went wide, "You don't remember?"

Awrosk shook his head, "I remember small moments with you but not much else."

Alpfeno frowned like he wanted to say something more but at that point they got in range of the other villagers and Awrosk was ripped from him and lifted above the group as they walked up the hill to town.

The day was a long one for Awrosk. He was forced to stay in his wet clothes as there were speeches from the mayor which was followed by a feast where people all over town provided the food. Even though all of it looked good, Awrosk could only eat a little of it. His stomach felt nauseous as if he hadn't settled yet.

Once the feast was done they brought him to his home but he frowned, he didn't remember much but he knew this wasn't where he lived. "This isn't my house." he said, turning to the Mayor.

The mayor smiled at him, "It is now." He waved to the house that was the most fancy on this street, "This is the House of Water. Made for you for whenever you arrived."

Awrosk frowned, "But I have my stuff back at my place ."

"We can get that for you later if you still want it."

With that, he was pushed into the house to get a tour. It was an hour later when he was laying in bed that he realized he didn't remember anything of the house and would have to find his way in the morning.

It took a few days of celebrating before the town calmed down enough to get his things from his old house. During those days he spent most of his time in his new house because anytime he stepped out his door, he would be crowded by people and dragged into the celebration. As fun as it was, it got tiring for him very quickly.

Because of this constant partying, he also wasn't able to see Alpfeno for a while.
Alpfeno announced his presence with the slamming of the front door.

"Those leeches," he muttered. "Acting like they cared for you your whole life."

He stomped into the room that Awrosk had been reading in. They had given him a bunch of books about water magic and he was hoping to read them all before trying anything.

"They hadn't?" he asked, making Alpfeno look at him with a heartbroken look.

"You really don't remember?"

Awrosk shook his head, "like I said I remember moments with you. I remember that you are my best friend and I am willing to do anything for you...but other than that... it's all blank."

Alpfeno sighed as he sat next to Awrosk, "I... didn't know this would happen." The two were silent for a long moment when Awrosk decided to go back to reading while Alpfeno stared at his hands. "Can I tell you something?"

"Of course. I don't remember anyone else so your secrets are safe with me."

"Actually it's about you," Alpfeno said with a sad chuckle. When Awrosk said nothing Alpfeno continued, "I was mad at you for what you did." When Awrosk still said nothing. Alpfeno covered his eyes and continued, "I was so mad that you took my place. It's an honor but it's more than that. You were going to die because of me. I didn't mind dying but I didn't want you to. I'm sorry you had to go through that."

Awrosk was silent for a long while before pulling Alpfeno close for a side hug. "that was why I had to do it. I felt the same and was determined to set it right. It might be an honor but that honor didn't matter to me, your life did." The two were silent after that. Awrosk went back to his reading, a little harder now with his arm still around Alpfeno, and Alpfeno crying for his lost friend.

It was the next day that staying in his house wouldn't be enough to keep him away from people. Outsiders who were interested in Children of the Elements started to come to town. They came to his house and knocked on the door to ask him questions. He answered what he could but with each answer they only got more interested.

Through these talks he heard that there might be other Children of the Elements, that two had been seen once or twice but he was warned against dealing with them as they had attacked their towns after waking up.

The other change that happened was a blacksmith had come to town. He seemed to stop Awrosk almost every day to test a cuff he was working on. Awrosk didn't understand till a month later when the cuff was placed on his wrist and he lost connection to the water around him. It was something he didn't even know he was noticing until now.

Awrosk frowned at the cuffs, "why are you making this?"

"Just a test to see if I can," the blacksmith muttered. Awrosk frowned as the man's eyes turned fully red. Awrosk had realized that this was only something he could see, that he was the only one who could see when people lied.

"I see..." was Awrosk's response as he stared at the cuff.

"Well, did it work?"

Awrosk was silent trying to figure out if he wanted to confirm or deny. "What is it supposed to do?"

The blacksmith was silent for a moment, "It's supposed to cut off your connection to your element."

"And why did you want to make this?" Awrosk looked back up at the man to watch him carefully.

The man shifted from one foot to another before standing up straight. "You heard about the other two, didn't you? How they attacked their towns the moment they could." Awrosk nodded, "What if they decide to attack others, people would be helpless."

"But they haven't," Awrosk watched as the man's eyes turned a full green.

"Yet."

Awrosk watched him for a moment longer before nodding, "yes they work. I can't seem to control any water once it was put on."

The blacksmith gave him a smile, "thanks for the help." he unlocked the cuff and Awrosk gave a small sigh as his contact with the water rekindled again. It didn't hurt when it wasn't there but it felt...empty.

The blacksmith seemed to pack up and leave soon after having gotten what he came for. Alpfeno spent a few days after he left complaining about how he used Awrosk but he didn't mind. It was true that he didn't know what the others were capable of and if those cuffs could help the town then he didn't mind.

Eventually the excitement started to die down and life went back to what he slightly remembered. Now that he had more free time, he started to head to the lake to practice, not wanting to cause any problems for the town members. He was slowly getting proficient with the different techniques. He tried to copy different spells that he read in the books. The one that he found the most interesting was one that allowed him to create weapons out of elements. There was a wide range of weapons to try. He was better at melee weapons rather than ranged. Melee would last four swings while ranged stuff only lasted one or two shots.

Most days he would practice until lunchtime when Alpfeno would bring him food for them to eat together. Alpfeno had to work, his father hoped he would take over the position of mayor. Lunch was the only time that the two could really hang out. Awrosk was wondering if that was a plan of some type. Alpfeno was the only thing he had that connected him to his past life.

One of these lunches was when Awrosk got the courage to ask Alpfeno about his past. Alpfeno really had two feelings when it came to talking about his past. Sadness at Awrosk's death or anger that it had to happen. This talk was surprisingly neither.

"I was wondering about my powers?" he said.

That made Alpfeno look up in surprise, "Your current ones? I thought the books were helpful enough?"

Awrosk shook his head, "No, I was wondering about my past life's magic. Did I have water magic?"

"No."

"Then why am I so good at it now?" he said, making a dagger out of water.

Alpfeno looked at it before sighing. He looked to the lake for a moment before speaking up. "It's because of what you used to have. You were a specialized mage."

"I was?"

"Yeah you could summon weapons. It's probably..."

"It's probably what?"

Alpfeno looked at him and sighed, "It's probably why the town let you stay here even though you were an orphan. If we got attacked you would have been really useful."

Awrosk frowned as he threw the dagger up and caught it on its way down, letting himself think about what Alpfeno revealed.

Time moved slowly for him, people came and asked him questions which he answered unless they were too personal. The town heard news about the outside from travelers who came to talk or learn about Awrosk.

He heard about some other children who had been seen. The two that stayed at their town had started to fight every other week. He didn't understand the reasoning but it seemed Pitydden and Whighridge were the ones that wanted the fight. Awrosk was happy that Harllpool wasn't interested in him fighting anyone. They seemed to mostly want to raise him above anyone else while also keeping him close. He hoped the two children that had to fight would eventually be free from that expectation. Maybe they could travel with the others he heard had been moving about.

It had been a year since the blacksmith had left town, they had taken everything with them. Awrosk thought that would have been the last that he saw of those cuffs. Then one day as he was walking back from the market a gang of men he didn't recognize pulled him into an alleyway.

Awrosk huffed at them, pulling his arm from their hold. "If you wanted to ask me questions you could have just talked to me. You didn't need to be rude and pull me here."

"Acting almighty because you think this town bows down to you huh? Think everyone will just because of that?" the man that grabbed him asked roughly.

Awrosk frowned at him, "No. Actually I wished that they would treat me how they used to, it's annoying to see so many lies said straight to my face."

"Well you won't have to worry about that soon."

Awrosk watched as the group of men moved to surround him fully. He frowned as he formed the water in the air into a sword, "Don't think just because we are in town I'm defenseless."

"You'll be defenseless for other reasons."

Awrosk frowned and was about to ask what he meant when he heard a click and the sword came apart in his hand. He looked to see one of the cuffs he helped to make and his eyes went wide. He was about to move away from them, trying to push through to get back to the street, when they charged at him. Grabbing him and tying his arms to his body and a gag over his mouth. They pulled him away from the main street and it turned out that what he thought was an alleyway was actually a small walking path between buildings.

They walked outside of town quickly and once there, they moved to the lake where this life had all started. He struggled against them trying to break free. He knew he wouldn't die but with how he was tied up he didn't know how long he would be down there and he didn't want to die of hunger.

In his struggles he thought he saw something white on the other side of the lake but before he could get a good look he was thrown in. Being tied up, he tried to stay afloat but the men wouldn't leave until he was under it seemed.

Eventually he got too tired and let himself slip under the water, even with the fear of starvation the silence was calming. He closed his eyes and let himself drift back to the bottom. He might as well take a nap while he tried to think of a plan to get out of this situation. He heard a far off splash but ignored it, thinking it was a rock that had rolled down the hill and had landed in the lake.

But as he laid there, he heard more sounds. They were muted like always in water, mostly talking but no one could talk that clearly in water. He felt the water near him move and heard a girl talking about a town to the left of him. He opened his eyes and looked hoping to see someone at the water's surface that he could convince to save him. Instead, what he saw was a group of three people, a boy and two girls, in what looked to be a bubble of air. He would have asked them what they were doing but the gag prevented him from doing so.

He looked to see if anyone else was around them, ignoring the people in the bubble since he couldn't really hear them anyways. When he saw that no one else was around, Awrosk looked back at the three. Eventually they seemed to agree on something and he was brought into the bubble of air. He shivered slightly because the wind made his clothing cold.

"Oh good, you're still alive." Gizlae said, moving closer to him. She touched the gag slightly and he turned his head to allow her to help him with it. "There, are you okay?"

Awrosk blinked at them, "Of course I am."

Gizlae frowned at him "You were tied up and thrown into a lake!"

Awrosk watched as they started to head to the surface.

"Yes." He looked at the others to find the two girls concerned and he frowned. "You all must be travelers since you don't know me."

"Are you famous?"

"You're outside of Harllpool talking to the Child of Water."

"Oh that's which one you are." Kihakso muttered.

"Why would someone throw you tied up into a lake then?" Ceaxtra asked as they got to the beach the three had entered from.

Awrosk sat on the ground while Gizlae untied him. Once he was free he held up his hand showing off the cuff. "They probably thought that cutting me off from water meant that I would drown."

"Do you want help getting that off?" Gizlae asked.

He looked over at them, "Can you help?"

Gizlae smiled, "I'm Gizlae Child of Light, this is Kihakso Child of Darkness and Ceaxtra is Child of Wind." she waved to each of them.

Awrosk frowned, moving away from them. He tried to form some water into a sword but when it didn't happen he glared down at the cuff, "So you were the ones to attack your own towns. Are you here to do the same to mine?"

Gizlae moved closer to Kihakso and Ceaxtra crossed her arms, "They deserved it and so does yours. I'm surprised you haven't done it yet." Ceaxtra said, moving a little closer to him. Awrosk frowned as he saw Ceaxtra's eyes turn green. It was the one flaw of his sight, the truth was based on what the owner believed as truth and was not based on what Awrosk believed.

"I chose to become this."

"Did you really?"

"My friend was chosen and I took his place." Three pairs of eyes went wide at his statement. Awrosk watched them for a moment before shaking his head and lifting his hand. "Can you get this off me."

Gizlae looked at the other two who were watching Awrosk carefully. She moved closer and took his arm. He watched her as she pulled him closer to Kihakso. "Yeah we can, Kihakso?"

Kihakso sighed, "You were complaining about Ceaxtra not being able to fight and yet you can't attack yourself." Gizlae rolled her eyes as she watched Kihakso used a spike created from darkness to strike the cuff off Awrosk's wrist.

Awrosk rubbed his wrist watching them all. He looked at the campfire for a moment. "If you promise not to attack the town you can stay the night at my house."

Gizlae smiled at the other two and Ceaxtra sighed, "They should die, but that's your choice."

Awrosk nodded his head then led them to the hill and up it. He moved quickly and the three quickly followed since he needed to make sure that the thugs that got him didn't do any harm to the villagers.

Once he got to the front gate he moved to one of the guards quickly. "There are some men that attacked me. I hadn't seen them before so they hadn't been here long. Maybe a day or two?"

The guard blinked at him, "did you leave?"

Awrosk shook his head, "not by choice."

The guards looked around him to see the other three coming up behind him, "and they are?"

He looked over his shoulder, Gizlae smiled at the guard while Ceaxtra looked around and Kihakso watched them carefully. "They're with me, so just let them in. I just need you to keep an eye out for who I mentioned?"

The guard nodded and waved the four of them though. They walked slowly, Awrosk leading the group as he pointed out smaller things quickly keeping an eye out. Ceaxtra frowned at how quickly they were moving. "You're doing a terrible job."

He turned to look at her, "what?"

"You're supposed to be giving us a tour but you're rushing us through the town."

"I'm trying to find the guys who attacked me," he growled at her. "What if they attack someone else?"

Kihakso shook their head, "if they attacked you they would only be aiming for other Children of the Elements, no one else."

Gizlae looked at them, "Do you actually want a tour?"

Kihakso shrugged, "He doesn't seem to want to do it."

Gizlae sighed and gave a small smile to Awrosk.

He glared at Kihakso before muttering to himself, "Fine…" He waved back the way they came. "That was the residential area. Nothing to really see there, the farther you go from the gate the poorer the area."

He turned back to the way they were going, "As we go forward we are going to hit the market area. Anything you need to buy is probably there."

He started to walk again, this time at a slower pace. Gizlae took Kihakso's hand and started to drag them along, giving them a once over before doing so. Ceaxtra stopped to look at something every once in a while, mostly at the art shops. Awrosk kept moving though, so she didn't have very long to look around each store. There were some smaller pieces that she wanted to buy but had to keep up with the group.

They entered a new section that was more open, it had an intricate fountain that was in the center of the plaza. It was that of a young kid, water flowing from both his hands upwards in a spiral before coming down into floating puddles. One at the kid's hip and one at their shoulder, created by a glass platform. Awrosk looked at it for a long moment before turning to the group, "a statue for the first version of the Child of Water."

Ceaxtra looked up at the big statue, "Something to work towards?"

Awrosk looked up at the statue, "I've never been good at pretty things like that. Never had an interest in it." He formed the fountain water into a sword in his left hand and a bow in his right. After he threw them behind him both deforming into water droplets even before hitting the fountain.

"Did you learn that from someone?"

Awrosk shook his head, "No, I read it from one of the books they gave me." He turned from then walking around the fountain and the others followed before they could ask anything more.

They walked through the rich area and Gizlae moved closer to Kihakso. They squeezed her hand and walked a little faster for her. Awrosk watched them for a moment before looking forward. "Was that good enough for you all?" He waved to the place that he now lived in, "Because this is where you will be spending the night."

The three looked up at the house, Ceaxtra's eyes were especially wide. "You live here?"

Awrosk shrugged, "They forced me to."

"Where did you live beforehand?"

Awrosk looked to the left before shaking his head, "It doesn't matter now. They knocked it down." He walked up to the door and opened it wide enough for the three to enter. He led them up the stairs and pointed out a room to each of them. "Just...stay..."

"Stay?" Ceaxtra said, "You can't control us."

"I just need...to be away from you." He turned away from them, "you can go where you want just don't follow me." He left after that. As soon as he was out of the house he moved quickly, going to a place that was now long gone. He took a deep breath as he entered the opening where his house used to be. Most of his memories were here, he had tried to fight the town knocking it down but they ignored all his requests. Even Alpfeno couldn't stop them, and most times, his requests were listened to.

He moved to where his backdoor used to be, it didn't look out to anything but it was the best place in the town to watch the sunset. He spent a while just sitting there, the sun was only just about to set when Alpfeno joined him.

"Heard you were a tour guide," he said with a chuckle.

"Also got attacked and attempted to be sacrificed again," Awrosk muttered.

"What!" Alpfeno turned fully to Awrosk. "Are you okay?"

Awrosk shrugged, "Even with my powers cut off I can still breathe underwater."

"Cut off power?"

"They had a cuff. Seems like that blacksmith made more of those, including ones for me."

Alpfeno tensed, "if he ever comes back here I'll...I'll..."

Awrosk chuckled, "I'll cheer you on." The two sat there for a while before Awrosk sighed, "we should head back. They probably need food."

Alpfeno chuckled, "Do you want help?"

"To deal with them or make the food?"

Alpfeno shrugged "a little bit of both." The two headed back, both were silent, just enjoying each other's company. Once they got to the house, Awrosk was surprised to see Gizlae and Kihakso resting in the yard. Gizlae was sitting, enjoying the sun with Kihakso laying their head on her lap. "So, are these the people you toured the town for?"

"There was another," Awrosk muttered, walking up to them.

Gizlae smiled up at them, however, Kihakso's eyes were still closed, "hello there."

When Awrosk didn't say anything Alpfeno spoke up instead, "It's nice to meet you, I'm Alpfeno, Awrosk's friend."

"And the mayor's son."

Alpfeno shrugged, "not that important. Do you have any preference for what you want to eat?"

Gizlae shook her head, "no but Kihakso likes spicy things. Do you need help?"

Alpfeno shook his head, "Nah we cook together all the time. You just stay here, you're a guest," he started pushing Awrosk to the door who rolled his eyes.

The two worked together to make something simple like a chicken dish. When they set up the table, they made sure that there was a bunch of spices for Kihakso to use. Alpfeno was the one to round up the three, finding Ceaxtra who had now joined the other two in the yard. It was a pretty quiet dinner even though Alpfeno wanted to ask a bunch of questions.

The next day Kihakso started the conversation during breakfast, "So since you knew about us do you know about any other kids?" he said to Awrosk.

Awrosk nodded, "easiest ones to find would be Fire and Ice. Their towns are fighting so they fight once a week."

Gizlae smiled at him, "Oh, do you know where their towns are?"

"They're kind of close so you can get there in two to three days. I can lend you a map."

"Or you could just show us," Kihakso said, tapping their plate lightly.

Awrosk shook his head, "No, I need to protect the town I can't leave."

"We need to stick together." Gizlae said with a frown.

"Why?"

"You were attacked already, we saved you this time but what about next time."

"I wasn't expecting the cuff, now I know."

"You should still come with us," Gizlae said, scooting her chair a little closer.

"I don't see any reason to do so."

Ceaxtra sighed, "you should probably just go along with it. They'll force your hand if not."

Awrosk looked at the three before sighing. "I'm only going with you till Pitydden, then I need to be back."

Gizlae and Kihakso shared a silent conversation turning to look back at Awrosk, "We'll agree to that. Maybe we can change your mind by then," Gizlae said with a bright smile.

Awrosk sighed and shook his head. He wasn't looking forward to this trip. He didn't have much to do but he did need to tell Alpfeno about him leaving. Awrosk stood up, "alright, I'll meet you at the entrance of the town in an hour. I need to go find Alpfeno and talk to him." He didn't give them the chance to say anything else as he left quickly.

He had a few places to look for Alpfeno but as he was making his way to the first location he found him looking up at the statue. Awrosk moved to stand next to him, "You know something?" Alpfeno said.

"I know a lot of things, what specifically did you wonder if I knew?"

"I always look at this statue every day."

"Why?"

"I'm trying to see how this is supposed to stand up against you."

Awrosk chucked, "You're the only one who sees me as better than this."

Alpfeno gave a sad smile, "What are you doing out so early?"

Awrosk looked up at the statue for a moment before crossing his arms, "I'm leaving."

"Oh, do you have something to do? Didn't think you would have plans for something?"

"...They need a guide to Pitydden"

Alpfeno turned to look at Awrosk for the first time since they started talking. "You're leaving town?"

He nodded, "For a few days, I'll be back though."

"You better be," Alpfeno said, crossing his arms.

"Want to come with?"

Alpfeno frowned and shook his head, "I want to but you know I have to stay here. Got my job."

Awrosk nodded, "I figured, don't get yourself hurt."

"Yeah, I'll keep the town safe for you." Alpfeno said with a smile.

Awrosk finally turned to Alpfeno, "No. that's my job. You should just worry about yourself."

"But what about the town, what about dad and everyone else?"

"Everyone doesn't matter. If I'm not here to protect the town then I don't want to chance you dying to keep it safe instead."

"I…"

Awrosk grabbed his shoulders and looked Alpfeno in the eyes, "I need you to promise me," he squeezed his shoulders. "If the town is in danger you need to keep yourself safe."

Alpfeno looked him in the eyes for a long moment then nodded, "I will try."

Awrosk sighed, "I need to accept that."

"And I need to get to my first job."

"I'll see you when I get back." Alpfeno waved before heading off. Awrosk nodded to himself, as he headed towards the front gate while the others should be waiting for him.

Awrosk sat at the front gate having a conversation with the guard as he waited. They didn't have a lot to talk about but the two did enjoy talking about different fighting techniques with the spear. Awrosk was expecting them to be early since they seemed eager to leave but the three definitely took longer than an hour to get to the gate.

He crossed his arms, "Do you actually want me to guide you or do you only want to waste my time?"

"We had to get supplies. It would have been nice to have a little longer than an hour to do everything that we wanted to do." Ceaxtra huffed.

"You took longer than planned because you were picking out artwork to buy." muttered Kihakso.

"Kihakso" Gizlae sighed, while Awrosk turned to glare at Ceaxtra.

"There were just too many good ones so it was hard to pick just one." She then turned to Awrosk "besides isn't that a compliment to your town?"

Awrosk was silent for a moment before nodding "You're forgiven." With that he turned and headed out of town.

Ceaxtra sighed as she followed him, "great another annoyance."

"Where are you going to put that anyways?" Kihakso asked.

"I'll find a place. When I pick somewhere to live, I'll find a perfect spot for it." she whispered the second part to herself. No one seemed to hear as no one made any further comments. They were following a road down the hill, it split with the right leading to the lake and the left back into the forest again. They took the left path. Once they entered the tree line Gizlae moved closer to Awrosk who was still in the front.

"So, will we be making a straight path to Pitydden?"

He shook his head, "we could but it would take more work since it would take us off the road." He pointed to the road they were walking on. "This will take us through two towns, the road eventually splits into two. With one going to Pitydden, the Town of Fire and the other going to Whighridge, the Town of Ice."

"And you said it will take two to three days to get there?"

Awrosk tried to see the sun through the trees but failed, "We started pretty early so we should reach the second town Gillabury by the end of the second day."

"Can you tell us anything about the towns that we will pass through?" Kihakso asked

"I know Gillbury is a craft town."

When he didn't say anything else Ceaxtra spoke up, "that's it?"

Awrosk frowned at her, "Seems I'm pretty useless, I might as well go back to town."

"No no" said Gizlae, stepping between the two. "It's fine, us three never have plans where we are going." Awrosk nodded and kept walking, Ceaxtra shook her head but didn't make any complaints.

After walking for a while, the trees started to thin out and they stepped out onto plains with a few hills here and there. The road went up and down them and when they got to the top of the hill, they could see a town in the distance. Every time they got to the top of another hill, Ceaxtra whined that they weren't there yet.

When they eventually got to town, Kihakso and Gizlae stopped outside town.

Awrosk turned to them, "aren't you coming in?"

"Well..."

"People are hunting us down, we shouldn't go into the town," said Gizlae with a sigh.

Ceaxtra frowned, "but if they are looking for you two then they probably don't know to look for four of us." She waved to them, "It will be fine"

Gizlae looked at Kihakso who nodded. She sighed, "alright we can give this a try."

The town was pretty similar to Harlpool so they managed not to get lost. They ate dinner at a small secluded restaurant but when they planned to go to bed, Ceaxtra stopped Awrosk. "Hey, could we talk?"

He watched her carefully. "What for?"

"I was hoping you could teach me how to fight?"

Gizlae gasped, "You agree with us that you should learn to fight."

Ceaxtra rolled her eyes, "yeah, yeah."

Awrosk looked between the three before nodding, "I can maybe teach you something, let's go to my room."

"Mind if we watch?" Kihakso asked.

Awrosk shrugged, "Sure."

They made their way up to his room and Ceaxtra sat on the floor while Gizlae and Kihakso sat on the bed. Awrosk frowned at the two before shaking his head and focusing on Ceaxtra. "What do you want to learn?"

"I don't really know." She looked at Gizlae and Kihakso "these two tried to teach me their fighting styles but one doesn't fight and the other isn't possible for me."

"I just don't think I explained it well," Gizlae said with a frown. Kihakso just crossed their arms.

"So," Ceaxtra spoke up before anything else could be said, "Just tell me how you use your magic and I'll see what is usable."

Awrosk frowned at that before nodding, "I can do the normal water magic but because of my past life I managed to create a new type of magic." Awrosk formed a dagger out of water in his hands. "I can make weapons out of water, I have tested them against actual weapons and they seem to be sharper and stronger. Though, when handling them I can't cut myself unless I will it." Awrosk looked around for something to cut but when he didn't find anything he sighed before turning and stabbing it into the door. It only went a little into the hardwood but it was still deep enough to hold it in place.

He waved for Ceaxtra to come over and she stood up to get a better look at the blade as he talked about it. "I start by forming the outline of the weapon I want to summon. Smaller weapons will obviously be easier but knowing the weapon or having handled it before is even better." He pointed to the handle before moving his finger along the blade.

"After that, I fill it with water to give it the proper weight and solidity." He tapped the blade "weight is important. Too light and the thing will shatter on impact, like hitting something with glass. Too heavy and you might not even be able to swing it or tire yourself out from using it or energy use."

"Energy use is the important one for us." Gizlae interrupted.

"It is?" Awrosk asked.

Gizlae nodded, "Yes if we use up all of our magic energy we die."

Ceaxtra's eyes went wide, "How do you know that!"

Gizlae waved to Kihakso "When we first met, Kihakso set up a spell that almost caused that to happen. The info I gained when I shook Kihakso's hand told me so."

"It was my first spell and I fixed it after you told me," Kihakso muttered.

"But that is why if you use too much magical energy you start to have side effects. It's your body warning you about your death coming," Gizlae said with a bright smile.

Ceaxtra blinked "so that's why..." she muttered to herself.

"Good to know," Awrosk said, thinking of ways to change his fight style now that he knew how truly limited he was. It was silent as Gizlae and Kihakso let the other absorb the information they just learned.

Eventually, Awrosk broke the silence turning to Ceaxtra, "do you want to try making something?" He didn't know how confident she was now after seeing it firsthand.

Ceaxtra nodded, "sound pretty useful if I can get it right, it would be nice to have a backup if anyone gets close." She moved back to where she was sitting to start working on a weapon, Awrosk moved to sit next to her.

Gizlae stood up "Well, I think I will be heading to my room. It's been a while since I stayed in a room for a night." They said their byes for the night to her and Kihakso left shortly after but not before he gave them a warning to not use too much energy.

The two decided that if Ceaxtra was going to use it as a backup then making a dagger would be the best option for her.

Awrosk formed another dagger for her to collect wind around trying to memorize the shape. That made it easier for her to get a similar outline even if it wasn't perfect.

While trying to get the weight right the two found that they had different preferences and Awrosk let her decide what was the right weight for her. After she had managed to make a slightly misshapen dagger with no help from Awrosk the two decided to call it a night.

The next morning Ceaxtra walked into the dining area to see that Awrosk and Gizlae were already at a table, "you're up early."

Gizlae smiled, "I get more energy when the sun is out."

Ceaxtra looked over at at Awrosk who shrugged, "I always get up in the morning early to try and spend some time with Alpfeno."

Ceaxtra looked back to Gizlae, "and Kihakso?"

Gizlae sighed with a small smile, "Kihakso has more energy at night so mornings are hard. Kihakso would prefer to be woken up close to when we're ready to leave."

Ceaxtra sat down, "so when are we leaving? And where are we going?"

Gizlae looked over to Awrosk who sighed, "We should leave soon, the town isn't too far away but since it is the major crafting town, you all might want to look around."

The three ate their breakfast slowly. Once they finished, Gizlae was the one who went up to wake Kihakso. They came down grumbling but took a bit of food to eat as they walked.

It took half the day to get to their destination, they spied it after climbing the last of crested hills that had blocked Gillabury from view. Awrosk sighing as they did so, "Do you know anything about this town?" Gizlae asked.

Awrosk shook his head, "only that this is a crafting town. One of the major ones from what I have heard."

"So you don't know anything else ?" Kihakso asked.

Awrosk shook his head again. The group looked at the town in front of them. It was bigger than most of the others that they had seen. Suddenly, they heard a rumble of thunder behind them. They turned to see a girl in a hat that covered her eyes who smiled at them.

"Oh...hello, most people don't come to the town from this direction. I'm usually the only one. What are you all doing here?" the girl said with a smile.

"We were coming from Harllpool."

The girl nodded, "Ooohhhh, not too many people come from that way."

Gizlae smiled, "Do you know much about Gillabury?"

The girl nodded, "yeah, I work as a delivery person for this town and Siverkept. Do you all not know about this place?"

Awrosk frowned, he didn't like that her hat was covering her eyes but he couldn't just ask her to remove it. "We are heading to Pitydden or Whighridge." He pointed to the others, "they wanted me to lead them there."

"But he doesn't know much about the town." Ceaxtra muttered. Awrosk turned to glare at her.

"Oh, going through the town shouldn't be too hard. They made it pretty easy to navigate," she said with a smile.

"Would you be willing to guide us through the town?" asked Gizlae. "If you aren't too busy."

She shook her head, "I'm not too busy." She pulled the strap of her bag a little tighter. "I do have a package or two to deliver but I can just do that at the same time."

"Wait, you really do deliveries between towns?" Ceaxtra said.

The girl nodded, "yeah, I like to run and Aphi says I have too much energy," she said with a chuckle to herself. "Since I'm your guide I should introduce myself, I'm Tesirew."

She felt a tingling all over her body, as if she had restless energy she wanted to use but found she couldn't move.

"You were the farthest one." A voice said above her. She could only slightly remember a challenge of some sort that she was trying to beat. "And she's already alive. You are a lucky one child."

"She? Lucky?"

"You will know her, and what she will mean to you when you see her. We know it."

"We?" She frowned, not liking the lack of answers.

"Hopefully your luck stays with you in this next one." She felt like someone was hugging her. "Your name is Tesirew, It is time for you to wake up." The tingling seemed to condense into her back and then she groaned. Blinking her eyes as she looked to the sky.

"Are you...okay?" A voice said to her left. She looked over still blinking trying to get her eyes to adjust. She saw a girl who looked her over for a moment before looking her in the eyes. That had been a mistake. She cries out as memories rushed through her head, of a life lived and lost and Tesirew couldn't help but cry now that it had ended.

Her crying seemed to draw the girl closer, since Tesirew felt a hand going through her hair. It took a moment for her to calm down but when she did she looked back up at the girl. "I'm so sorry."

The girl frowned, "for what?"

"For...how your life went."

"You know?"

"You don't?"

"Do you remember yours?"

Tesirew was silent for a moment, "oh...no..."

The girl smiled, "Then don't worry about it." She kept running her fingers through Tesirew's hair. She closed her eyes for a moment just enjoying the feeling for a while going once again over the memories she had just gained.

When she reached the end of them, she knew what Lightning had wanted. The girl had been betrayed by her sister, something Tesirew had experienced personally that she could never forgive. She opened her eyes to look up at the girl who smiled at her.

"I'm Tesirew, Child of Lightning."

"Nice to meet you. I'm Aphiqalena, Child of Earth." Aphiqalena frowned, "Are you feeling better?"

Tesirew sat up and turned to Aphiqalena. She was about to say something when her shirt started to fall off. Both of their eyes went wide while Tesirew crossed her arms to stop it from coming off.

Aphiqalena took off her jacket and offered it to Tesirew who put it on and zipped it up. "Thanks."

Aphiqalena nodded her head, "You were going to say?"

"I am feeling better. It's weird. When I looked into your eyes I saw all the memories of your last life."

Aphiqalena looked above her head for a moment before looking back to her, "so you don't see a number above my head." Tesirew shook her head.

"I see…We should rest here for a while. I don't know much about us but if we need food we should find a town."

Tesirew looked around, "I think Mithfield, the town of lightning is near here…we could go there if we need food."

Aphiqalena frowned, "Do you want to go there?"

Tesirew shook her head, "Not really."

Aphiqalena nodded, "Do you know what way it is? We can go the opposite way." Tesirew pointed behind her and Aphiqalena nodded before putting her hand on Tesirew's shoulder. "Then once you get some more energy we can move."

"Energy?" Tesirew stood up, "I have ssssoooo much energy. I could run laps." She ran the way they were planning to go and Aphiqalena had to close her eyes from the flash as well as her ears from the rumble of thunder. When she opened her eyes

Tesirew was gone. Aphiqalena looked around her before in the distance there was another rumble. Aphiqalena started to head that way when there was another rumble in the distance, after a moment there was another flash and Tesirew was now next to her. Aphiqalena rubbed her eyes

"I'm sorry," Tesirew said.

Aphiqalena shook her head, "No it's fine. Could you always do that?"

Tesirew shook her head, "Not that I know of."

Aphiqalena sighed but then smiled, "alright just don't leave me for good okay?"

Tesirew nodded her head, "Yeah I can do that. I can also do scouting for us."

Aphiqalena frowned, "Will we need that?"

"Maybe not..."

Aphiqalena chuckled, "I'll leave it up to you then."

The two traveled slowly away from Mithfield, with Tesirew taking off every once in a while to see what else was around them. The two didn't see anyone else as they walked, which they didn't mind.

As they were walking, Aphiqalena was the one to speak up, "you know about my past life right? Can I ask about it?"

Tesirew bit her lip, "depends on what you are asking about."

"Why?"

Tesirew thought about how she was going to say her answer, "You get this chance of a new life. I don't want the bad things from your past to come back and affect you."

Aphiqalena thought about it for a moment before nodding, "Alright I understand."

Tesirew smiled, "Then what do you want to ask about?"

"I don't remember anything but there is one person." Tesirew held her breath wondering who Aphiqalena would bring up. "A boy my age, he seemed to be like me though I don't know what we did? We kissed so I know we were close." Tesirew breathed out slowly as Aphiqalena blushed. "I think his name was Ko-"

Tesirew covered her mouth quickly, "You can't say that name."

"Why not?" Aphiqalena asked after her mouth was uncovered.

"They have two names. That's their real one that they only tell people who are close to them. You can never say that name." Aphiqalena nodded her head, "What did you want to ask about him?"

"What happened to him? To us? I only have the one memory with him."

Tesirew sighed, "I don't know. You two parted ways before you went to Termouron. He's probably still out there. We should keep an eye out but because of what you both did, he's good at disguise so it won't be easy."

"What we did?"

Tesirew chuckled, "You two were thieves. You met him when you both tried to steal the same thing."

They talked about the boy that Aphiqalena loved in her last life. It made the travel quicker and before they knew it they were standing at the entrance of the town. The town seemed a little busy as Tesirew looked around, she saw Aphiqalena looking at something over people's heads with a frown.

"What is it?"

"It's just...you and probably me have positive numbers above our heads. Everyone else has a negative number. And I don't know what that means."

Tesirew smiled, "we'll figure it out." They started to head into town and Tesirew enjoyed looking around until she met eyes with someone. When she did, their memories rushed into her head. She covered her eyes with a groan, she waited until the pain passed. It felt like there were now two folders in her head, one for this new person and one for Aphiqalena .

"You okay?" Aphiqalena asked. Tesirew nodded and tried to keep walking but again she looked into someone's eyes accidentally and groaned again as a third folder entered her head. "Are you sure?"

Tesirew sighed "I don't mean to but every time I look someone in the eyes their memories flood my brain."

"Then you should look at the ground so that doesn't happen," Aphiqalena muttered. Tesirew frowned but nodded. They walked down the main street for a while longer, Aphiqalena noticed that the farther they walked the sadder Tesirew became.

"What's wrong?"

"It's...nothing."

Aphiqalena frowned but didn't say anything, as they walked along she saw a shop that had the perfect item. She pulled Tesirew over before picking out a dark blue floppy hat. She placed it on Tesirew's head and watched as it flopped over her eyes. "There you go." Tesirew looked up and Aphiqalena adjusted it so the hat's brim blocked her eyes. "That should stop you from looking in others' eyes.

Tesirew gasped and looked around them quickly, her smile growing as she didn't gain any more memories. "It works." she pulled Aphiqalena into a hug, "How did you know it would?" She still couldn't see everything but being able to walk around without worry was nice.

Aphiqalena hugged her back, "I didn't know for sure but I'm glad it helped. We don't have much so hopefully we can arrange something with the owner to get it."

"You could always pull on your old life experiences and steal it," Tesirew whispered with a chuckle.

"I don't remember any of it though,"

"Well let's go check what they want for it," Tesirew said finally letting Aphiqalena go. Aphiqalena walked up to the main desk and smiled at the man, "Hi...this is going to be a weird question," she waved to Tesirew who was still wearing the hat. "We don't have much money, and we were wondering if we could do some type of trade?"

"What type of trade?"

Aphiqalena nodded her head, "We could clean, or organize?"

"or do a delivery" Tesirew offered.

"A delivery?"

Aphiqalena looked at Tesirew quickly before looking back at the man "yes. If you need something dropped off in town we can do it."

The man thought for a moment before nodding his head, "alright I need something dropped off a few streets over but you need to leave the hat."

Tesirew gripped the brim of it, "leave the hat?"

The man nodded, "I'm not letting you leave with both my stock and the hat. What would stop you from keeping the stock and the hat and running off."

Tesirew bit her lip and started to remove it when Aphiqalena touched her shoulder. "You stay here. I'll do it okay?"

Tesirew nodded as Aphiqalena took the items, got the location and headed off. waving at Tesirew as she left.

Tesirew looked around the store seeing different kinds of hats but none interested her like the one Aphiqalena picked out.

"Why don't you have any money?" The man's question pulled her interest back to him.

"What?"

"Why don't you have money? Everyone does. So why don't you?"

Tesirew thought for a moment trying to think of something before looking at the exit. She remembered what Lightning hopped for her and ran with that, "Our parents kicked us out." When he didn't say anything she kept going "my older sister," she waved to the door Aphiqalena left through, "our parents loved her," she knew that wasn't true for Aphiqalena but it was all she could think up, "but they hated me."

She pulled on the only memory she had of her life. She didn't know why she remembered that moment but it was probably her promise to herself to see the world. "They liked to beat me. Aphi only found out about it recently."

"I'm sorry to hear that kid."

Tesirew shook her head, "It's okay. Now I have Aphiqalena," she fidgeted with the brim of the hat. "I have really sensitive eyes, so...we need this hat so I can travel without problem."

"Ah so that's why you came here rather than figuring out lodging." Tesirew nodded. By that time they heard the door open and Aphiqalena walked forward handing a paper to the man.

"What's this?"

"A letter from the person I dropped off to. Just to prove I did."

The man looked over the note nodding his head. "I see, that was a big help for me."

Aphiqalena looked at Tesirew, "You were a huge help for me too."

The two started to head out when the man spoke up again, "If you need money I can help with that." They turned back to him, "I know a few other shops that regularly need things delivered and would be willing to pay."

Aphiqalena smiled at him, "Are you sure they'll pay us?"

The man nodded, "If you don't help they will have to wait at least a week till one of the usual messengers returns back to town."

Tesirew bounces on her toes looking at Aphiqalena, "Could we? We need money." she whispered.

Aphiqalena moved back over to the man, "Alright, can I have those names then?"

The man nodded and wrote them down, giving her a second paper. "Show them this as well," he said pointing to the second paper. She looked it over to see that it was just a note by the man stating that he was the one that gave them their information.

"Thank you," Aphiqalena said, taking both notes.

He nodded, "You did good as a big sister," Aphiqalena blinked at him before looking back at Tesirew who gave her a small smile.

Aphiqalena looked back at him with a smile, "Thanks." She turned back to Tesirew and the two left quickly. "What was that about?" Aphiqalena whispered to Tesirew .

"Well…we needed a reason why we didn't have any money. So I told him you're my older sister and you saved me from our abusive parents."

"And he believed it?"

"Well…I pulled on my only memory so it was easy to act appropriately."

Aphiqalena rubbed her shoulder, "I'm sorry."

Tesirew smiled up at her, "You have nothing to be sorry for." She then pulled on Aphiqalena's arm holding the papers, "Now, let's look at these names?" Aphiqalena nodded and the two looked over the names on the sheet. Each name had their store name next to it. There were only seven names but that should be enough for now.

They planned it out where they would go to one place together, Tesirew would then take the item to the shop while Aphiqalena would go to the next shop to pick up the next item.

After a day of running around town, they had enough money to stay for a week. They decided to move on to the next town after they were done to find more delivery jobs.

It took a few days for them to get to the next town. As they were walking along Tesirew heard a lady crying. She grabbed Aphiqalena's hand and started to lead her closer to the sound. The two found her in a small side path between two buildings. Aphiqalena stopped but Tesirew smiled at her and pushed Aphiqalena towards the lady.

Aphiqalena sighed before moving closer to the lady, "Are you okay?"

The lady sighed, wiping her eyes before she held up her bag, "I was trying to get this over to Bredsty but no one is heading that way."

Tesirew gasped, "Oh we just came from there, do you want me to bring it there?"

The lady frowned, "it's a few days travel from here. I wouldn't want to make a child take that trip."

Tesirew shook her head, "No, no, I got this." she held out her hands for the bag.

The lady sighed, "alright."

Tesirew smiled, "Where do you need this to go?"

The lady shook her head, "There is a blue house, right next to the main gate."

Tesirew nodded her head, "I'll be right back." there was then a rumble of thunder, before she was gone. Tesirew laughed as she started to run, one hand holding the bag tight and the other on her hat to make sure she didn't lose it. She would have to add a drawstring to it just in case there was a moment where she forgot to hold it down.

She loved the feel of the wind going through her hair and running was just so freeing. It only took a few minutes to get back to Bredsty, she stopped outside the town since the lady said the house she was looking for was just past the gate. She skipped through the gate and was glad to see that there was only one blue house in sight. She walked up to the door and then stopped, she didn't ask the lady her name or who she was supposed to deliver it to.

Thinking about it for a moment before shrugging and knocking on the door. A man answered the door and she smiled at him. "Hi there, are you waiting for a package from Whadenne?"

The man blinked at her for a moment, "Yes my sister lives there and wanted to send me something."

Tesirew held up the bag, "Wonderful this is for you." She held it out for him. He took it and looked inside to sigh in relief. "I suppose that means it's for you?" when he nodded she clapped her hands together, "Great. I'll go tell her." With that she ran off leaving a rumble of thunder behind her.

She made it back to Aphiqalena soon after that. She stopped in front of Aphiqalena with a smile "I did it. They told me to tell you thanks." They hadn't but Tesirew felt it was fine, they would have probably told her if she had stayed longer. She looked between the two when no one said anything. "What's-"

She was interrupted when Aphiqalena grabbed her hand and the two moved away from the lady.

"Guards!" the lady shouted. Tesirew frowned as she let Aphiqalena drag her away. She could see some guards run up to the lady and she was pointing to them while talking quickly. They were too far away for Tesirew to hear them, so she would have to rely on Aphiqalena. She wanted to ask but Aphiqalena was running and Tesirew didn't want to distract her.

They ran through the town and Tesirew could hear the shouting increase behind them. Aphiqalena pulled her through side paths and Tesirew got lost quickly since she couldn't see where they were going.

When the shouting got quieter Aphiqalena started to slow down. While they hid in some side path, Aphiqalena started to breathe heavily. "What was that about?" Tesirew said, rubbing Aphiqalena's back.

"That lady, you helped her and she thought that you had kidnapped me."

Tesirew frowned, "Why did she think that?"

"She realized that you were the Child of Lightning and that made her think I would only spend time with you if I was forced to."

Tesirew sighed, "We might want to hide the fact we are Children of the Elements then. I didn't know people would hate us."

Aphiqalena stretched, "Neither did I."

Aphiqalena looked around to make sure they were still unseen. "We probably shouldn't stay here. We still have some money left over from the last town so we should be okay for a while."

Tesirew bit her lip. "Once we get out of town I'll scout ahead to see which way we should go. We could go back to Bredsty but that might be annoying to go backwards."

Aphiqalena chuckled, "Yeah I want to keep moving forward."

Tesirew gasped, "I'll go check now." Before Aphiqalena could stop her Tesirew ran off again. She took her time making sure she knew exactly what town they would go to as well as which direction they needed to go.

She made her way back to where she left Aphiqalena. "I found it." She looked around but found that Aphiqalena was no longer there. "Oh no." she looked around quickly but saw no sign of her. "Where could she have gone?" she muttered. She passed back and forth before a shout pulled her attention.

"Hey!" a guard shouted walking up to her.

She looked up and accidentally met his eyes. She gasped as she held her head, his memories created another folder in her head. While she hated it he did have memories of Aphiqalena being taken away.

Tesirew shook her head before starting to move away from the guard, starting to take the path Aphiqalena had taken. "Hey!" The guard grabbed her arm and Tesirew crossed her fingers before turning to him. As he opened his mouth she spoke up first "What!" she shouted at him.

The guard blinked at her "Mama I-"

"I'm sorry I can't hear you!" she shouted at him.

"Mama you-"

"My ears are ringing from the thunder." She didn't think her thunder was that loud but she needed to get away from the guard and this was all she could think of.

"I-"

"Can I go? My head hurts from the thunder! You should catch that person, they're a menace."

The guard frowned when he looked at her and she waited.

After a moment he nodded and let her go. She smiled at him "Thanks!" she waved at him and turned the way Aphiqalena had gone in the memories. She could have jumped to the end but wanted to check if Aphiqalena dropped anything on her path.

As she walked along she couldn't help but beat herself up. They had decided to hide who they were and yet almost immediately she had caused Aphiqalena problems.

By the time she finished walking the path she wanted to cry but knew doing so wouldn't help her. She was currently waiting till it was nightfall so she could get Aphiqalena out of the building that they had locked her in. There were two guards in front of the door but she hoped there would only be one later or maybe someone who didn't seem to be as experienced.

When night fell, she waited till the guard changed before moving forward. The two guards looked at her before looking back forward as she came over to them.

She bit her lip not knowing if this would work. "Excuse me," she said with a smile at them

They looked at her for a moment before looking at each other, "what's a kid doing here?" the one on the left asked his partner.

His partner shrugged before turning back to Tesirew "what do you want kid?"

She held out her hands for them "I need help finding my parents," she said with tears building in her eyes. The guard on the left took her hand and she gave him a sad smile.

"We can't leave, we're guarding a dangerous person," the guard said with a frown.

She reached out at the other guard but he didn't take her hand. "They aren't far, I just saw them a few minutes ago." She looked up at him and held out her hand again. The guard looked at his partner who nodded, he sighed and took her hand as well. She took a breath covering it up as a sniffle before closing her eyes forcing lightning through her hands and into theirs.

They cried out in pain and tried to pull away but she held on even tighter. She waited till they fell to the ground. She didn't know if it meant fainting or death but she didn't care or have time to check. She needed to break Aphiqalena out before the guard change happened again.

She walked up to the door and knocked on it. "Aphiqalena?"

There was shuffling behind the door "Tesirew? Are you okay?"

Tesirew laughed, "Am I okay? You're the one that's locked up." Aphiqalena didn't say anything but Tesirew could imagine her shrugging.

"I'm sorry."

"Sorry?"

"We said we would hide and then I ran off which led them right to you."

"How did you...?"

"...I saw the memories of one of the guards that caught you."

Aphiqalena was silent and Tesirew looked at the ground resting her head on the door. "I don't mind. You were excited to help, I should have gotten away. I'm not mad at you, so don't worry."

Tesirew sighed before looking back up. "How do we get you out? Can you break the door down?"

"I could but it might draw attention and we might not be able to get away."

Tesirew looked back at the guard who she took care of.

"Hold on, let me check something." She looked through their pockets and soon found the key, holding it proudly above her head. "I can get you out." She quickly unlocked the door and sighed when she saw Aphiqalena smiling at her. Before either said anything Tesirew rushed forward and hugged Aphiqalena.

Aphiqalena rubbed her back, "we shouldn't stay here long." Aphiqalena looked around them but didn't see anyone. "We have but a few moments." She rubbed Tesirew's back with a small smile.

Eventually, Tesirew sighed, pulling away from Aphiqalena, rubbing her eyes, "I'm sorry."

Aphiqalena rubbed her head, "It's okay. Let's move from this town before people find out you let me out."

With no one else walking the streets the two made it out of town quickly. Tesirew led the way since she knew which town they were heading to next. It took them a day to get there, but it was the closest that they could go to. As they were walking along the main road, Tesirew frowned when she heard a kid crying.

"Do you need help with that?" Tesirew asked, pointing to the letter the kid was holding.

The kid looked up at her and she smiled at him. "I want to send this to mommy but I don't have the money."

"Well, where does it need to go?" Tesirew asked.

Aphiqalena moved over to them and grabbed Tesirew's arm, "What are you doing? Don't you remember what happened last time?" she said, pulling her away from the boy to whisper to her.

Tesirew smiled, "don't worry I have an idea," she whispered before looking back at the kid "So where does it need to go?"

"My mom lives in Gillabury," he said, holding the letter out to her.

Tesirew nodded her head, "I see. Do you know where that is?" she asked the kid taking the letter. Aphiqalena still didn't know what Tesirew's plan was but didn't speak up.

The kid nodded, and he pointed in the direction they were heading. "It's that a way," he muttered

Tesirew nodded before turning to Aphiqalena, "think you could find an inn for us while I do this for the kid?"

Aphiqalena frowned, "how long do you think it will take? We don't have much money left."

Tesirew frowned, "I'll bring some money back with a return package," She turned back to the boy with a smile, "Could you show her an inn we could stay at and you should return tomorrow so I can give you a return message?"

The kid nodded before moving down the street, looking at Aphiqalena expectantly. "Are you sure?" Aphiqalena asked. She started to move down the street and Tesirew followed since they were going the same way.

"Yeah, don't worry. I've been thinking about this while we traveled." The two saw the kid take a side road and they waved as they parted ways. Tesirew skipped as she made her way through town. She looked around as she did. There were some shops that looked interesting that she wanted to visit when she came back.

Once she left the town she kept walking for a while. Once she could still see the town but no people were present she started to run leaving the thunder behind her. She looked around to make sure she didn't miss the town just in case it wasn't directly in front of her.

After a few moments, she saw buildings appear on the horizon to the left. She turned in that direction hoping it was the right town. Once she saw the buildings a bit better, she slowed down. She started to walk towards the town taking out the letter to look to see if it had an address that she forgot to ask the kid about.

Smiling when she saw that it did, she moved a little quicker to the town. Once she got to the gate she moved over to the first guard she saw. "Excuse me?"

The guard nodded at her, "what do you need?"

She held the letter out to him, "I'm here to deliver a letter for my friend but I've never been here before, could you please tell me how to get there?"

The guard took the letter and looked it over. "This will be easy to get to," he said as he pointed down the main road. "You need to go past all the artisans' shops. After that there is a big building that splits the road in two. You want to take the left road. It should be on your left after a few more houses."

Tesirew took the letter back before skipping off down the road. Since she had arrived earlier in the day, she didn't need to rush and spent some time looking at each of the artisans shop. She hoped she could show Aphiqalena this place. Eventually, she made it to the big building and her eyes grew wide when she saw that it was a huge trading market. The building was really just a roof with a bunch of pillars.

She sighed before turning left, watching the numbers on the house to find which one she needed to stop at. She moved quickly when she found her destination, knocking on the door a little harder than she probably needed to. On the third knock the door was opened by an older woman. "Yes?"

"Um…are you…" she looked at the letter to read her name, "are you Vipdrea?"

Vipdrea nodded slowly, "yes?"

Tesirew smiled, "Oh great." She held the letter out to her. "This is a letter from your son." Vipdrea slowly took the letter with wide eyes before opening it quickly. Tesirew looked around as the women read the letter, wanting to give her a little privacy.

Once she finished, she pulled it to her chest and sighed. Looking at Tesirew, "He's such a sweet child. I miss him so much. Thank you for this."

"No problem. I'm glad I could help." Tesirew turned to leave when Vipdrea spoke up.

"One last question."

Tesirew turned back to her, "are you planning to go back to Gillabury?" Tesirew nodded, "then could you wait for me to write a reply?"

Tesirew nodded again, "I'll be here till tomorrow morning, so you can find me at the inn sometime before then. My name is Tesirew." Tesirew thought for a moment, "actually could you tell me where the inn is?"

Vipdrea nodded, "If you make it back to the market," she pointed the way Tesirew came. "It's at the end of it, so you have to go through all of them."

"I see. I did want to look through that place as well so that's perfect." She waved as she went back to the market. She made it to the inn after rushing through the market, she then counted how much money she would have left after paying for the one night she would be staying here.

She went back to the market after she was done and spent a while looking at different booths. She was looking for something she could buy for Aphiqalena. She spent a few hours before moving over to the crafters hoping she could get another delivery to Gillabury to make some money for them. Since she wasn't thinking she wasn't looking where she was going when she suddenly ran into someone. Her hat was knocked off and she covered her eyes. "I'm sorry," she heard Chabnorl. Before she could stop him, he grabbed her arm to help her stand. When she was standing up, she accidentally looked him in the eyes.

She flinched as the memories flowed into her head, grabbing it as she watched and remembered all of it. Her throat squeezed tight as she found out about the death of Rohgren.

The two were silent as she steadied herself. She took a few slow breaths, "I...I need my hat...Do you know where it is?" she said, looking at the ground.

He looked around, seeing it a little bit away from them. "Let me get it." When he was sure that she could stand on her own, he went over and grabbed it. Tesirew was still struggling to breathe. She knew what Rohgren went through, having lived it through as Aphiqalena. She needed to say something, she just had to.

She looked up when she heard his footsteps approaching. He held her hat out for her and she took it slowly, still trying to think of what to say. She held the hat tightly in her hands, "Sorry,"

"For running into me? It's fine."

"Not for that," she whispered.

Chabnorl frowned, "what for then?"

"For what you had to go through." She looked up at him with tears in her eyes. She placed her hat on her head and took off as quickly as possible. She didn't mean to but she ran too fast, needing to get away from him. She left in a rumble of thunder and flash of light. She ran to the edge of town, only stopping when she could only just see the buildings. She was breathing heavily once she stopped, not because of the running but because of the memories she just saw. She felt bad for him but at the same time, he wasn't someone she wanted to associate with. His current goal of destroying the different towns of elements was something she was okay with, but she was worried that his anger would eventually turn to Aphiqalena and her.

She sat down on the hill she had stopped on and watched the sunset in an effort to calm down. She didn't know what they would do but she would have to inform Aphiqalena tomorrow. She waited till nightfall before sneaking back into town and going back to the inn.

When she was walking by the front desk, she was stopped by the innkeeper. "You're Tesirew right?" Tesirew nodded her head, "this came for you as you were out." He placed a letter on the desk and she nodded, picking it up and putting it away. She wanted to make sure she didn't lose it.

She went up to her room and frowned as she lay on the bed. She got freaked out by bumping into Chabnorl which had distracted her from getting another delivery. Now that she had the letter, she'll have to try and get something else tomorrow.

She woke up with the sunrise but stayed in bed for a while, enjoying the comfort of the bed. After an hour or two of just lying in bed, she begrudgingly got up, deciding to skip breakfast to look for other deliveries before she left town.

She started with the marketplace but when no one needed a delivery to Siverkept so she moved on to the artisans' shops. After checking out each place she was able to set up two deliveries. They gave her a bag full of items and told her she would get paid after she dropped them off. She was more than happy with that arrangement, since Aphiqalena was the one who held most of their money anyways.

She walked outside town fixing her grip on both bags. She would need to get a bag to hold stuff on later if this worked out and Aphiqalena agreed with her plan. It was a quick run and she made sure to stop outside of town. Once she was walking again, she went along to the two locations that she was supposed to deliver to.

She didn't get as much money as she hoped but she got just as much as they did in the first town. After that, she started to look around town to see what it had to offer before the town actually woke up. She didn't know where she would be meeting Aphiqalena but she knew how to draw her attention later today.

She was heading to the entrance of Siverkept again, feeling a little hungry when she heard Aphiqalena's voice, "You're back pretty early."

Tesirew smiled and turned to her, "I got here earlier and already dropped off two deliveries. I made as much as we did in the last town, take a look." She handed the bag over to Aphiqalena before going in for a hug.

Aphiqalena seemed to stiffen then relax, rubbing her back. "Good, we can use these for supplies once we figure out where we are going."

"Where did you stay last night? And do you know where that kid is?"

Aphiqalena nodded, "Seems his dad owns an inn. They let me stay there cheaply. It's this way."

The two walked in silence for a while, Tesirew looking around. "Hey, Aphiqalena?"

"Hmm?"

"Do you like it here?"

Aphiqalena shrugged, "Well it's quiet. The people seem okay. I've only been here a day though, why?"

"Well, I was thinking. We should find a town we like and buy a house. I can do deliveries between towns and you can do them inside the town, or maybe take another job that you find interesting."

Aphiqalena watched Tesirew as she bounced in place, "you okay with that? You have so much energy I don-"

"That's why the deliveries between towns would be my job, it's the best. It means I can run pretty much every day and if we live in a house, I won't have to fake a day's travel. I can just do it in one day and go back home without either town knowing."

Aphiqalena watched her for a moment more before heading towards the inn again "I'll think about it."

Tesirew smiled as she skipped along. Her smile grew when she saw the happy tears from the Gemhidl after getting a letter from his mom.

After spending a week there the two did decided to live there permanently. They had made friends with the Gemhidl and his father, Rujthij who then helped them out by introducing them to people around town. Aphiqalena went through the work of buying the house, since she was the older of the two, while Tesirew did at least one delivery a day or more, depending on how many were available.

The two had gotten into a pattern. Both would wake up around the same time. After breakfast, they would split ways, with Aphiqalena going for her deliveries while Tesirew headed off to Gillabury to drop off the deliveries she picked up the night before. Usually, after checking all the stalls to see if there were any return deliveries, she would go back to Silverkept but this day, things went slightly differently.

Tesirew was walking along the aisles looking for another delivery or two for Silverkept when she saw a group of people at a specific booth. This one was known for selling the works of local artisans that did a mix of crafts. They used the store only for custom orders and the booth for their bulk items.

Tesirew walked up, smiling at the lady who ran the booth. She was one of the two owners. "Such a big crowd today. Are you having a sale?"

The lady chuckled but shook her head. "We are trying to come up with a new bulk item but haven't heard anything good." Now that Tesirew got a good look at them, she could see quite a few people standing there were employees of hers.

"Well, what are you trying to use?"

"Something metal we got a big stock of and would like to use it somehow."

"Not a lot of custom orders with it?"

The lady sighed, "It was for a custom order but we ordered the wrong amount."

"Oh, sorry to hear that."

"It will be okay if we can figure out something else that we can make with it."

Tesirew looked along at their booth. While she couldn't think of a whole idea she could maybe come up with a new idea of something they already sold. Her eyes landed on the suncatcher and she blinked, "What about butterflies?"

"Hmm?"

Tesirew took a moment to think of how best to word what she wanted to say without giving too much away. "The children of the elements have a butterfly on them right?" the lady nodded slowly. Tesirew pointed to the light catchers they already had on display, "Well, why don't you make a butterfly pattern like his."

"We could, but what about the other kids?"

Tesirew shrugged, "Just guess the colors or maybe pick ones that look good together. Personally I like dark green and blue or maybe iridescent and white." Tesirew frowned, "that second one might be hard."

The lady smiled, "Since you've given us such a good idea, I'll make sure we make it, even if it's only just one for you."

Tesirew's eyes went wide, "really?" When the lady nodded, she gave her instructions on which wing she wanted what color, so she would get exactly what she wanted. The way home seemed to be twice as quick as normal since she was so excited.

Aphiqalena started as a delivery person for in town deliveries but also took a side job of babysitting since she enjoyed spending time with the kids. It took them a few months of them working their new jobs to eventually afford a house of their own. Soon after, because of Aphiqalena's babysitting, their house became the local hangout. Even if it was only the two of them they got a big house with five bedrooms in case they needed to watch kids overnight.

Tesirew seemed to be the only one to take her path between towns. It seemed to be a side path that most didn't take, which meant that she was surprised when she stopped running and four people stood in front of her looking over Gillabury. She held her bag tighter, agreeing to be their guide while making the two deliveries that she had to do today. "Since I'm your guild I should introduce myself I'm Tesirew."

The older girl smiled at her, "I'm Gizlae," she then waved to the boy standing next to her, "this is Kihakso." Then the two standing a little farther away, "the girl over there is Ceaxtra and that is Awrosk." Tesirew nodded her head at them.

"Well then I'll need to stop at some of the artisans to drop off my stuff and get paid." The group nodded letting her take the lead.

"So this is Gillabury. It's where a bunch of artisans got together and created their own town." They went through the entrance of the town and she pointed to places as they passed them. "The very first places were the blacksmiths and things to go along with them." She pointed to the blacksmith on the left and then to the stable on the right.

She pointed to the right after the stables, "There are a few different seamstresses and the town put them all in the same place to make it easier for them to work together on bigger projects." She turned left after the blacksmith shops, "This is the main leatherworker. They mostly deal with armor while the others all work on clothing and furniture." She then entered the leatherworkers place holding the door for the four to follow her.

The others dispersed to look at the armors around the shop while Kihakso followed her. She walked up to the counter with a smile, "Got a delivery for you."

The clerk smiled at her, "Another one?"

"Yeah, you seem to be getting a lot of things from Siverkept. Are you making a big order?" Tesirew took her bag off and started to dig into it.

"A very custom order."

"Oh that makes sense," she said, taking out a dark black leather. "This is a really pretty color though." She placed it on the shelf and the clerk started to carefully look it over.

"And we just asked for this three days ago." Once the clerk was satisfied, she moved over to the cash register, pulling out some money and placing it into a bag before handing it over to her, "Fastest service around."

"Glad to be of service. Do you happen to need a return delivery?" she said as she put the money into her bag.

The clerk shook her head, "No but I think you'll have another delivery in a few days since we have a few more colors coming in."

Tesirew nodded as she put her bag on, "Then I'll see you in a few days." She waved as she walked away, Kihakso followed her again.

"Do you do many deliveries here?" he asked, watching Gizlae look at the different pieces while the two waited by the door for everyone.

"Not normally. Usually it is only once a month. Though I sometimes do have some deliveries every few days. I still have another delivery to the glass blowers."

Ceaxtra's eyes went wide and she moved closer to the two, "Glass blowers? What do they do?"

Tesirew smiled, "You can watch them while I drop off the supplies." Ceaxtra's eyes went even wider. "Can you get the other two so that we can go there right away?" Ceaxtra nodded and they left, not having anything else to look at.

After they left, they continued down the road. They passed a few buildings and Ceaxtra walked quicker than the others. Tesirew stopped by the first build on the right after the seamstresses. She chuckled as she watched Ceaxtra, whose back was turned to her.

"Why did you stop?" Ceaxtra pointed down the street. "I want to go see the glass blowers."

Tesirew nodded, "Yep that's here." Tesirew opened the door for them to go inside. Ceaxtra ran quickly inside, Gizlae chuckled before grabbing Kihakso hand and pulling them inside. Tesirew followed the group in, waving to a fenced off area where a lady was currently making a rainbow-colored vase. Ceaxtra leaned against the fence to get a better look, her eyes going wide when she saw them using their breath to expand it.

Kihakso watched Tesirew as she walked over to the desk and talked to the clerk before trading a box for some money.

Gizlae moved closer to them, "Don't trust her?"

Kihakso shook their head, "Too nice, deciding to guide us after just meeting us for nothing?" he whispered.

"It's not like we're causing her trouble by asking her to do this," Gizlae whispered. Kihakso frowned as they watched Tesirew talk to the clerk. They stayed like that until the artisan was finished with the vase. Ceaxtra sighed as she watched them place the finished vase on the shelf.

Tesirew walked back over to them with a chuckle, "Are you learning how to make them?"

Ceaxtra turned to her, "No...not that I know of," she said with a frown.

"Oh, but you seemed to really like it, though. I had assumed you were learning about it."

Ceaxtra shook her head, "No this is the first time that I've even ever heard of it."

Tesirew smiled, "Well if you plan to spend time in this town, the clerk is usually willing to talk about the craft. And all the guys when they aren't working are willing to talk as well." Ceaxtra turned to look at the vase once more.

Gizlae smiled at Tesirew, "So, have you finished your deliveries?"

Tesirew nodded, "I have but I need to check the marketplace for any return deliveries. So you can follow me there and I'll show you the best inn in town." Before they could say anything she waved at the clerk and then left for the door. Ceaxtra sighed and followed Tesirew out of the building.

Gizlae pulled Kihakso along with her to catch up with Tesirew.

"So, are there any stalls you always check?"

Tesirew nodded, "Aphi really likes some of the bread made here, so I try to always get some for her."

"Aphi?" Gizlae asked.

"Aphiqalena. She's my older sister; we live together. She doesn't come here often, so I want to get her stuff to make her smile when I go back home."

"Why doesn't she leave?"

"She doesn't like to travel as much as me, so she keeps the house clean and I bring her stuff."

"That reminds me, I need to get something for Kympilej," Kihakso muttered.

Gizlae turned to them, "Oh, what should we get him this time? He loved the book we got him."

Kihakso turned to Tesirew, "Are there any stalls that sell unique stuff in this town?"

Tesirew laughed, "With so many artisans here there are multiple unique items that mix more than one together." She walked them along aisles of merchant stalls pointing out items that were made by one or more artisans. Gizlae was listening for the most part but her eyes were drawn to one booth. She let go of Kihakso and moved over, looking at what they had for sale.

"What are these?" she asked Tesirew. They were little metal butterflies with wings in different colors that were filled in with glass.

"Oh," Tesirew moved to her side, noticing the merchant talking to another customer. "You know how it is well known that the Child of Water has a butterfly tattoo after he woke up?" Gizlae nodded, "Well, this is what I recommended when asked what this stall should make next."

"And these are?" she looked them over carefully.

"Well, I thought maybe the colors meant something, so I suggested just a bunch of random colors to guess what the other children of elements might have." Tesirew was looking at a pair next to each other, one had the left wing dark green and the right wing was blue. Another butterfly had the left wing iridescent and the right wing white. "Even if they aren't right, it's been a big hit." She looked up with a smile.

"I see," Gizlae looked over them more carefully. Eventually she found what she was looking for: a butterfly with the left wing lilac and the right wing black, the second had the left wing that was white while the right wing was light green. She smiled as she held the two up, looking at the colored beams of light that passed through the wings. The wing patterns weren't right but she felt Kympilej wouldn't care about that.

She waited for the merchant to finish up before paying for both, asking that they be packed extra carefully so that they would be safe during travel. She hoped Kihakso would love the two just as much.

Once her gifts were in her bag, she hurried to catch up with the group again, taking Kihakso's hand right away.

They looked at her, "Found something?"

Gizlae smiled, "Yep, I hope you both love it."

"He probably will."

Gizlae chuckled at them "And you're a harsher critic?"

"My brother deserves the best, so of course I am." That made Gizlae laugh loudly, ignoring what was being said around them.

Once they were done looking through the marketplace, Tesirew led them to the inn behind it.

"And here is the best inn in Gillabury...Well really the only one but still the best."

Ceaxtra opened her mouth to ask something when an explosion in the distance interrupted her.

"What was that?"

Tesirew sighed, "Probably the Child of Fire and Ice fighting again."

"Why are they fighting?"

Tesirew shrugged, "From what I heard, the towns hate each other and make them fight."

Awrosk frowned, "It shouldn't be that way."

Another explosion happened, and Tesirew shrugged again, "They can't all be lucky like the Child of Water I guess."

"We have to stop them before they get hurt," Gizlae said running off down the street to the left

"Wait Gizlae...you'll..." Kihakso huffed before following after her.

Ceaxtra looked at Awrosk with a sigh, "Come on, you still need to guide us to the fight at least," she said before running off after the two.

"I..." but she was gone before he could even finish his sentence. He turned back to Tesirew, "Where is the fight happening?"

Tesirew smiled at him, "Either street will take you there since they fight in the middle. Once you leave town you'll be able to see it. Their fights have left the area pretty barren."

Awrosk sighed but nodded, "Thanks for guiding us."

He then took off the other three. He didn't want to be there but he wasn't the type to go back on his word either.

"Be safe!" Tesirew shouted, waving at his retreating back.

Once she was at the edge of town, Gizlae stopped, letting the rest catch up to her. Kihakso grabbed her arm, "What are you thinking?"

"What if they hurt each other?"

"What if they hurt you?" Kihakso asked her, holding her arm tighter.

"It will be fine." She looked at the land around them to see pillars of ice jutting out of the ground everywhere. The ground was soaked from all the water while some places were scorched from the fire. "No one is here now."

Ceaxtra looked around for a moment before pointing, "Actually there is someone here." The others moved closer to see a girl lying on the ground with her eyes closed.

"Are you okay?" Gizlae asked.

The girl sat up quickly, turning to them with her arms raised, "You are here for round two already."

She blinked at them, "wait...you're not Aylnivi...but..."

She looked at them more carefully, "you're like us...are you here to fight me?"

Gizlae shook her head, "No, we were here to stop the fight."

"How did you know we were like you?"

"You all have a colored filter just like Aylnivi...though it isn't the same color."

She woke up feeling a warmth, it made her want to squirm but her body wouldn't move. "Hush now child. You don't need to fight it any more." Hands were placed on either side of her face. Whoever was touching her sat in front of her head.

"What was I fighting?"

The voice sighed, "A town that wanted to honor me."

"Did I take any out?"

"The one that caused you to be picked."

"Did they deserve it?"

The voice was silent for a moment. "You seemed to believe so." She tried to nod her head but it didn't move. The voice chuckled, "I hope you keep that spirit in the next one."

"When will my next life happen?"

"Your name is Vadixas and it is time for you to wake up." was the last thing she heard before the warmth was gone and she was looking up into the clouded sky.

She looked around her as she sat up. The ground around her was burnt black in a ring around her body. She could see people looking at her and whispering to each other. She couldn't tell what they were saying but with their eyes were wide as were the smiles on their faces; based on this she assumed it was good.

She stood up and looked around but no one came closer to her.

"Hello?" she shouted to the group but that made them take another step back. She frowned at them, wondering if she had done something to make them mad. She looked around her at the burn marks, "Oh did I do that?" she looked up but no one had moved, "I'm sorry?" she shouted to the group. Suddenly the group parted and an older woman walked forward. She looked at Vadixas as well as the burn marks around her before giving a small smile.

"You are awake. I am glad to see it."

Vadixas took a step towards her, "I...I seem to be yes." She looked at the group around them who were all looking at the old women.

"Um...who are you?"

The lady moved closer to her, "I'm Gihmea, the ruler of this town."

"This town?"

Gihmea frowned, "Do you not remember?"

Vadixas shook her head, "No...I remember..." She looked at her feet, she remembered the pain her father had caused her and what she did to him to get herself freedom. She didn't know how long it's been since then or what has even happened since.

Gihmea frowned and Vadixas moved away from her before Gihmea sighed. "Then I will inform you. If you would please follow me."

Before the Vadixas could say anything, Gihmea started walking away. Vadixas looked around once more at the crowd that was still watching them before following the older women.

The walk to Gihmea's house was silent, Vadixas not wanting to make her angry. The house Gihmea lived in was the biggest she had seen by far, being four stories while all the other houses were only two stories at most. Gihmea led her to a living room and indicated where she should sit. She sat across from her.

The two sat silently staring at each other for a while, "um..." Vadixas started but Gihmea interrupted her.

"So you said you don't remember stuff from before?"

Vadixas nodded, "Not much...just moments with my father and they weren't..."

Gihmea nodded, "We are deeply saddened about what happened to you. Had any of us known what was going on, we would have stopped it."

Vadixas knew that all of her memories were just her and her father so she nodded, "No, that's...okay..."

Gihmea nodded "Now then," her smile dropped as she sat up straighter, "This is the town of Pitydden. You are the Child of Fire."

Vadixas nodded, "Yeah I talked to the Element of Fire. Though I don't know how that happened or why I woke up in the center of town."

Gihmea shook her head, "That doesn't matter." Vadixas sat up straighter with how sharply she said that, "You are here because we need a defender for our innocent town."

Vadixas' eyes went wide, "A defender?"

Gihmea nodded, "Yes, from Whighridge the Town of Ice. When they received their child, they sent a warning that they would be attacking once she was ready. We immediately started praying for a Child of Fire to be chosen to save us."

Vadixas stood up, hand raised, "I can do it. I can keep us safe."

Gihmea nodded, "Wonderful. I will leave that to you." Vadixas nodded quickly. "I will lead you to where you will be staying. Come along."

They left the house and once again, it was a silent walk to the house. As they walked, the houses got smaller and smaller. Until finally Vadixas was looking at a house from her memories. Gihmea smiled at her, "And this is where you will be staying." She turned to Vadixas, "We hope that the familiarity will be comfortable."

Vadixas looked to the left of the house where her father's life had ended not too long ago. She wasn't planning to go into that section but thankfully the only thing there was her father's room and the living room, which she didn't need. She looked back at Gihmea who was watching her with a careful look. "Um…yeah…great…"

Gihmea nodded, "Good. We will leave the Child of Ice to you."

Gihmea then nodded once more before turning and leaving her alone in front of the house. Vadixas reached out for her but when she saw others looking at her, she shook her head and headed into the house. Once she could no longer see anyone, she slid down till she was sitting on the floor.

She had her eyes closed, desperately trying to calm down. All she could remember was the pain, and she didn't want to let the town suffer as she had. She sat there for a while, not knowing how much time had passed. Eventually, her stomach rumbled and she stood up to make food.

After she ate, she moved to lay on her bed, trying to make sense of everything that had happened today. She had died somehow and now she was alive again and different. She could feel a strange power flowing through her. She assumed that it was fire energy considering everything she now knew.

If she was going to protect the town she was going to need to practice so she could fight against the Child of Ice. She didn't know the first thing about magic and didn't know where she could learn either.

The next morning she wandered around the town until she came to the entrance. She walked out for a bit and found a big clearing. On the other side of the clearing, she could see another town. She stood on her tippy toes to try and see it better but it was too far for her to get a good look. She started to walk towards it when someone grabbed her arm. Vadixas looked back at the guard "Where do you think you are going?"

Vadixas frowned, "I was planning to go check out Whighridge," she said pointing to it.

"Do you want to get killed?" he looked like he was about to say more but cut himself off.

"What do you mean?"

"You're the only thing keeping them from attacking us. If they find out who you are they will kill you."

Vadixas frowned, "But if I can't go to the town how will I challenge the Child of Ice."

"You'll figure it out."

He pulled her back to town and pushed her back inside of it. She stumbled but managed not to fall. She sighed as she walked back to her house. She realized that behind her were only one or two other houses before the edge of town. An idea popped into her mind as she looked around to see if anyone was about.

"Alright this should do," she said to herself.

She planted her feet shoulder length apart and started to breathe slowly. She could feel the magic in every part of her. If she focused, she could see a translucent layer of red covering herself.

She took a deep breath, and she gathered the energy in her mouth. She slowly blew it and along with the air came fire. Her eyes went wide and she dropped her concentration, covering her mouth until the fire was gone.

She slowly removed her hands and looked at them. She brought them together and started to concentrate her energy into them. Once she did, a little flame formed on her hands. When she pushed more energy there, the flame grew. She formed her hands into a circle and the fire turned into a ball of fire that was spinning slowly in her hands. She brought them closer to her face to look at it. Watching as it slowly turned, folding into itself but still keeping a ball shape. She moved it back to waist height and changed her hands to a cupped shape facing upward. She immediately had to move her head back as the ball that had formed in her hands flew upwards. She watched as it went higher and higher until it exploded into a rain of fire that thankfully fizzled out before it reached the town.

Vadixas was still looking up at the sky when Gihmea and a few guards arrived.

"What do you think you were doing!" Gihmea shouted.

"I'm sorry I was-"

"Do you know what damage you could have done!"

"I didn't mean to it just-"

"People could have been hurt!" Vadixas just looked at the ground, realizing she wouldn't get heard.

"you need to think about your actions and the well-being of those around you. What if the fire had touched someone or something. You are the one who was given to us to save us. Don't betray us by becoming the very thing that destroys us."

Vadixas kept looking at the ground but when there was only silence, she looked up to see Gihmea watching her expectantly. Her eyes went wide and she spoke quickly, "I'm sorry, I really didn't mean to do that. It won't happen again."

Gihmea nodded, "You are forgiven but don't do it again."

"But how will I practice fighting?"

"My staff will inform you where and when you can practice."

Gihmea waved her hand at Vadixas. Vadixas blinked at her, not knowing what it meant but when she did it more slowly, Vadixas took a few steps back. She kept sweeping her hand until Vadixas's back hit her back door. When she put her hand on the handle Gihmea nodded and Vadixas entered her house, going right to her room to lay on her bed. She spent the rest of the night just laying there, not even bothering to get up when she got hungry.

The next morning she looked in her kitchen to see if she had some food. She eventually found some but her supplies were getting low. Vadixas bit her lip, she didn't remember if she had any money in the house but she would need some soon enough. After eating some of the food she found, she headed out looking for a job, even a side one, to get some money.

She spent the whole day looking but no matter who she asked, they all refused her offer. They all claimed that she was too special to work for them, even the blacksmith who she could have helped to maintain the fire with relative ease, turned her down.

When sundown came, she still had no luck so she was forced to go to Gihmea's house. She didn't want to talk to her after yesterday but if she was too special to work for anyone then Gihmea might be able to pay her since she was the protector of the town.

She made her way to the door and knocked on it.

It was answered by a butler, "Yes?"

"I'm here to talk to Gihmea?"

He looked her up and down, "I will see if she will see you."

"Please tell her it's important," she shouted before he could close the door on her. She paced back and forth while she waited for him to come back. Time flowed slowly as she stood there outside the closed door waiting, it was getting dark as the sun slipped below the horizon before he opened the door for her again

"She will see you now."

Vadixas nodded and followed him to the room she originally talked to Gihmea in.

She sat down and waited a little longer before Gihmea came to join her.

"I'm busy, so this must be quick."

Vadixas nodded, sitting up straighter, "I was hoping you could hire me."

Gihmea frowned, "Why?"

"I need money for food, but everyone else said I was too special to work for them."

"And you want me to..."

"Well..." she shifted for a moment before continuing, "Since I'm supposed to protect the town from the Child of Ice, I was hoping you could pay me as protector of the town so I can get food."

"I can't just pay you to do nothing."

"Oh"

Vadixas looked at her feet

The two were silent before Gihmea spoke up again, "But I can pay you on the days that you do fight or protect us."

"Well that helps," Vadixas muttered

Gihmea sighed, "I don't want you to suffer."

Vadixas looked up at her, "I'll arrange two meals to be sent to your house until you start fighting the Child of Ice. Once you do, the food will stop and you'll get paid instead."

Vadixas smiled up at her, "Thank you."

Gihmea nodded, "now as I said before, I'm very busy," she remarked as she waved to the door and Vadixas stood up

"Oh right, I'll let you get back to what you were doing. Will you be bringing the food or..."

"I'm much too busy for that. One of my servants will."

"Of course. That makes sense."

Vadixas left soon after that with a wave. She didn't get her first meal until two days after that conversation but she had food in the house that lasted until then.

It was smaller plates causing her to be hungry most days but she still hadn't been told when she could practice so could only spend time walking around town.

Then one day she tried to spend the day in her house by midday a guard was banging on her door. When she opened the door he glared at her.

"Yes?" she asked, looking up at him.

"What do you think you were doing?"

"I...I was staying home?"

"When we needed you?"

Her eyes went wide, "I didn't know." She whispered and that only made him frown more.

"Of course, you didn't." He grabbed her arm and started to pull her, she only had enough time to close her door. He dragged her to the far corner of town where a pile of wood was. He pushed her towards it and then just stood there.

She looked at it then back at him, "um..." she said looking back at the pile.

"Well?" the guard said.

"What am I..."

The guard rolled his eyes, "I was told you want to practice so." he waved to the pile.

She bit her lip but turned back towards the pile. She brought her hands together to form a ball of fire. She looked at the pile before throwing the ball at it. When it hit the pile it exploded, the first bits of wood shattered a part while the pieces under it started to burn. The parts of the wood that had shattered rained down on the two.

"Can't you be more careful?" the guard shouted at her.

She turned to him with wide eyes, "but you said…"

"Who said to make an explosion? You should have just burned it."

"But I-"

"Just get out of here."

Vadixas left quickly, she wanted to go back home but didn't want to get yelled at again so took her normal lap around town avoiding where she could still see smoke rising.

After that day, she finally figured out how she was going to fight with the Child of Ice. She rushed back home and wrote a note. It took her half a day to find someone willing to go to Whighridge. She was worried that she hadn't given Aylnivi enough time to get ready for their battle. She was able to convince the guards to let her out when she promised she would stay within their sight.

A few days later, it was time for her fight with Child of Ice. She was excited enough that she was bouncing in place at the gate, waiting for the guards to let her go out. Once the guard nodded his head, she skipped out into the no man's land between the two towns. She turned around to walk backwards so that she could get as far from Pitydden but could still see it. When she thought she was far enough, she stopped and turned, waiting for the Child of Ice to arrive.

After a while, another girl could be seen headed toward Vadixas.

"So you're the Child of Ice?" Vadixas said, standing straight.

Aylnivi looked down at herself before looking back at Vadixas, "Who else would accept your invitation to battle."

"I don't know? I've never met you."

Aylnivi curtsied, though the bored look never left her face. "Well, now you've met me."

Vadixas pointed at Aylnivi "I will beat you and save my town from your attacks." Aylnivi frowned but didn't move. Vadixas's finger dropped a little "Well aren't you going to say anything?"

Aylnivi shook her head "I'm waiting for your attack."

Vadixas puffed up again "So you're so scared you can't

speak."

"Terrified."

However, the boredom was still present.

"You're so mean!" Before she could think of anything else, she threw a fireball at Aylnivi. Aylnivi watched it approach before making an ice ball the same size and throwing it. The two balls of opposite elements met midair and steam formed. Aylnivi had to quickly dodge a smaller fireball that had made it through the flame.

Vadixas pointed at her again "Ha, I'm stronger than you. This will be an easy fight."

Aylnivi stood up with a sigh, "So, that's what the coloring means."

"What coloring?"

"On the left wing of my butterfly tattoo."

Aylnivi watched as Vadixas touched her left thigh, "It's red, like the color following you."

Vadixas looked behind her for a moment, "I don't have any red following me, but you have an iridescent color covering you."

"Covering me?"

"Yeah, it actually looked really pretty. Like a fire surrounding your whole body. It went down, it's now at eye level for you. It actually matches your hair color."

Aylnivi shifted, crossing her arms, "It went down? When?"

"When you...attacked..." Vadixas gasped. "Ha ha. I now know what it means. It shows how much energy you have left to use." She stood up straighter again "This will make your defeat even faster."

"You think."

"I know."

Aylnivi shrugged, "Let's see then."

It wasn't Aylnivi's defeat that stopped the battle but Vadixas's. While she had the advantage, she had only been awake for a week at this point. Aylnivi had better control of her magic and could stop Vadixas's attacks using less energy.

While Vadixas was able to throw multiple fireballs at Aylnivi, Aylnivi was able to make each fireball explode before it got close to her, unlike the first time. At the end of the battle, Vadixas was breathing heavily while sitting on the ground. Aylnivi was leaning against one of the pillars of ice that she had used to defend.

"Well..." Aylnivi looked over at her, "You lasted longer than I thought you would."

"I...I can...still...fight..." Vadixas said.

She raised her hand but dropped it soon after with a groan. "I...I just...need...a nap." She blinked a few times before fainting.

Vadixas didn't know how long she was out, but when she regained consciousness, she kept her eyes closed, just hoping her headache would go away.

"Are you awake now?" a voice said over her. It was then she noticed that her head was a little raised and wasn't on hard ground. She blinked her eyes open to see Aylnivi looking down at her with boredom.

"Wha-"

"You should probably not use that much magic again."

"I...what?" Vadixas kept blinking up at her, noticing she was currently resting her head on Aylnivi's lap.

"I think we need to watch how much magic we use, if your fainting is any indication."

Vadixas blinked at her for a moment before suddenly sitting up and moving away from her. "What are you doing?"

"I was making sure you didn't die?" Aylnivi said, watching her.

Vadixas pointed to her, "But you are my enemy. You shouldn't care."

Aylnivi frowned before standing up, wiping herself off, "Well if you died that way you would have been killing yourself which is not the same as me killing you."

"Oh, that makes sense," Vadixas said with a nod.

Aylnivi nodded, "When you've practiced some more, I will fight you again."

With that Aylnivi left, and Vadixas stared at her back as she walked away. She stayed there a while before she slowly walked back to her own town, her head dropping.

The guard huffed as she made it back to the gate, "You're late."

"I...I'm sorry," she whispered.

He huffed again but didn't say anything else. Vadixas then just walked back home, going to bed as soon as she arrived.

The next morning, she made her way to Gihmea's house. She figured that since she had fought Aylnivi, she would be able to get paid and would be able to buy her own food. She knocked on the door to have it answered by the butler again.

"Yes?" he asked.

"I'm here to talk to Gihmea again."

"I will see if she will talk to you now."

She nodded and paced back and forth in front of the door once again. Eventually, he came back and let her in.

"You will have to wait for her to be free but you may wait inside this time."

She nodded and let him lead her into the waiting room once again. It was a few hours before Gihmea joined her.

"You needed me?"

Vadixas played with her fingers for a moment before smiling at her, "I came because I fought the Child of Ice yesterday and I was hoping to get my pay so I can get some food."

Gihmea frowned at her, "is the food I offered not good enough?"

Vadixas shook her head, "Nothing like that...I just wanted to support more people."

Gihmea sighed, "I see. And how did the fight go?"

Vadixas's eyes went wide "What?"

"Did you win?"

"Oh...no...she had more experience than me...so she won."

"I see. I am glad she didn't kill you."

"oh...I..."

"Well then. It will be a reduced amount since you didn't succeed."

"I...okay..."

Gihmea nodded, "The butler will give you your money. Is there anything else you need?"

"Oh...no..."

"Then I will be leaving. You can head to the door and the butler will give you the money there."

Gihmea left the room before Vadixas even stood up. She walked over to the front door, knowing the path by now, and waited there until the butler came over. He handed her some money and pushed her out the door before she could count how much she was given. She stared at it for a moment before counting it.

The total would only last her about a week if she used it sparingly. Which means she would have to fight Aylnivi sooner than she wanted to. She walked to the market to look for the cheapest thing to eat for lunch.

She sent a note quickly telling Aylnivi she would fight her again on the same day. She hunted down the man who had sent the letter before. He refused to go again without pay, so she had to give up a meal to pay his fee but she figured she could manage missing one meal.

She spent the next week planning out some new attacks while not actually practicing them since she wasn't called on by the guard for training. She got disapproving looks for walking around town but she couldn't do anything about it. When she went to ask the guard he just glared at her silently till she left again.

When the week was over, she was again waiting at the entrance until the guard told her that she could leave. Making it to the same area where they fought before and luckily she didn't have to wait long for Aylnivi to meet her.

"Are you ready to fight again?" Vadixas pointed at Aylnivi.

"I've come here haven't I?"

"Did you practice? Because if you didn't then this time, I'll beat you."

Aylnivi crossed her arms, "I wasn't the one who needed to practice after our last battle."

"I did so much practicing since then that you'll be the one who'll need it."

"Then show me," said Aylnivi, letting her arms drop to her side to get ready for what Vadixas would throw at her.

Vadixas took a breath before blowing it out in a giant breath of fire. The speed was quick but petered out before it got halfway to Aylnivi.

Vadixas frowned "Aww it wasn't long enough."

"Did you actually practice?"

Vadixas pulled at her fingers, "Well last time I did but I was yelled at so...no." She then stood up straighter, "but my magic is strong against yours, so I can beat you without it." She brought her hands together to create a fireball bigger than she had last time.

Vadixas smiled as it headed towards Aylnivi but it dropped as it blew up midway to her.

"What?"

"I figured out that your fireballs explode when they hit something sharp. Which means that if I throw an ice spear," she created one by forming her left hand into a circle and ice growing out from both sides in a sharp shape. "Into your fireballs, they explode on impact rather than lessening their size like an ice ball does."

"That's no fair!"

Vadixas brought her hands up, and the remnants of fire around them flew into the air. She then stomped down, causing the rain of fire she created to head right to Aylnivi.

Aylnivi's eyes went wide and she brought the spear up, grabbing a part of it and pulling its side out to protect herself. She kneeled, sticking the ice into the ground and using both hands to repair the ice as it melted under the assault to keep herself safe until the attack had finished.

Once it was done, Vadixas gasped and moved closer to the now cube of ice around Aylnivi.

"Are you okay?"

She stood in front of the block and watched as the front split like a zipper being pulled open to see Aylnivi sitting on the ground.

"We are fighting."

"I know, I'm so sorry I just had an outburst. I wasn't planning to rain fire on you and hurt you."

"You are supposed to hurt your opponent when you fight."

"You haven't hurt me yet and this is our second fight."

Aylnivi frowned, "You are weaker than me. It would be a cowardly move to hurt you."

Vadixas stood up straighter, "Well, that just proves that I'm right and not supposed to beat you by hurting you. I'm the stronger one of us."

Aylnivi watched her for a moment, "I'll believe that when you beat me."

Vadixas nodded, then looked back down at her

"You're really not hurt right?"

Aylnivi shook her head, "I was able to guard against it. Not a bit of fire touched me."

Vadixas breathed a sigh of relief, "Good."

She then frowned, "I need to plan more for our next battle. I thought the fire breath would beat you since it uses such little energy."

Aylnivi collapsed the box and stood up, brushing off her clothing "If you had been closer I wouldn't have known how to deal with it. It just means you have both close range and far range attacks."

Vadixas turned to her with wide eyes, "Oh that's smart."

"Anything you come up with can be used in battle. You just need to know when or how."

"Okay, I got it. When I think up a new attack for our next battle. I'll also think about how to use it."

Aylnivi nodded, "I'll plan for a defense against your rain of fire and your fire breath too."

Vadixas blinked at her, "Okay, then I'll use that in our next battle as well to let you try them out."

Aylnivi chuckled, "You'll need all your stuff to beat me anyway."

"I'll do it next time."

"We'll see."

"Same time next week?" Vadixas asked slowly, watching Aylnivi carefully.

Aylnivi frowned before looking over to Pitydden.

"You better be prepared," Aylnivi said with a nod.

Vadixas smiled.

"You too!" She watched as Aylnivi walked away before skipping back to Pitydden.

By the time she was back in town though all her excitement was gone. The guard glared at her as she made it to the gate.

"And what were the results?"

She blinked at him before asking, "What?"

The guard frowned, "Gihmea told me that you should tell me the results of your battle. I will then inform her of it and one of her servants will give you your money the next day."

"Oh..." she said, pulling on her fingers.

"So what happened?"

Vadixas was silent for a moment, "I lost."

The guard sighed, "Of course you did."

Vadixas looked up at him, "But I got her to agree to fight me next week. And I'll win that time."

He glared at her but still let her into town. She sighed and walked along the marketplace. She was about to get the same soup she always did but frowned when she found that the price had doubled. Her eyes went wide as she looked up at the merchant who was frowning at her.

"Why is it so much today?"

The merchant shrugged, "The price went up so I had to charge more money."

"Oh..." she looked at the amount of money she had. She would have to wait until tomorrow for more money.

She sighed as she walked away, looking for something cheaper to buy. After getting a sandwich, she ate it quickly and went to bed because she did not have anything else to do. The next day, she snuck out of town to practice since the guard hadn't gotten her since the first time. She had thought up a new attack before she went to bed the night before.

She noticed that her bigger fireballs were slower so she wanted to test if a smaller version could move faster. She walked far away from Pitydden before she felt comfortable enough to start practicing. Once she could only barely see the town, she took a big breath. She formed a fireball of normal size and tried to squeeze her hands together. While it condensed, it also shot out in front of her without her meaning to. It exploded in the distance and she hoped no one was hurt.

She took a breath and lowered the energy going to her hands. This time she made a circle in only one hand and the fireball formed again. This time the smaller size was easier to handle. She took a slow breath before letting it go. The fireball went faster than any of her others had.

She cheered at her success. She straightened up and took another breath. This time, making the same fireball but one in each hand. She let them go and gave another cheer when they both went in the direction that she wanted. She made two more and flung her hands out to the side and the two fireballs flew out in opposite directions before turning midair and hitting each other some distance in front of her, causing an explosion when they hit.

She bit her lip a little, worried if it would hurt Aylnivi but ignored the concern as she moved to the location where they exploded to see the effects. She was pretty sure Aylnivi would survive, it might just hurt a little.

Having succeeded with her practice, she snuck back to her house, not wanting to get in trouble with the town again. She wanted to go back to bed but knew she had to do a few laps around town before that. The next day she was given the money she was promised, thankfully it was the same amount as last week. Some of the food she always bought had become more expensive in the last few days so she had to limit what she could buy. She decided to get all her meals rather than what she liked to eat.

A week later, she was walking up to their battle area to find pillars of ice all around. Her eyes went wide, "What are those?"

"You said you wanted me to practice."

Vadixas turned to look at Aylnivi, who was leaning against one of the pillars, "How did you make those if your magic isn't affected?"

"I just need to use a little bit of my magic every day to keep them from melting. I've just been working on these for the last week."

"You really did practice?"

"I heard your explosions earlier in the week."

"I thought I was far enough away. No one in Pitydden seemed to notice or say anything."

"I was here at the time, so I was much closer than they were."

Vadixas pouted, "Fine, can we start fighting?"

"If you're ready." Aylnivi said.

Vadixas smiled and threw a fireball at Aylnivi. Aylnivi moved behind the pillar, and when the fireball hit the pillar it exploded. Vadixas waited for the steam to clear and her pout only increased when she saw that the pillar was still standing.

"You're going to have to try harder than that," said Aynlivi, moving back to the side of the pillar.

"I have more than that." She formed her two smaller fireballs before flinging them to the side. She then threw her normal fireball at Aylnivi. Aynlivi moved behind the pillar again and Vadixas gasped as the two smaller fireballs exploded behind the pillar.

Vadixas moved closer to where the explosion happened to see an ice box attached to the pillar. It zippered open and Aylnivi climbed out of it.

"Wait, you guarded against that?"

"Have anything better?" Aylnivi said, fixing her tousled hair.

"Yeah." Vadixas took a breath before blowing fire at Aylnivi.

Aylnivi swung her hand at the pillar, cutting it into two and causing it to fall between them, blocking the flame breath. Vadixas threw a small fireball and when it hit the pillar, the explosion caused it to go crashing backwards. Vadixas looked where Aylnivi had been but the spot was now empty. She looked to where the pillar had landed but Aylnivi wasn't there either.

"A little too slow.," Aylnivi said from behind her.

Vadixas looked over her shoulder to see Aylnivi standing behind her with an ice spike, waiting to stab her. In her surprise, she raised a pillar of fire around herself. The spike turned to steam when it hit. Once the spike was gone, Vadixas stopped the flame pillar only to flop to the ground breathing heavily.

"Why aren't you even winded?" she asked, kicking her feet.

Aylnivi stood a bit away, having jumped back from the cascade of steam formed from the melted spike.

She shrugged, "I'm just better than you."

Vadixas turned her head to pout at Aylnivi, "You know, I can see that you have the same level of magic left that I do."

"And yet I'm the one that's still standing."

"I could stand if I wanted."

"Of course, you can."

Vadixas huffed looking back at the sky again, "Why can't I beat you even though I'm stronger."

Aylnivi watched her for a moment "You just need to keep practicing"

Vadixas huffed at that.

"Your move with the two smaller fireballs was very smart," she said with a small smile.

Vadixas looked at her with a smile, "Really?"

Aylnivi nodded, "Had you not shown what you were doing with your arm movements, it would have caught me off guard."

Aylnivi copied the move by throwing out her arms and then bringing them close to her chest like Vadixas always did before throwing out a big fireball.

"If you hadn't done that then I wouldn't have had time to guard against it."

Vadixas frowned but nodded, "Got it."

Aylnivi nodded before turning back towards the path to Whighridge.

Vadixas sat up, "Same time next week?"

Aylnivi chuckled, "I'll be here."

She heard Vadixas flop back into the dirt before she left.

Vadixas lay there staring up at the sky, dreading going back to her town when another voice sounded from behind her.

"Are you okay?" Gizlae asked, moving closer to Vadixas.

Vadixas smiled up at her, "Oh yeah just tired. Aylnivi doesn't hold back."

She sat up, "What are you four doing here then?"

She frowned suddenly, "Did we bother the other town with our fighting? I didn't do as many fireballs as I could to keep the sound to a minimum."

"Was that the explosion we heard?"

Vadixas nodded, "yeah they're my main form of attack but they do make a lot of noise."

She looked at the group, "So is that why you're here?"

"No, we're here to meet you and Aylnivi."

Vadixas looked at them for a moment, "Oh, that's why you've all got the same covering like me and Aylnivi."

"Covering?"

Vadixas nodded, "Yeah I can see the same translucent covering over you, each in a different color though. Aylnivi and I figured out that it represents our magical energies. So since you have one as well, you must be like us," she said with a smile.

"Like you?" Ceaxtra asked.

It took a moment before Vadixas was able to stand up, "Sorry that was rude of me. I'm Vadixas Child of Fire."

"If you're the Child of Fire, then Aylnivi would be…"

"Child of Ice," Vadixas said with a nod.

"Oh, wonderful. We wanted to meet you both," Gizlae said, her smile growing wider.

Vadixas looked in the direction of Whighridge "you want to meet Aylnivi?"

She then looked at the sun, which was now close to setting.

"She might not be up for it right now."

She looked back at the group, "But you can stay at my place for the night and meet her tomorrow."

"Are you sure?" Gizlae said, moving a little closer. "We can just camp outside."

"Yeah, my place isn't the biggest but you should all be able to fit."

Vadixas started to walk to Pitydden without giving them a chance to argue. She was slow since she was still tired from her fight, but the others didn't complain. Once they were at the town entrance, Vadixas stood a little straighter. The guard watched Vadixas enter and she nodded at him. She walked through without any complaint from him but he glared at the others.

"And who are these?"

"oh, just some town guests that bumped into me while I was coming back. I figured it would only be proper to house them and guide them."

He watched her carefully, "You aren't bothering them?"

Vadixas shook her head quickly but Kihakso quickly stepped in.

"No, she was kind enough to offer her own place for nothing in exchange. If anything, you stopping us is the only thing that's bothering us."

The guard glared at them for a moment more before letting them through.

The group started to walk into town but Vadixas turned around to walk back to the guard quickly "Um…about the battle?"

"You beat her this time right? That's the only way you would be bringing guests."

She pulled on her fingers, looking over to see the group waiting for her, "No, I didn't…but I didn't bring these guests. They were coming here either way."

The guard huffed, "I will inform Gihmea."

Vadixas nodded, taking that as her cue to leave. She moved back over to the group.

"What was that?" Awrosk asked.

Vadixas blinked at him, "Oh…I get paid to fight Aylnivi and I have to tell the guard what the results are each time."

She then turned to Kihakso, "You didn't really need to do that," she whispered.

Kihakso shrugged, "I don't like that type of person."

Vadixas blinked at them, "What type?"

Kihakso just shook their head, "Don't worry about it."

The group started to walk towards her home when she stopped at the marketplace. "Oh wait, I don't have any food at home."

She looked around at the stalls and frowned, "I also don't have enough money to pay for enough food to feed you all," she muttered to herself but since Awrosk was standing closer to her, he heard.

"I could get an advance payment from Gihmea but she doesn't usually pay me until the day after," She started to pace but didn't realize it, "and the stalls might charge extra since I'm taking food from people who need it."

Awrosk reached out to lightly grab her arm, "I'll pay for it."

Vadixas gasped, "I can't have you do that. You're the guest."

Awrosk shrugged, "I got a lot of money from my town and nowhere to use it since they refuse to let me pay for food there."

Vadixas frowned at that.

"So, it would just be going to waste."

"If you're sure it's okay..."

Awrosk nodded, "What would you recommend?"

Vadixas gasped, "I don't know. I haven't tried half the stuff since it's usually too expensive for me to buy."

"Well then, let's pick out a bunch of stuff that you've always wanted to have."

Vadixas's eyes went wide before she started to drag Awrosk along, pointing to things that she liked and didn't like. When Awrosk looked back at the other three, he saw Ceaxtra chuckling at him and Gizlae giving him a small smile.

After they had picked out their food, the group made it back to Vadixas's house. She let them in and led them right to the kitchen, giving them a quick tour that didn't go anywhere near the left side. The group didn't say anything or even ask about it.

There was some small talk while they were eating but Kihakso asked the important question "So Awrosk, are you going back today or tomorrow?"

Awrosk had been talking to Vadixas so it took a moment before he responded

"What?"

"You said you were only guiding us to Pitydden. And you've done that now."

"Oh right," Awrosk said with a frown.

"I will be sad to see you go," said Gizlae, her smile didn't fool him, though her eyes going green did surprise him.

"But we can't force you."

Awrosk looked back at Vadixas, "I can stay for a little longer."

Gizlae chuckled but didn't say anymore, she just continued to eat. Once they were finished, the group slept in the guest room, the closest one to the living room. Once Vadixas pointed it out, she moved quickly to her own room.

The next day Vadixas walked the group to the front gate.

"You should be able to find Aylnivi fast...Well, I assume you should."

"We will," Kihakso said with a nod.

"Good," she was about to step out of the gate when the guard stopped her.

"Where do you think you're going?"

"Oh...well...I..."

"Why does it matter to you?" Kihakso said, moving in front of her.

The guard glared at them, "My job is to make sure that she is safe."

He looked down his nose at Kihakso, "I can't do that if she is just messing around with some strangers."

"Messing around? You-" Kihakso started to get upset but Gizlae stepped forward and took their hand.

"I'm sorry for making your job harder. It's just that we found Vadixas so interesting yesterday that we were hoping she could talk to us longer by walking us to Whighridge." she said with a bright smile.

The guard looked her over, before quickly glaring at Kihakso, who glared back. He then turned to Vadixas, "You can go but remember to not enter that town. If they know who you are they'll kill you."

Vadixas shivered but nodded, leading the group out of town.

Once they were out of earshot, she spoke up again, "Sorry about him. They're just protective of me."

Kihakso rolled their eyes, "Protective...sure," they muttered.

Gizlae gave a sad smile and rubbed their shoulder.

It wasn't a long walk between the two towns but Vadixas stopped when she reached the edge of their battlefield. She looked back to Pitydden before taking a slow step closer to Whighridge. She was shaking till Awrosk reached out and took her hand. She looked at their connected hands and he squeezed it. She looked up at him and gave him a small smile before taking another step forward, this one was a little easier for her.

Eventually, they stood at the gate entrance of Whighridge. Unlike Pitydden there weren't any guards but there were two towers by the gate where they could see a few guards watching from windows above.

"Well, here it is," Vadixas said, waving to the town.

"which means I shou-"

Awrosk squeezed her hand. "You're not going to leave are you?"

She blinked at him, "I...you heard the guard...if they know who I am, they'll kill me."

Awrosk moved a little closer so he could brush his shoulder against hers.

"We'll keep you safe," he said, a little quieter.

"Promise?"

"Yeah."

Vadixas nodded before looking at the rest of the group. "I've never been here, so I don't know where Aylnivi is."

"How did you challenge her if you haven't been here?"

"I always sent a messenger," Vadixas said, shifting from one foot to the other.

Gizlae smiled before looking at Kihakso, "So, where are we going?"

"This way."

Kihakso started through the gate and down the main road. Gizlae and Ceaxtra followed right away, Vadixas took a moment longer before following them. As they walked along the road, Vadixas looked around her, her eyes wide. The farther they went in the tighter she held Awrosk's hand.

Eventually, they made it to a big house that had two guards protecting the stairs leading up into it. The group stood a bit away from the house while Vadixas stood in front with Awrosk still next to her.

"Do you want me to talk to them?" Awrosk asked, waving in its direction.

Vadixas shook her head, "No, I can do this."

She walked up to the front door and stood up straight.

"We are here to see the Child of Ice," the two guards nodded and let them in. Vadixas was surprised that there weren't any arguments like she normally got from guards back in her town.

The room on the other side of the door was connected by tight hallways. There weren't any other doors besides the double doors on the other side. Once they made it through, they found a ballroom with a throne in the center. Ceaxtra moved a little closer to get a better look at it. She could tell that it was made from stone but the carver had managed to make it look like a chunk of ice that had been shaped into a chair.

"Is she here?" Kihakso asked, Since the throne was empty.

"Would they let us in if she wasn't?" Gizlae asked.

"Aylnivi?" Vadixas shouted out to the room.

For a moment, there wasn't any sound before they heard footsteps coming from the side door. It was thrown open by Aylnivi who was standing there with eyes wide open.

She opened her eyes and shivered, the cold that she remembered before closing her eyes for the last time. She tried to sit up but she seemed to be held tight by the hole she had jumped in.

"So confident," a voice said.

"That you would pick me? Of course."

"And why did you think that?" She couldn't open her eyes but she had a good guess who she was talking to.

"You're talking to me now, aren't you?"

"And what if I talk to everyone?"

"Do you?" The voice was silent for a moment and she smiled to herself. "So does my confidence get me a special meeting? Or more?"

The voice chuckled, "No I just decided to give you your wish. Hopefully, it is everything you wanted."

Her throat and lungs hurt from the cold that she was breathing in. She was going to ask about that when Ice spoke up again

"Your name is Aylnivi and it is time for you to wake up."

With that, she opened her eyes to find herself in the box that held the ice but the ice was no longer there. She looked up to see that the door was still closed, so she had to pull herself up and open the door, which was difficult. When she looked out, a few people were milling around. They all looked at her when she climbed out of the box, dusting herself off when she stepped onto the ground.

She glared at the long sleeves she remembered being forced to wear. With a sigh, she moved over to the closest person.

"So I succeeded," she said, crossing her arms.

The person just stared at her without saying anything. She frowned at them before looking around. No one else was saying anything either.

She sighed, "I'll be in the town square when you need me."

With that she left the group behind walking back to town.

It was only a moment after she sat down that someone rushed over to her. People started to get excited around her but she didn't care. The crowd led her to the house of the Child of Ice. She wondered if she had been in it before she became the Child of Ice when they led her to a throne room. They then forced her up the stairs and onto it. She wasn't allowed off the throne for the rest of the night while the town celebrated. She didn't even get a moment to eat. She fell asleep on the throne after surrounding herself with walls of ice to keep people away from her as well as keeping the noise down.

When she woke up in the morning she zippered the wall open, and looked around to see the hall empty. She sighed as she stood up, stretching her poor muscles and looking around. She saw a few other doors besides the entrance ones. Since she didn't get it the day before, she decided to take a tour of her new house. Her memories from her old life didn't include a house, so she didn't care what happened to it herself and would leave it to the town to deal with.

In her tour, she found that the kitchen was fully stocked though there was only one bedroom in the entire house. Most of the other rooms were filled with artwork which was more of a show than anything, just like the party from yesterday. They didn't care about her. They just wanted to use her for their own purpose.

After making herself some food, she decided to take a look around town. Even if she didn't remember anything, seeing something in town might spark a memory. She went to the town center again, looking around to see it had a sculpture similar to the throne. It was a giant block of stone carved to look like a wall of ice. It had been carved to look like children of different ages slept inside of it. She looked around her to see that people were watching her. They were looking at the sculpture then back at her, she could feel her anger building, she knew she would come back but none of those other kids had.

She turned from the sculpture and headed back home, forgetting the tour. She had some training to do. Once she got home, she looked through each of the art-filled rooms until she found one filled with more sculptures, they were many different types.

She started to figure out what shapes she could form, testing out all that she could think of.

She found that spikes were the fastest to form and their flexibility could change depending on how she needed or what was useful.

Once she figured out what shape she wanted, she started experimenting with the ice itself. Making it faster and slower to see if the time made the ice stronger. With each spike she created, she threw it at one of the sculptures frowning when they only chipped.

She then turned to the ability to manipulate coldness, she wanted to see if she made the air around the spike colder and if it would improve its strength. She only got to do two tests before she started to feel dizzy, going to bed soon after.

The next day she repeated the same routine. She would wake up and eat then go to the sculpture room, testing out spike after spike changing its conditions each time to see what accomplished her goal. When she got dizzy or tired she would go to bed, usually after grabbing a snack to nibble on so she wouldn't sleep hungry.

It took a few months but she had finally completed what she wanted, going to bed with a smile on her face. She ate like she normally did but instead of going to the sculpture room, she left the house for the first time in months.

She made her way to the main square. She stood in front of the sculpture, close enough that no one could stop her but far enough away that she couldn't touch it.

She closed her eyes before taking a deep breath. She breathed out onto her hands, starting to form the spike, using all her knowledge from her training to make the perfect spike.

She knew people were watching but they wouldn't know what she was planning before it was too late.

Once the spike was fully formed, she smiled at it. Taking a moment to admire her handiwork before taking a step towards the sculpture throwing the spike as hard as she could at it

The spike hit the sculpture and penetrated halfway before it started to expand at the tip slowly breaking the sculpture apart from the inside.

She stood there watching every moment as cracks started to appear everywhere on the outside. as the rocks started to chip away and small spikes of ice started to poke out in random areas.

Eventually, the sculpture started to crumble, turning into small rocks and a pile of dust with only the now ice wall standing in its place. Aylnivi stepped forward, placing a hand on the part of the ice that was still a spike.

"Rest in peace now," she whispered.

Once her show was done, she looked around at the people that hadn't moved. All were wide-eyed staring at the wall of ice that she had made. She left the ice and went back home, deciding to make herself a feast to celebrate her victory.

The next morning she was planning to head to town again when she found people standing in the throne room.

"Where have you been? We have been waiting for you!"

Aylnivi looked them over. All of them looked older with fancy clothing

"Did you knock?"

"Of course but since you didn't answer, we came in to find you."

Aylnivi shrugged, "You shouldn't have put me in such a useless house."

The gentleman glared but decided to change the subject, "What you did yesterday-"

"Was exactly what I needed to," Aylnivi said, watching as his frown deepened.

"That sculpture was made by this town's founder. It took him years of practice just to get it right."

"And it only took me months to get it taken down right."

The gentleman's face went red at that, "You must pay us back for the damage you did!"

His shout echoed in the empty hall.

"With what money?"

"What?"

"I haven't been paid. I'm surprised I still have food but you seem to be willing to give me that for free."

The gentleman glared at her, "You will take out the Pitydden. They threatened us as well as you."

Before Aylnivi could make a comeback he turned and left.

She found two guards stationed at her door after that day whose job it was to always know her movements. It just meant less time in town which she was fine with. She spent the time working on other ways she could use her ice powers instead.

It was sometime later when she heard the word of the Child of Fire having woken up. The gentleman started to visit her once a week. They demanded that she finally took care of Pitydden but she kept pushing it off, making claims that she wasn't strong enough to take out the whole town.

One morning she heard a knocking that she ignored. Usually, the knocking would stop and the gentleman would come in on his own but this time, the knocking just continued. This told her that it was one of the guards that wanted her to come to the door. She let the ice she was working on fall to the floor and made her way to the door before opening it to see that it wasn't one of the guards that were banging on it.

"What is it?" she asked.

The guard waved to a man standing next to him.

"You have a messenger."

Aylnivi watched the man standing at her door. It was obvious with how he was constantly looking over his shoulder that he didn't live in Whighridge.

"What did you need?" her speaking made him jump and he turned to her quickly holding out a letter.

Aylnivi just stared at it, not taking it. His hand shook before he spoke up, "it's for you." When she still didn't take it he licked his lips before continuing, "It'sfrom the Child of Fire," he whispered watching the guards carefully.

Aylnivi took it. As soon as the letter left his hand the man turned and fled the way he came. Aylnivi didn't give him another thought as she looked over the letter. The two were going to fight eventually, so she was surprised the child had decided to contact her in such a formal way.

She opened it to read the contents.

We're supposed to fight, so I challenge you to a battle in three days. We will meet in the middle of our two towns to fight. Bring your strongest spells because I will beat you otherwise.

Then in a smaller script close to the bottom was another line

If that day isn't good for you, just send someone to meet me that day to tell me when would be a better day.

Aylnivi frowned at the letter. It was challenging but courteous. She knew that the Child of Fire had only woken up a week ago. Challenging Aylnivi who had been awake for a few months, was overconfident. Aylnivi shrugged wondering what their first meeting would be like.

When Aylnivi first saw Vadixas, she was sure it wasn't overconfidence that brought this fight about, but a desire to prove herself. While Vadixas stood confident when talking to her, the first poke at her town made her deflate. After the first battle, Aylnivi was surprised to get a message the next day from Vadixas requesting a fight at the same time next week. It slightly concerned her, but they were technically enemies and it wasn't something she was supposed to be worried about.

She was surprised by how fast Vadixas was able to improve. With only a few words from her, Vadixas was able to come up with new techniques and spells. She couldn't help but be proud of the other girl even though they were meant to be enemies.

Once again, she was making her way back to her house after a fight. She felt sore and was planning to sleep once she got home but she wasn't planning to let Vadixas know about that. While she walked home, most of the people in town ignored her. They hated her after the destruction of the sculpture but she didn't want to talk to them anyways. As she was getting to her front door, one of the guards spoke up, "you went to fight that child again?"

Aylnivi didn't bother looking at him, she just stared at her closed door.

"She requested it. Why shouldn't I humor her?"

"You should stop playing with her and end her life."

"It is my choice to decide and I will do so when I grow bored."

She glared at him and he huffed, opening the door for her finally. She didn't know how long they would wait. She hoped that eventually Vadixas would learn enough from her to keep herself safe when the town decided to go through with their threats. Her reluctance being the only thing keeping Pitydden, and more importantly Vadixas herself, safe.

One day after their last battle, she woke up to make food. She was still a little sore from her fight with Vadixas. She had used more magic energy than she had in previous battles. It definitely showed that Vadixas was getting stronger. She would need to figure out a new move to use against her.

She almost dropped her plate when she heard Vadixas shouting her name. She thought that she was imagining it but couldn't trust that, so she put the plate down and ran to the throne room, throwing the door open to see Vadixas standing there with a group of people.

"So you were here," Vadixas said with a smile.

Aylnivi looked between the group and Vadixas before moving over to Vadixas.

"So these are-?" she was interrupted by Aylnivi.

"Are you okay?" Aylnivi asked quietly but since there wasn't any other sound the group also heard.

"Huh?"

"Are you hurt?"

"No, why would I be?" Vadixas said with a frown.

Aylnivi frowned herself, "It isn't safe for you to be here. The only reason you would be here is if they threatened or hurt you..."

"We wouldn't," Gizlae said, taking a step towards them.

Aylnivi moved Vadixas behind her to watch the group carefully.

"What do you want?" she said.

Vadixas poked her shoulder, "I was getting to that when you interrupted me."

Aylnivi sighed but didn't move, "Sorry, what you were saying?"

"I was saying. Aylnivi, that these people are just like us," she waved with her hand over Aylnivi's shoulder, which was a little awkward since Aylnivi was a little taller than her. "They call our group children of the elements."

"And what do you want?"

"We wanted you to travel with us," Kihakso said as they had moved closer to Gizlae when Aylnivi had moved to protect Vadixas.

"And why should I?"

"Someone is hunting us down. His name is Chabnorl."

"My town wouldn't let him."

"It still would be safer."

Aylnivi was about to refuse when Vadixas spoke up, "Awww I'm going to miss you Aylnivi."

Aylnivi looked over her shoulder at Vadixas, "You aren't going?"

"Well...the town won't be very happy if I do so-"

"We were planning to ask her tonight."

Aylnivi looked over to Awrosk, "she can't go back to her town, so we were figuring out how to convince her later tonight."

"I said I can't go. My town needs me."

Aylnivi watched the group for a moment before looking back at Vadixas again, "Too bad. If you went, you would be able to stop me if I did something evil."

The group gasped, except Awrosk, Vadixas took a step away from her. Gizlae looked like she was about to say something when Awrosk stopped her by shaking his head.

"You can't do that Aylnivi."

Aylnivi shrugged, "If you stuck around, you could have a say but since you're just going to go back to your town…"

Vadixas looked between the group and Aylnivi for a moment, "If…if you're with them they'll stop you."

Aylnivi looked back at the group with an eyebrow raised.

Gizlae wanted to speak again but Ceaxtra had caught on and interrupted her, "Why should we? It isn't our job to."

Vadixas just stared at her for a moment before looking back at Aylnivi. She then stood up straighter "Then I must go with you all to make sure that you don't do anything evil."

Aylnivi nodded "alright."

She turned back to the rest of the group, "Looks like we'll be going with you." Before anyone could say anything else, Aylnivi spoke up again, "Are you all ready to go?"

"Go where?" Gizlae asked, she wasn't comfortable with the previous conversation and she hoped they would move on from it quickly.

"We need to leave as soon as possible."

Gizlae frowned, "But we didn't get supplies."

Aylnivi shook her head, "We can get them at the next town. We need to get out of here as soon as possible."

"Why?"

"If the town finds out Vadixas is here. They will kill her."

"The guard wasn't lying about that?" Vadixas said with a gasp.

Aylnivi sighed, "Pitydden and Whighridge have been fighting for years. When I woke up, that tipped the balance and the only thing keeping Pitydden from being destroyed was due to me delaying it. Then Vadixas woke up and that shifted the balance again. Thankfully Vadixas was determined to fight me solo and the town was fine with me delaying her death since they think I was taunting and torturing her."

The others' eyes all grew wide.

"So, we need to get her out of here as fast as possible."

"We can go back to Gillabury, it isn't far from here and we know where the inn is."

Aylnivi nodded, "I was worried that our battles would continue till my death."

"I wouldn't have killed you Aylnivi," Vadixas said, looking nervous.

"Of course, but you're being used by your town. I believe they would have pushed you to the point where you had to."

"What...no they," Vadixas pointed to Aylnivi. "Your town uses you too."

Aylnivi nodded, "They do. But I knew that going in. They could only use me as far as I would allow them to." she looked Vadixas over, "You on the other hand, didn't know, and would have given your life for a town that didn't care about you."

"I..." Vadixas curled into herself and Awrosk moved over to her, lightly placing a hand on her shoulder before glaring at Aylnivi.

She gave a small smile, "Seems like it won't be a problem soon."

Vadixas looked up at her with wide eyes "What?"

Aylnivi looked at Awrosk, who also had wide eyes and removed his hand.

She nodded at Vadixas, "Since you won't be dealing with your town while we travel. I figured you will be able to realize the problem with it." She then turned to the rest of the group. "Since we don't have time to get supplies from town, do you want to take what you can from the house? The town supplies it, so I don't need it."

"They supply you food?" Vadixas whispers.

Aylnivi looked at her with a frown.

Ceaxtra frowned, "You all can grab stuff. I want to look at the throne." She turned to it, "It looks like carved ice, but it has to be made from stone."

Aylnivi nodded before leading the rest of the group to the kitchen leaving Vadixas with Ceaxtra.

Once the Ceaxtra was finished looking at the chair and the group collected all the food they could take, they headed towards the door. as Aylnivi stepped out the guard stopped her.

"Where are you going?"

Gizlae and Kihakso were ready to step up when Aylnivi spoke up first, "Vadixas has challenged me to our final duel with this group of people." She waved at them, "They will watch over as witness, so I need to go and defeat her."

The guard nodded and let them all through. As they moved through town, Vadixas moved closer to Aylnivi "But I didn't though, is that what you want?"

Aylnivi shook her head, "That was the only way I could get out of town without being watched." She looked at the rest of the group before turning back to Vadixas "As for practice fighting, it would be better for you to fight others to improve."

"I see." Vadixas said as she looked at the others, before looking back at Aylnivi.

"Would you ask for me?" Aylnivi just shook her head leading the group out of town.

When they got to Gillabury Vadixas had stuck close to them. But once they got to the marketplace, Vadixas gasped before running off, trying to look at everything at once.

"Wait!" Gizlae said following after her.

"No Giz-" Kihakso sighed as the two ran off. "I need to go after them," they muttered.

"Let me go with you," Ceaxtra said, looking down the main street.

Kihakso sighed, "You just want to check out the glassblower again," they muttered but headed off after them.

Ceaxtra waving at the two as she followed after him.

Awrosk turned to Aylnivi, "Are we going to follow them?"

"In a bit," Aylnivi turned fully towards him. "We need to talk."

"What about?" Awrosk said but decided to keep looking at the crowd in front of him instead of at her.

"Your interest in Vadixas."

Awrosk turned his head away even more from Aylnivi, not wanting to look at her, "I don't know what you're talking about."

"I'm sure you don't," She said, taking a step closer towards him. "But I feel you should know that anyone who hurts her will be taken care of by me."

Awrosk gulped.

"Do you understand?"

Awrosk nodded.

"Good let's go find the others."

"I know where the glassblower's shop is."

He started to head that way. As they were walking through the busy street, they were suddenly dragged into an alley and thrown against the back wall.

Awrosk glared at the group that had brought them here, "Who are you?"

"We saw you arrive with the others. We have them, so tell us who you are and you can see your friends again."

Awrosk saw their eyes flash green and reigned in her first instinct to attack. He saw Aylnivi step forward but grabbed her hand.

She pulled it away with a glare but he spoke up first, "I'm Awrosk Child of Ice."

The leader turned to one of his men "you got those cuffs?" the men started to look between a bunch they were holding before pulling out one and throwing it to Awrosk

"Put that on."

He then turned to Aylnivi.

"Who are you?"

Aylnivi ignored him to look at the cuff that Awrosk was putting on.

"What are those?"

Awrosk sighed, "so you hadn't seen them before. They're cuffs that were made to stop our connection to our powers." He then looked her in the eyes, "they only work for a specific child, so mine won't work for you and yours won't work for me."

Aylnivi watched him for a moment longer. The leader spoke up getting annoyed that she hadn't answered him "I said wh-"

"I'm Aylnivi, Child of Water." She saw the slight nod from Awrosk before looking back at the leader. He glared at her but pulled out the correct cuff and threw it to her. She clicked them on her wrists and tried to act like she did when she was low on energy, which meant a slight droop of her head and shoulders.

With them both cuffed, the leader grabbed the chain and started to pull them through the alleyways. Having no knowledge outside of the main road they got lost quickly in the twists and turns.

"Who are these guys?" whispered Aylnivi.

"They were hired by someone, I haven't met him yet but Gizlae, Kihakso, and Ceaxtra said they did."

"They did mention that someone was hunting us down at my place."

"Wonder if we'll meet him?"

The leader spoke up with a laugh, "We're bringing you right to his side base, you'll meet him for sure."

He pulled the cuffs a little harder, "now be quiet."

The rest of the walk was silent until they got to a building that seemed like any other. They knew if they had been looking for it, they would never have found it.

They were quickly brought down to a basement where indeed, the others were being kept in a cell. There were guards along the other wall watching them. Ceaxtra was off to the side, seemingly trying to pull her hand out of the cuffs but they were too tight.

Gizlae and Kihakso were on the other side. Gizlae had her head on Kihakso's shoulder and they were glaring at the guards. Kihakso looked like they were ready to attack the first person that came near them. Vadixas was looking out the window, seemingly ignoring everyone else. Awrosk and Aylnivi were shoved in with the others. Aylnivi managed to keep her footing while Awrosk fell to his knees, he glared at the leader as he laughed while heading up the stairs.

Aylnivi looked around quickly before looking at Vadixas. "You okay?"

Vadixas looked over her shoulder before looking back out the window, "Oh you're here Aylnivi. I'm fine."

"You seem to be taking this pretty well."

Vadixas shrugged, "Well they said he was our enemy. And you're my enemy but you haven't hurt me." She looked at the cuffs, " Although it is weird that he wants to weaken us, maybe he wants to teach us a different fight style?"

"Oh…Vadixas…no…" said Ceaxtra who was listening.

Vadixas looked over at her "Huh?"

"He wants us dead," Kihakso muttered, Gizlae flinched when they said the word but didn't move otherwise.

"But…that's not what enemies do. That's not what Aylnivi does," she said, pointing to Aylnivi.

"I'm different."

Vadixas turned to her with wide eyes, "What?"

It was then that Chabnorl came down the steps. He looked over the group and sighed, "Not the ones I was hoping for," he muttered then shrugged.

"I'm sorry to drag you into such a situation but our last meeting didn't go how I wanted."

"What do you want?" Aylnivi said, turning to glare at him.

Vadixas moved up to look over her shoulder at him, which she preferred.

"It should be obvious at this point but I will state it for you."

He then looked Aylnivi directly in the eyes, "Your deaths."

"Why?" Vadixas shouted, holding her shoulder tighter. "We didn't do anything."

When he looked at her, he actually looked a little sad, "You are correct, you didn't."

Vadixas started to smile but then he shook his head, "That still doesn't mean you should exist though."

Aylnivi couldn't stop herself, she started to form ice around her hands and the cuffs where they touched.

"What!" Chabnorl took a step back, "The cuffs should be working."

Aylnivi looked down at her hands, as if surprised she was making ice. She started to form her spike using her anger, doing her best to make it her best one.

"They would if they were for me and not for Awrosk."

With that, Awrosk formed a dagger next to her and used it to cut the chains between the cuffs, giving him full range of movement.

Chabnorl turned to glare at the leader, "You put them in the wrong cuffs."

"They told me she was a Child of Water and he was a Child of Ice!"

"Everyone knows the Child of Water is a boy!" he shouted at the leader.

"I didn't-" the leader muttered as Awrosk moved around, cutting the chains for everyone. While it didn't remove the blocking effect it would have taken too long for him to completely remove the cuffs.

Once he was done, he turned to Aylnivi, who was still forming an ice spike.

"Are you going to help? Or are you going to make me do everything?"

He asked with a glare, changing the dagger into a sword to make it easier to cut the bars.

"It takes time," she said as she held the spike carefully.

Her eyes met Chabnorl's and she smiled before throwing the ice spike at him. His eyes went wide and he formed a hole under himself, falling inside quickly to dodge it. When the spike hit the wall, it sank halfway into it. The men looked at the ice spike, then at Aylnivi and they immediately ran from the room.

Chabnorl pulled himself out of the hole and glared at the men running away "you can't find good help anymore."

He looked back at the kids, "So, I just have to take care of two of you? I can-" there was a rumble behind him, "What was that?" he looked back at the spike in the wall.

"That was the ice expanding, I wonder how long this house will remain standing with the foundation crumbling."

"You did what!" shouted Kihakso, glaring at Aylnivi. By now all the kids were standing up.

Chabnorl was about to say something when another rumble sounded. He huffed before falling back into his hole it closing once he was fully inside.

"Why did you make this harder?" Awrosk shouted as he started to swing at the bars. The chains were very thin, so it was easy to cut through but he hadn't cut through bars this thick before and he didn't know how long it would take. Aylnivi walked up to the bars on the other side and wrapped a hand on bars next to each other. She took a deep breath before blowing down on them while pouring cold energy through her hands. This made the metal rapidly freeze allowing her to put enough weight on the bars that they broke and let her fall through them.

Vadixas gasped "Aylnivi that was so smart!"

"Compliment me later, I wasn't lying when I said the house was coming down."

She held her hand up for Vadixas, who ran over and took it immediately, seeing how much energy she used. The others used the hole to get out and up the stairs. Awrosk moved over to Aylnivi and put her arm over his shoulders, and with some help from Vadixas, he managed to get the three out. They took a few minutes to catch their breath when suddenly the house crumbled, only spikes of ice poking out of the rubble showed any indication that they were there.

They decided to move out of town before they were blamed for the house falling. Vadixas had to be dragged away from town since she didn't get to see all that she had wanted to.

Once they had found a place where they could rest for the night, Awrosk worked on slowly cutting off everyones cuffs. Aylnivi offered to help but Vadixas told her no since her magical energy was so low. When Gizlae reached to touch her hand she agreed, forcing Aylnivi to lay down.

Later that night, Vadixas and Ceaxtra were the ones on watch. Vadixas was there because she was worried about Aylnivi while Ceaxtra was there because she wanted to get the chance to talk to Vadixas.

Ceaxtra waited until she was pretty sure everyone was asleep before she spoke up.

"Vadixas? May I ask you something?"

"Sure?"

"Could you teach me how you fight?"

Vadixas gasped, "You want to learn how to fight from me?"

Ceaxtra nodded, "I want to know how you fight."

Vadixas frowned, "A practice battle would be too much noise. We would wake the others," she said, biting her lip.

Ceaxtra nodded, "That is why I was asking, telling me should be enough."

"I don't think I have a style. I don't know what I could teach you."

"She's good at energy control. It might be her eyes that cause it, though," Aylnivi said, sitting up suddenly making the two jump.

"Aylnivi, you should be sleeping."

Aylnivi just shrugged "I'll be fine." She moved to sit beside Vadixas with the two looking at Ceaxtra. "I've fought her multiple times. It's obvious that she still doesn't understand battle and that she is still adjusting but what she is very good at is energy control."

"What do you mean?"

"She can cast the same spell, one after the other but the power behind it will be different."

"I just know how much energy goes into my spells. you both probably can do it better if you practice too," Vadixas muttered.

Ceaxtra shook her head, "No, what are you talking about? I just imagine what I want to happen and then it does."

"Well, can you feel the flow of energy inside of you?" Ceaxtra and Aylnivi closed their eyes to concentrate for a moment before shaking their heads.

"oh...um..."

Vadixas looked at Aylnivi who just sighed.

"We should use examples, but" she looked to Ceaxtra. "That would lead to using what I am strong at."

"Which is?"

"Variety, I practiced with my ice so much that I can change the ice depending on what I want to do. Whether I make the air around it cold or let it form fast or slow. Whatever decisions I make, changes the abilities of the ice."

She waved to her side where Gillabury was, "That was how I was able to take down that house with one spike. It took months, but I was able to create an ice spike that could destroy rock, which you saw"

The two wanted to know why but figured from the rare look of anger Aylnivi had that now wasn't the time to ask.

"Since my knowledge will help us figure out Vadixas's abilities we should work together."

She formed a small spike of ice, the normal one that she would use in a battle. Once Vadixas told her how much energy that took, she formed a weaker one and then kept repeating the process.

Ceaxtra used the bubble she was still working on and Vadixas helped her figure out that the reason it kept speeding up was because she put too much energy into it. With Aylnivi's help, she figured out that she could change the wind using the environment around her and that there were different types of wind depending on the speed and power behind it. They spent the rest of the night working on this.

In the morning with the arrows pointing the way, the group headed to what seemed to be the closest town. When they were on the outskirts they heard a rumble of thunder behind them. The group turned around to see Tesirew smile at them again, "What are you doing here?"

Ceaxtra crossed her arms, "Us? What about you?"

Tesirew gave a weak smile and shifted from one foot to the others. "Well....you know...this is my home? Remember I told you all?"

Gizlae smiled, "Oh, is that so?" Gizlae looked back at the town.

Kihakso frowned, "Was it a long trip between the two?"

Tesirew shrugged, "I like to run, though I was slowed down because a house crumbled yesterday and that delayed my departure. Hopefully Aphi wasn't too worried."

The others looked at Aylnivi, who didn't even bother to look at any of them.

Vadixas frowned, "Have you met her before?" she asked, looking to Gizlae knowing she would be the most likely to answer.

Gizlae turned to her, "Oh yes. This is Tesirew, we met her back in Gillabury. She does deliveries between the two towns."

Vadixas blinked at Gizlae, "You were okay with her leaving but didn't want to leave me and Aylnivi in our towns?" She looked back at the town. "Did you have plans to meet her here?"

"What?" Kihakso asked, looking at Vadixas.

Vadixas waved at Tesirew not bothering to look at her, her sights still lingering on the town. "Because she's a Child of the Element like us?"

The rest look at Tesirew with wide eyes.

"What?"

They couldn't tell if her eyes were as wide as theirs because her hat covered them but she was standing a bit straighter.

Vadixas turned and pointed at Tesirew, "She's got the same filter over her that shows that she has magical energy just like all of us."

Tesirew stood there for a moment before there was a clap of thunder and a flash of lightning and she was gone. Everyone stared at where she once was for another moment, not knowing what to say.

"How did we not notice?" Kihakso shouted as he looked to Ceaxtra and Gizlae, "How did I not notice."

Gizlae sighed, "Well, when she met us, she was behind us just like this time. Which means that when you weren't looking, her arrow disappeared and then after that since you didn't trust her, you didn't let her out of your sight. Meaning her arrow never came back. Then we were distracted by them," she said as she waved at Vadixas and Aylnivi. "It makes sense that you couldn't tell."

"Let's just go find her," he said with a sigh. They didn't need to run since Kihakso knew where she was going but they did walk a bit faster, not wanting to give her time to flee. Aylnivi had to pull Vadixas along with her since Vadixas wanted to keep looking at everything they walked by.

Eventually, the arrow pointed to a house. Kihakso walked a little up and down the street to make sure but the whole time they were frowning.

"What is it?" Gizlae asked.

"There…" Kihakso shook their head. "No, don't worry about it, let's just go talk to her."

They walked up to the door and knocked. Waited a moment or two before they knocked again, this time, a little harder than needed. They were about to knock again when the door opened. Kihakso looked at the ground for a moment before looking up at Aphiqalena.

"Oh, there was another one here."

The person that opened the door stared at them for a moment before shutting the door in their faces.

She could feel a pressure all around her but there wasn't any pain. She also felt something petting her head making her want to just fall asleep again.

"Poor child." A voice whisperer.

She was too sleepy to say anything so she just decided to listen to the voice instead.

"You suffered too much. I can't make it right, but I can make it better."

"Better?" She croaked, just realizing that her throat was sore.

The voice chuckled, "You will forget the pain you suffered. You will be given a better life. One that loves you more than the old one ever did."

"I don't understand."

"You won't for now. But she will."

Suddenly the pressure was gone, along with the head petting. She opened her eyes to see a bright sky above her. She stood up and looked around. Behind her was a mountain range that seemed to fill her with dread and in front of her lay a plain that seemed to pull her forward. With a shrug and not wanting to confirm what her dread meant she headed forward.

She didn't know how long it took but after a while she saw a person passed out on the ground. She winced when she saw a crackling red mark down her back. She moved closer to check on her and when she turned her over she shouted and moved away immediately realizing that the girl was already dead.

Aphiqalena spent a moment just staring into her blank eyes, trying to calm down before holding her breath and moving back over to her. She turned the girl over on her back and closed her eyes.

Aphiqalena didn't know what to do, she knew she should probably bury her but Aphiqalena didn't have a shovel.

She started to pace next to the girl when she noticed a building pressure. She couldn't place where it was coming from but she could almost taste the lightning on her tongue.

Before she could move away the pressure seemed to condense into where the girl was and static started to arc over her body as she became so bright that Aphiqalena had to look away. Then there was a rumble of thunder and Aphiqalena was able to see that the girl had changed. Most notable was her hair, which was now a dark blue with crackling streaks of lilac along it.

Aphiqalena stood there for a long moment not knowing what had happened when the girl suddenly groaned. That made Aphiqalena take a step back knowing she had been dead only moments before. She watched as a number one formed over her head. Aphiqalena watched as the girl's eyes opened

"Are you...okay?" she asked.

Aphiqalena watched as the girl looked at her but did not actually see her. They met eyes for only a moment before the girl cried out, clutching her head. Aphiqalena moved closer, kneeling right next to the girl running her hand through the girl's hair. She kept going until the girl seemed to calm down a little and looked up at her.

"I'm so sorry." the girl whispered.

The following conversation confused Aphiqalena but that didn't stop her from comforting the girl by running her hands through her hair. Eventually the two started to head to a town since they had no food or money.

As they were walking, Aphiqalena started asking about her past wondering what Tesirew would be willing to tell her. It was interesting to know that they were both thieves.

Suddenly Tesirew changed the subject, "Do you remember what you talked about in the conversation with him?" Tesirew asked, looking over at Aphiqalena.

Aphiqalena thought about it for a moment. "It was a pretty weird conversation, but it had to be important if I remembered it."

Tesirew nodded, "I think so."

"We were talking about how we were going to make roots together?" Tesirew froze but Aphiqalena didn't see her and kept walking while thinking. "How it would be our secret and only those in our family would have the key to the root nest."

"Oh...that...that was..." Tesirew's weak voice made Aphiqalena notice that she had stopped walking. Aphiqalena turned to look at her and saw she was almost crying "Tesirew?"

"That was the last time you two spoke." she whispered.

Aphiqalena frowned, "What happened?"

"You were forced to leave town before giving him word of where you were going. You were confident that he would find you as he had done so many times before." Tesirew was silent for a moment. "You ended up in the Town of Earth and..."

Aphiqalena pulled her into a hug, she might not remember exactly what happened but she knew whatever had happened next wasn't pleasant.

Eventually they made it to a town where they got a nice hat for Tesirew and some money. Before moving on to the next town to get more money for supplies.

The two having entered the second town, Aphiqalena were surprised how fast they were able to find someone to do a delivery for. Aphiqalena wasn't too happy that it was out of town but she knew Tesirew could handle it. She looked away because she knew the flash of Tesirew was going to happen. She looked back at the lady to see she had stepped back with a hand on her chest.

"What was that?"

Aphiqalena smiled, "It's just an ability Tesirew has. It should be a few minutes for her to get there and back."

The lady's eyes went wide, "Is she..." she looked over at Aphiqalena.

"Is she what?"

The lady moved closer to Aphiqalena, "Is she holding you hostage?" she whispered.

Aphiqalena glared at her, "What are you talking about?"

The lady moved close to her again to whisper, "It's obvious that she's the Child of Lightning. Why would you follow her if she wasn't holding you hostage."

Aphiqalena pushed her away, "What are you-"

The two were interrupted with another rumble of thunder and lightning and Tesirew standing there.

"I did it. They told me to tell you thanks."

Tesirew looked over to the two, the hat still blocking her eyes. "What's-"

She was interrupted when Aphiqalena grabbed her hand and the two moved away from the lady.

"Guards," the lady shouted.

Aphiqalena started to run through the streets, dragging Tesirew with her. She started to take side paths trying to be as confusing as possible so the guards couldn't find them.

Eventually, they stopped to plan where they were going but before Aphiqalena could stop her, Tesirew ran off again. Aphiqalena had to blink away the spots in her vision from looking so closely at the flash of lightning. Once they were all gone she looked up to see guards turning the corner, they were brought here by the sound.

She couldn't run for very long, since she was still tired from before, but she still decided to give it a try. She just hoped that she would be able to find Tesirew later. She turned and ran, doing her best to take turns when she could. Her lack of knowledge was her downfall as she eventually ran into a dead end.

She was captured and brought to a room which she was locked in. They didn't talk to her so she didn't know what was being planned for her. She paced back and forth in the room. Until there were cries of pain and a knock on the door. She was so glad when Tesirew opened the door.

The two were able to get out of town before any guards came after them. She let Tesirew lead the way since she was the one who had found another town for them to stay in.

Once they got to the next town, Aphiqalena sighed. They needed to figure out a way to make money in a manner that wouldn't reveal themselves as Children of the Elements. She was about to look around when she heard Tesirew speak up "do you need help with that?"

Aphiqalena looked over to see Tesirew talking to a young kid.

"I want to send this to my mommy but I don't have the money."

"Well where does it need to go?" Tesirew asked.

Aphiqalena moved over to them and grabbed Tesirew's arm, "What are you doing? Do you remember what happened last time?" she whispered to her, pulling her away from the boy.

Tesirew smiled, "Don't worry I have an idea," she whispered before looking back at the kid, "So where does it need to go?"

"My mom lives in Gillabury," he said, holding the letter out to her.

Tesirew nodded before turning to Aphiqalena, "Think you could find an inn for us while I do this for the kid?"

Aphiqalena frowned, "How long do you think it will take? We don't have much money left."

Tesirew frowned, "I'll bring some money back with a return package." She turned back to the boy with a smile, "Could you show her an inn we can stay in and return tomorrow when I can give you a return message?"

The kid nodded before moving down the street looking at Aphiqalena expectantly. "Are you sure?" Aphiqalena asked, she started to move down the street and lighting followed since they were going the same way for a while.

"Yeah don't worry. I've been thinking about this while we traveled." The two saw the kid take a side road and they waved as they parted ways. The kid kept running forward but stopped to wait for Aphiqalena. Aphiqalena frowned when she heard the tell-tale sound of thunder but hoped whatever Tesirew had planned would work, she was led to an inn on the outskirts of town. The kid ran up to the front desk as Aphiqalena walked in.

"Dad, I sent the package."

He frowned as he looked up at Aphiqalena , "Did he bother you?"

Aphiqalena watched him for a moment, "It wasn't a bother, my friend Tesirew likes to travel so took the package. She'll probably be here later today or early tomorrow."

"That seems fast."

Aphiqalena shrugged, "She likes to run." She tried to keep it vague so no one would look into it.

The man sighed, "well either way. Thank you for the help, we can't pay you for your services, though."

Aphiqalena shrugged again, "Neither can I. I was planning to spend time here and try to figure something else out."

The man looked at his son again before looking back at Aphiqalena , "As payment for the package would you stay here for the night?"

Aphiqalena watched him, "Is that fine?"

The man smiled, "We couldn't pay for my son's package to get to his mom so you did a major favor for us."

Aphiqalena nodded, "Then I'll accept."

It was the next day, early morning before Aphiqalena heard the familiar rumble. Aphiqalena made her way casually to where Tesirew last saw her. It only took a few minutes for Tesirew to find her.

"So?" Aphiqalena said.

Tesirew smiled, holding out a bag. "I got a note for that kid and a pretty good pay when I drop this off."

"And no one...realized anything?"

Tesirew shook her head, "No one saw me so there wasn't any problem. Did you find a place to stay?"

Aphiqalena nodded, "Turns out the kid's dad runs an inn, they're letting us stay there as payment."

"Great, lead the way, I have a letter to give."

The two made it back to the inn with Aphiqalena leading the way. The innkeeper greeted them as they entered the inn again. The man's eyes went wide when he saw Tesirew "You're back already?"

Tesirew shrugged, "Yes I like to run," she said with a smile. "Is that kid up?"

Rujthij sighed, "He likes to sleep late. Have some food, you must be hungry."

Aphiqalena frowned, "But we don't have any money."

"You can pay me later," he said with a smile.

Tesirew moved closer to Aphiqalena to whisper, "I have a delivery here so we can pay for everything quickly." Aphiqalena nodded as she sat down. After a while Rujthij brought them their food. While they were eating, Gemhidl came downstairs from wherever his room was.

He blinked at the two of them before moving to their table. "Can I join you?"

Tesirew nodded her head, "Sure." She then pulled out the letter and put it on the table in front of him, "Before you eat why don't you read this?"

"What is it?"

"A return letter from your mom."

Gemhidl gasped and immediately opened the letter and started to read it. Once he was finished he ran over to give Tesirew a hug.

After that day, the two decided to stay in the town and live in the inn while they worked on collecting enough money to get a house of their own.

Aphiqalena woke up to find Tesirew not in her room. As she made her way down stairs she was practically tackled by both Gemhidl and the friend that had been playing with him.

"You're up already" they both shouted.

She nodded, "Couldn't sleep the whole day away. How else would I be able to play with you today?"

The kid's eyes shined "Really?"

Aphiqalena nodded, "Can you tell me where Tesirew is?"

"She went out to deliver something over in Gillabury. She said she would be back tomorrow."

Aphiqalena sighed, today was the day she was going to take a final look at the house that she had been eyeing. The two had raised enough money a week ago to get the house. They wanted to wait a while because Tesirew had some important deliveries that she couldn't delay. Sadly if Aphiqalena waited any longer they would lose the house so she had to buy it on her own instead.

"Are you okay?" Gemhidl asked.

Aphiqalena smiled at him, "Just thinking. I need to go."

"Without eating breakfast?"

"The faster I finish what I need to do, the faster I can play with you."

Gemhidl gasped, "Then go, go, hurry," he said, practically pushing her out the door.

"I don't know," she said, purposely walking slowly. "I might be hungry enough to have a full feast. Eating breakfast might take hours."

"Nnnoooo" he said as they made it to the door.

Aphiqalena laughed as she stepped outside looking back to see the kids smiling triumphantly about getting her over the threshold.

"Alright, I'll be back later today."

They waved at her as she headed down the street. It had taken the two a while to get enough money to buy a house. The houses weren't too expensive in this town but they wanted a bigger one to allow Aphiqalena to watch kids there and give them room to be kids. The two had agreed that Aphiqalena would buy the house since she was the older looking of the two.

They had been wondering where to live when the owners of the house started talking about leaving town. Aphiqalena had made her way over to talk to them as soon as she heard the rumors. She wanted to convince them to sell to her and no one else. Her reputation was good considering both her delivery job and babysitting job, so it wasn't hard to convince them to wait for her to gain the money.

When she got to the house she couldn't help but stand outside of it and just look at it. It was a two-story building with a big living room. The upstairs was all bedrooms, there were five of them. One for her and Tesirew and the other three would be just in case any of the kids she was babysitting needed a nap or had to stay the night. The front yard was big with plenty of room for the kids to run and play, it was also open to allow parents to check on their kids with only a look. In comparison the backyard was small with high walls leading to an alleyway. It was actually perfect for the two in case Tesirew needed to stop running in town somewhere that no one would see her.

It took half a day for Aphiqalena to actually buy it. They gave one more look over the house and then she was worried when they talked about raising the price but with her jobs from the week before she had enough for the raise. She wasn't happy about it but didn't want to lose the house either. This meant that she didn't have enough funds to furnish the place as yet but Tesirew had wanted to help pick out stuff anyways, so she would just have had to wait.

She gave a happy little sigh as she locked the front door of their house. She brushed her fingers along the keys just staring at them. For some reason Tesirew's jokes of her finally being rooted somewhere sprang to mind. She didn't know what they were for but Tesirew always said it was a joke from her past life.

Aphiqalena had a little extra money and she knew just what to do with it.

Tesirew arrived back in town the next day. She moved quickly to give Aphiqalena the gift she had secured in her bag. She wasn't running full speed but she was definitely running through town.

When she opened the door to the inn that the two had called home for the last month, she saw Aphiqalena having breakfast with the kid.

"I'm back!" she shouted, skipping over to the table.

"Tesirew!" Gemhidl said as he jumped off his seat and Tesirew just barely caught him.

"Oof, aren't we always saying you need to be more careful?"

Gemhidl nodded but didn't look sorry, giving her one more squeeze before climbing back on his chair to eat more food.

Tesirew looked over at Aphiqalena who smirked.

"Catch!"

She threw something up in the air and Tesirew took a step back to catch it. Seeing that it was a pair of keys that were in her hands.

"Now we both have roots to support us."

Tesirew looked at the keys for a long moment before moving quickly to hug Aphiqalena.

"I'll keep the root nest safe," she whispered into her ear.

Aphiqalena blinked for a moment before realizing what she was saying. With the context she could understand how important her last conversation was with Kovnegh.

She now knew neither of them had ever had a home in their last life but here they were, planning to make one together. She wondered if he would still like her now, if he would want to share this home she had made with her sister. She wondered if he would still love her or her him.

Instead of focusing on the sadness she felt for her loss, she focused on Tesirew who was still giving her a hug.

She held her tight for a moment more before saying, "I don't have much money left but we should go furniture shopping since you're here today."

"I have money from my last job that I can use to pay for it," Tesirew muttered into her shoulder. Aphiqalena nodded expecting that to be the end of it when Tesirew suddenly pushed herself away.

"Oh, I have the first thing to go into our house."

"hmmm?"

"I got it as a gift for you but this is perfect."

"You didn't need to get me a gift."

"I didn't have to but I wanted to. Think of it as payback for the hat."

Aphiqalena sighed but held out her hands, "alright." Tesirew smiled and got the wrapped package out of her bag, placing it carefully into her hands. Aphiqalena slowly unwrapped it, not knowing what to expect.

Inside were two metal butterflies, their wings filled in with colored glass, one of them was a butterfly where its left wing was iridescent and the right wing was white. The other butterfly had the left wing dark green and the right wing was blue. Aphiqalena blinked at them "where did you...?"

Tesirew's smile grew, "Gillabury was looking for some new ideas and I offered up this one."

"They had fun trying out all sorts of color combinations." She moved closer so that only Aphiqalena could hear her whisper, "When I saw they got ours, I just had to buy them."

Aphiqalena held one up to see the light coming through the glass.

"We'll need to stop by the house and find a place to hang them."

She wrapped them up again and placed them on the table. "Have you eaten?" Tesirew shook her head, she had left Gillabury as soon as she had woken up. Aphiqalena waved at the food still out. "We'll go after you eat something. Wouldn't be good for you to go shopping hungry."

Tesirew nodded and moved to the empty chair, listening as Gemhidl told her how pretty the butterflies were and how excited he was to play at the new house. Tesirew just nodded along as she ate, giving a small smile to the keys every once in a while

It was a few months of their life being perfect. Aphiqalena still wished she would meet with Kota someday but she hadn't yet. Aphiqalena was having a day off and spent the time cleaning the house.

Aphiqalena suddenly heard the thunder right outside their back door and frowned. Tesirew would only do that if she had a problem or was running late, but they had no plans for today. As she walked to the living room she heard the back door open and slam shut in quick succession. Entering the living room, she saw Tesirew throwing the clothes out of the basket before turning it over and hiding under it.

"Those were clean clothes."

"I didn't know, I didn't know. I never looked into their eyes. How would I know?" Tesirew muttered.

Aphiqalena moved over to the basket and went to lift it up but Tesirew grabbed the edge and pulled it down back over her.

"What's going on?"

"They shouldn't have followed me. I went too fast, I left right away."

"Who?" Before Tesirew could answer, there was a knock on the door.

Aphiqalena stood up, before starting to head to the door, she could hear some shuffling behind her. Looking over her shoulder she saw that Tesirew had shuffled herself to face the door.

Aphiqalena watched her for a moment before there was another knock on the door, this time a little louder. Aphiqalena sighed before moving to the door and opening it. She looked at the group and her frown grew as she only saw positive numbers over their heads.

"Oh, there was another one here," said a boy standing in front of the group. Aphiqalena watched them for a moment before slamming the door in their face. She locked the door before turning back to the hidden Tesirew.

She went over and kneeled next to her.

"Was that who you were talking about?"

Tesirew lifted the basket high enough for Aphiqalena to see her nod her head.

"Well that makes sense."

The person started to bang on their door again, she looked over her shoulder before looking back at Tesirew.

"Do you want to just leave through the back door till they go away?"

Tesirew looked at the door for a moment before nodding her head and slowly lifting the basket off herself. Aphiqalena chuckled before heading to the door and opening it for Tesirew. The two moved quickly down the street before taking the left to the market area. They waved to their friends as they moved along wondering how long it would take for the strange people at their door to get bored.

"Where should we go?" Tesirew asked as she looked around at the various stalls.

Aphiqalena sighed, "We shouldn't leave town, but we need to hide somewhere."

Tesirew smiled at her, "We should go to the inn. Gemhidl and Rujthij would help us."

Aphiqalena frowned, "We might not be able to leave right away."

"Sleepover!" Tesirew shouted with a laugh before running towards the inn. Aphiqalena chuckled before following after her. Tesirew and Aphiqalena were so close to the inn that they could see the sign down the street. The two were running down the street until suddenly Kihakso stepped in front of Tesirew. She tried to stop but couldn't in time and slammed into him.

Her hat now had a string so it didn't drop to the floor but it did fall off her head. she looked up at him with wide eyes and he looked down. Before she could look away their eyes met and the stranger's memories entered her head.

"Tesirew!" Aphiqalena ran over to her as she grabbed her head with a groan. Aphiqalena glared up at Kihakso before she picked Tesirew up in a bridal carry and headed back to their home. Getting Tesirew into her bed was more important than dealing with these bothersome people.

As she was heading back Gemhidl ran up to her.

"Aphiqalena are you and Tesirew okay?"

She stopped to talk to him while looking back to see if the others were still following them.

"we will be."

Gemhidl looked up at the group, "Are they bothering you? Do you want us to deal with them?"

Aphiqalena's eyes went wide and she shook her head.

"No, they're just annoying but I don't know if they would hurt you so just leave them alone. Tell the others okay?"

"Okay I'll talk to the others."

Gemhidl quickly ran off before Aphiqalena could say more. She wasn't confident he would listen to what she said. The group moving closer to them during their conversation she shook her head and went back home.

She smiled when she saw the house coming into view but it dropped when she saw two of the group waiting by her door.

"Oh, you made it back." said Vadixas with a wave, Awrosk watched her carefully next to her.

"Would you move so I can get back in?" she asked, shifting Tesirew slightly.

Vadixas shook her head, "No can do. The others said to wait to see if you returned."

"We just want to talk," said Gizlae behind her. Aphiqalena turned so that she could see both groups. It backed her into a corner because her fence was behind her but it was better than being surrounded.

"And what if we don't want to talk?"

"Those two," Ceaxtra said waving to Kihakso and Gizlae. "Don't really take no for an answer."

Aphiqalena frowned, "So you're just going to-" before Aphiqalena could finish her sentence a shout interrupted them.

"Leave them alone!" ten of the older kids she usually watched over rushed the group. Most of the group looked confused, but a few were visibly annoyed, as the kids shuffled them away from the front door and onto the sidewalk. Aphiqalena took a breath of relief as she was able to get to the front door having a small smile as the kids made a wall between her and the group.

"Kids you should-" she tried to lead them into the house where it was safe when the parents came up.

"Is everything okay?" asked Rujthij, the kids letting him through to get next to Aphiqalena.

Aphiqalena nodded, "Yeah. It will be."

"No, it won't!" shouted Kihakso, taking a step forward.

Rujthij watched him carefully, "They'll come after you, that's why you need to leave."

"No," muttered Tesirew.

Aphiqalena looked down at her.

"Who will come after them?" Rujthij asked.

"Chabnorl," Ceaxtra said as the group nodded.

"No," said Tesirew a little louder this time the group could hear her and Kihakso frowned.

"He will, he's gone after all the Children of the Elements so far," Kihakso nodded as Rujthij's eyes went wide

"Even if they know and try-"

"No!" shouted Tesirew trying to stop them from revealing their secret.

Gemhidl looked up at his father, "What's a Child of the Element?"

"I don't think anyone knew," Aylnivi whispered, noticing how stiff Aphiqalena was now standing watching Rujthij.

He looked at the two next to him before looking at his son, "It's someone who was blessed by the elements."

Gemhidl's eyes went wide "How were they blessed? Can I be?"

Rujthij looked at the kids around him with a sad smile, "They were hurt really badly," he said not wanting to go into details just yet.

The group of kids gasped moving over to Aphiqalena, "Are you okay?" they all asked, looking up at her.

She looked over the parents before giving them a small nod, "Yeah like Rujthij said. We were blessed and that made us all better." She looked at the three groups before looking at Tesirew.

"Can you stand?"

Tesirew nodded slowly and Aphiqalena put her legs down before letting her lean on her.

She got her key out and unlocked the door before pointing at the group.

"We'll talk but go to the backyard."

Kihakso opened his mouth to say something but Gizlae pulled them along, "She needs to talk to them, let's not make more of a mess."

Once the group had all entered the house, she looked at the kids. "I need you guys to do me a favor."

All the kids nodded their heads, bouncing in place, eager to help.

"Tesirew is tired and needs a nap. Could I leave you all to set up the living room for her to rest?" When they all nodded, she smiled. "Great. Get that started and we'll join you after I finish talking to your parents, okay?" Once the kids rushed into the house, she closed the door with a sigh looking up at the parents who had moved closer with a frown.

She looked at Tesirew who was shivering, before standing up straight. "I'm sorry we didn't tell you." She didn't let them say anything before continuing, "The last time it was found out the town attacked us."

She took a breath, "If you want us to leave-"

"Our root nest," she heard Tesirew whisper but continued on.

"We can do so."

All of the parents looked at each other before Rujthij spoke up, "if you left, the kids would be devastated."

Aphiqalena frowned, "But...I'm the Child of Earth" she then waved to Tesirew. "And she's the Child of Lightning."

"That would explain all the recent thunder," one of the parents said. Some of the others chuckled at that but it died when Aphiqalena and Tesirew didn't join in.

Rujthij gave her a smile, "We didn't know that but you aren't at all what the kids have been described as."

Aphiqalena frowned, "What have they been described as?"

"Weapons for the towns to control others with."

Tesirew looked up a little then, "But...we never entered our towns."

"That might be why you are different."

Aphiqalena frowned looking up at the closed front door.

"What does it mean with them all coming here then?"

Rujthij shrugged, "I don't know but if you decide to go with them, me and Gemhidl can watch your house for you until you get back."

Tesirew gasped, "We really don't have to leave if we don't want to?"

"Temporarily sure. But if you were trying to leave for good you have to deal with the crying children before you go, not us."

Tesirew was too shocked to say anything, so she just nodded.

Aphiqalena gave a small smile, "Thanks."

"The root nest stays," Tesirew whispered with a smile.

Aphiqalena looked back at the house.

"We should talk to those people."

"Will you two be fine?"

Aphiqalena sighed, "We'll see. Wait here, I'll send the kids out. I'll inform you about what's going to happen after we figure it out."

The parents nodded and Aphiqalena smiled, helping Tesirew back into the house and towards the couch. Tesirew laughed as she saw the state of the couch, which was now just a pile of blankets and pillows.

"I think they brought every blanket in the house."

Aphiqalena let her flop onto it while she turned to the kids.

"Alright, your parents are waiting for you outside. We need to have a talk with our guest, so you can all go home now."

"But what if they are mean to you?"

Aphiqalena gave them a smile, "We know just who to run to if they do."

Gemhidl smiled, "No go on."

The kids all whined till they could give Tesirew a hug before heading out the door. Aphiqalena sighed before heading to the back door to let the group inside to talk.

"Alright, I'll let you in but there are some rules."

The group didn't move or say anything, they just looked at her.

"This is my house, if you say something that I don't like, I'm throwing you out. The town will help me." She waited for them to nod. "Tesirew isn't feeling good, so even if we do leave with you it won't be till tomorrow. Also don't think it will be forever. We'll go with you for some amount of time but we will eventually return home."

Gizlae nodded, "We'll figure that out."

Aphiqalena looked over at the group who all nodded. After a moment of just staring, Aphiqalena nodded.

"Come on then." She left the door open and walked back to the living room to see that Tesirew had buried herself under the blankets.

"Do you have your hat on?"

"No," Tesirew whispered.

"I won't let them move the blankets then."

With that Aphiqalena sat on the arm of the couch and watched as the group moved in. Ceaxtra sat on the floor, Vadixas moved to the window, looking at the two butterflies. Awrosk sat on the stairs and Aylnivi, Gizlae, and Kihakso stood around the room.

"So…" Aphiqalena started the conversation. "You said someone was hunting us?"

"Yeah, Chabnorl."

"I took care of his base in Gillabury but there are probably others." Aylnivi said, standing straighter.

"So where is he located now?" Aphiqalena asked. The group looked amongst themselves but they all shrugged.

"Alright, so we have no idea where he is or when he will attack."

"We thought it would be safer if we were a group instead of staying solo."

"We haven't needed the help," said Tesirew, the blankets shifting.

"And how long do you think that will last?" Kihakso muttered.

Tesirew sighed but didn't argue.

"So you just want to travel around?" Aphiqalena asked.

Gizlae shook her head, "We wanted to get everyone together so we can plan what to do about Chabnorl. We can also figure out how to communicate after we split up."

"So you don't have a plan yet?"

"We only have the Child of Nature to meet up with."

"Do you even know if the Child of Nature has woken up?"

Kihakso nodded, "I do, I can see arrows on the ground that point to other Children of the Elements when they are out of my sight."

Aphiqalena sighed, "So that's how you were able to find us once we left the house."

"That's cheating," Tesirew said.

Aphiqalena chuckled while Kihakso frowned, "Are you going to just stay under the blanket for this whole conversation."

"Why shouldn't she?" Aphiqalena watched Kihakso with a frown, they opened their mouth to say something but Gizlae pulled their hand

"It's alright," Gizlae said with a smile to Aphiqalena.

Aphiqalena sighed, she looked at the pile of blankets that was moving a little closer to her. "Alright, Tesirew needs to nap, you all can stay the night but we only have three rooms."

"We actually have four." Tesirew said.

Aphiqalena looked at her, "What?"

"I can just stay in your room. They can also use mine to spread out comfortably."

Aphiqalena looked at Kihakso then back to the blanket pile.

"Alright," She said as she stood up. "I can show you the rooms and you can all figure out where to go." She led them up to the rooms to see that all the beds had no blankets. Aphiqalena sighed "I'll get those, pick your rooms," she pointed to the three guest rooms and Tesirew's room. She then went down-stairs and lifted Tesirew off the couch, still covered in blankets. She brought her up the stairs into her room.

Once in her room she closed the door and placed her on the bed

"I don't need a nap."

"I know, but you've got a headache now. Just lay down, I need to get the blankets back to the beds."

Tesirew nodded and handed the ones she was using to cover herself back.

"I'll take care of our guests, you just rest."

The night was quiet. Most everyone stayed in their rooms, though Aphiqalena made dinner for the night. Placing plates for them at their doors, eating in her own room with Tesirew.

After eating, Ceaxtra was slightly bending the wind around her while sitting on the roof of Aphiqalena and Tesirew's house. She kept trying to practice but she didn't have any shape or form she wanted to make right now. she was gazing out, just moving the wind around her when she froze and sat up a little straighter.

"Enjoying the view?" Gizlae asked.

Ceaxtra turned to see her climbing up a ladder.

"I was wondering how you got up here." she turned back to the sunset. "How did you know I was up here?"

"I heard you land," Gizlae said with a chuckle

Ceaxtra sighed, "I still haven't managed to perfect the landing bit yet."

"What were you doing?"

"Oh, I was trying to get used to moving wind like Kihakso suggested, but without a shape to form it seems pretty pointless so I was just moving it around."

"Would you be up for a separate lesson then?" Ceaxtra looked over at Gizlae. "I figured out how to explain getting information to wind."

Ceaxtra shook her head, "Will it work?" She knew that Gizlae hadn't given up trying to teach her.

"It'll be different than how I do it, and you'll need to work on it to make it a better fit for you but I think if I give you the basic idea, you'll figure out what you need."

"Am I that impressive to you?"

Gizlae nodded, "I think we all are. It's what makes us a Child of our Element rather than just a user of elemental magic. I believe if all of us were willing to learn, we would be able to do each other's powers."

"And yet you haven't been trying to learn?"

"I'm content with my powers. But I have noticed you watching other people, not just the rest of the group and trying to copy them."

Ceaxtra shrugged. She wasn't ashamed of her desire to learn. "I see. Alright, tell me about this lesson."

"So, first I want you to make a ball of air," Ceaxtra copied what Vadixas had taught her and focused on moving her energy to her hands which she made a circle.

She started with a small ball and slowly grew it in her hands, "How big does it need to be?"

"No bigger than our heads. I only want to show you the concept and let you work on it. Let you have more fun that way." Ceaxtra nodded and made it the size Gizlae requested. She then cut off most of her energy to it only giving it enough to keep it going at a slow pace.

"Now then, this." Gizlae waved to the ball, "Is what you would feel most of the time when you do this."

"I don't feel anything."

"That's correct but then," she slowly moved her hand towards the ball, pressing her hand into it. Ceaxtra frowned as she adjusted the shape to accommodate her and Gizlae. She smiled when she stopped feeling the wind press against her hand.

"Could you feel the difference when I touched it?"

"Yeah it was like pressing up against something. Because it was." Ceaxtra said frowning at Gizlea.

Gizlae chuckled, "yes. That's the concept. You want to use the wind to brush up against everything in an area. If you can do it well enough then you might be able to tell people apart."

"I think...I think I get it."

Gizlae smiled at her.

"When you were climbing up here the wind patterns behind me changed, so I knew someone had come up...but not who."

"I knew you were smart. You managed to understand the concept without even getting a clear explanation."

"The explanation helped. It made me understand that something I was doing from time to time was what you were talking about."

Gizlae smiled and shifted to get more comfortable to enjoy the sunset.

Later that night Vadixas was twisting and turning in her bed, she dreamt that the people of the Whighridge were chasing her down. Cries of help for Aylnivi and Awrosk were ignored or only increased the anger of the people. When one of them grabbed her she woke up with a start. She sat there breathing heavily covering her mouth while trying not to wake Aylnivi.

After getting her heart to slow down a little, she decided to head to the kitchen to get some water. Instead, she found Awrosk pacing the room. She watched him make a lap or two before speaking up.

"Are you okay?"

Awrosk jumped, forming a dagger in his hand. He turned around and saw that it was Vadixas. He then sighed and threw the dagger into the sink. There was a splash of water when it landed.

"What are you doing up?"

"I had a nightmare. What about you?"

Awrosk moved closer, holding out a hand for her, "Do you want to talk about it?"

Vadixas shook her head, "Right now, I want to talk about you. What's wrong?"

Awrosk sighed, dropping his hand and going back to his pacing. He lapped another time before he spoke up.

"Have you ever had a gut feeling but didn't want to listen to it?"

"What do you mean?"

"Like there is somewhere you needed to be but...you don't want to leave where you are?"

The two lapsed into silence as Awrosk started to pace again. Vadixas moved a little closer so she stood right next to his path.

"Where do you need to go?"

Awrosk sighed, he looked out the window for a moment before looking back to his feet as he moved "I feel like Harllpool needs me."

"And...why don't you want to go?"

This time Awrosk stopped his pacing in front of her. He looked at her for a moment before speaking softly.

"Reasons."

She blushed lightly with how intensely he looked her in the eyes.

"Am I...." she couldn't finish the thought, making her blush more.

"I... don't know yet...but I feel you could be..."

Vadixas watched him. He looked as nervous as she felt, and that calmed her.

"If I'm the thing holding you back-"

"You're not holding me back," he said quickly and she smiled at him.

"If I'm keeping you from where you should be. Then I give you permission to go there, as long as you come back. Think of it as a temporary release from duty."

She stood up straighter, "As long as you promise to come back. It isn't safe for you to be out there alone."

Awrosk took her hand and gave it a squeeze, "I promise." He leaned in and gave her a quick peck on the lips.

"Sealed with a kiss" he whispered which only made her blush more.

She moved away, fanning her cheeks, "How...how long do you think you'll be gone?"

Awrosk had a small smile on his face but didn't make a comment about her, "I need to go back to Harllpool for a few days. I'm going to take the route we took back but I might take a faster route to come back, more straight forward."

Vadixas nodded, "You know we're heading to Willedale the Town of Nature," he nodded, "when are you leaving?"

"I should head out soon. I don't think Gizlae or Kihakso would be happy with me leaving."

"Do you have to go right away?"

He moved closer to squeeze her hand again, "I can stay for a little longer."

The two ended up talking for a few hours before Awrosk left. Vadixas waved him off and headed up to bed flopping onto her pillow. She didn't even think she fell asleep again before Aylnivi woke up. She hoped the pillow absorbed her tears.

She walked down the stairs to sit at the table.

Only Gizlae was awake, "What would you like?"

"Whatever," Vadixas muttered, leaning her head against her hand. Eventually everyone else joined them getting their own breakfast, Tesirew being the third one up helped everyone get their food.

Aphiqalena was the last one to join for breakfast, coming in through the front door rather than from upstairs. "so...I cleared with all the families I babysit for the next two weeks. Do you think that will be long enough?"

Gizlae frowned, "we didn't really have a plan except get everyone together. We can work something out after we do."

"Mentioning together, where is Awrosk? Isn't he one of the first ones to get up usually?" Ceaxtra asked.

"Yes, usually he would be helping me," Gizlae said, looking around, counting everyone.

"He...left..." said Vadixas, pushing her food around. She still hadn't looked up since sitting down.

"What do you mean he left?" Kihakso asked.

"He said he has been having a bad feeling about his town for a while now, so he wanted to go check on it. He left last night." She looked up quickly, "But he knows where we are going and he promised to meet us there."

Kihakso sighed, "We know where he is going at least," they muttered.

Vadixas nodded, looking over everyone to ensure no one was mad at her. When she looked at Aphiqalena she blinked, "are you always different?" she muttered.

Aphiqalena looked at her, "What do you mean?"

"I..." Vadixas looked around to see everyone looking at her.

"Never... nevermind."

She looked down, Tesirew looking between her and Aphiqalena. With Tesirew's help, Kihakso was able to identify which of the two arrows was Awrosk thanks to her knowledge of local towns.

With that determined, the group headed in the direction of the last arrow. As they walked along the way to the last town, Tesirew kept running ahead to check the way for them. With that, they were able to find out that the town was surrounded by a wide lake, essentially making it an island. She hadn't seen any bridges to connect the two.

Eventually, the group got to where she had been and stood at the beach, looking at the lake in front of them.

"Can we swim through it?"

Aphiqalena placed her hand in the water and concentrated for a moment. When she pulled her hand out she shook her head.

"Water seems a little fast. Also the closest earth is pretty far down."

"Can we make a bridge across?" Gizlae asked, looking at Aphiqalena.

Aphiqalena shrugged, "I could but it would take a moment." She stood in front of the water, ready to start when Vadixas suddenly spoke up.

"Wait. Why doesn't Aylnivi do it?" Vadixas asked, taking a step forward.

Aylnivi looked at her, "Why can't she do it?"

Vadixas bit her lip, "she's different. I don't think it will be a good idea," she said quietly. The only people who seemed to hear were Aylnivi and Tesirew.

Aylnivi sighed, "Alright but walking will be slow. I can't help it if it is slippery."

Tesirew moved over to Vadixas, "We can hold hands."

She held her hand out to Vadixas "Will you hold mine?"

Vadixas smiled "Sure."

After that Tesirew moved over to Aphiqalena to take her other hand.

Vadixas held her hand out to Aylnivi who shook her head, "I won't be slipping like all of you. It doesn't affect me."

Gizlae pulled Kihakso over to Ceaxtra to hold her hand. Ceaxtra sighed but didn't fight it.

They started to make their way across the lake. First was Aylnivi who was making the platform as she walked. Gizlae, Kihakso and Ceaxtra followed with Gizlae pulling the other two along. Then finally Vadixas, Tesirew, and Aphiqalena with Vadixas leading them.

Tesirew took a breath before taking a larger step. She slipped for a moment before landing on her behind.

"Are you okay?" Vadixas asked leaning over slightly to look down at her, having managed to keep standing even with the pulling on her hand.

Tesirew looked up quickly, causing the brim of her hat to fling up. At that moment the two eyes met and Tesirew cringed as she nodded.

"Yeah...I'll...I'll be okay."

Aphiqalena frowned at that, helping her up and keeping a stronger hold on her.

"Are you really okay? Do you need to rest?" she whispered to her.

Tesirew smiled, "Yeah. Everything is fine." She hugged Aphiqalena with how Aphiqalena was holding her up. "I just...needed to check something."

Aphiqalena frowned but didn't say more, trusting Tesirew with her own powers. Eventually, they got to the island going slowly to make sure Tesirew didn't fall again. Once they got to the island, they took a moment to relax. Aphiqalena fretted over Tesirew who was rubbing her head but shaking her head at any offers of help. After walking for a bit, Gizlae and Kihakso declared that they should stop for a bit to give Tesirew some time to deal with her headache.

"I said I'm okay," Tesirew whined but she let Aphiqalena push her to sit on a log.

"I know what's going on and you need to sit for a bit."

"What's going on?" Gizlae asked.

Aphiqalena looked down at Tesirew, who gave a small shake of her head. Aphiqalena sighed but placed her hand on Tesirew's head.

"Don't worry, I've got it handled."

Aylnivi looked at the group before looking to the town "I'm going to look ahead. You all stay here."

Before any of them could say anything she started to walk away from the group.

She looked around as she walked, seeing plants she had never seen before. Pretty flowers and sharp looking bushes. After walking for a while she eventually found a town.

She was about to enter the town when a guard stopped her

"Who are you!" he shouted glaring at her.

"I'm Aylnivi," she was glad the others weren't here. They wouldn't have taken this guard's attitude so easily.

"And why are you here?"

Aylnivi looked around, she figured the truth would be the best "I am looking for the Child of Nature."

The man's look of indifference turned into one of anger "And why would you want to talk to her?"

She took a step back, "I just need to say something to her."

He took a step towards her his hand on the weapon.

"No one wants to just see her." he growled, "you're like her aren't you?"

Aylnivi's eyes went wide and turned to try to make it back to the group to warn them. She started to run back to where she left the group, as she ran she made a sheet of ice between her and them. Because of a mix of not having the time and the temperature it was pretty thin and she heard the ice shattering and whatever group the guard formed coming after her.

She heard shouting behind her and she growled looking behind her quickly. She could tell they were going to catch up to her since they knew the terrain. She formed another wall, making it a little thicker. She started to blink as her vision was fading in and out but she had to keep running to get to the others.

She made it back to the group breathing heavily "you…need…to…run…" With each word she took a breath.

The group all stood up at her entrance into the clearing.

"Aylnivi, why are you so low?"

"Go!" she pointed behind them. She turned around to face the men coming towards them. She made a third wall that was thicker than the last two. She blinked for a moment before fainting.

"AYLNIVI!" Vadixas reached for her but Ceaxtra grabbed her arm to pull her away, the group broke through the wall and watched as the kids ran away leaving Aylnivi behind.

"What should we do?" one of the guards asked the leader.

The leader glared at the retreating backs of the others, "She was telling them to run, they are probably like her. After them!" The mob followed after the kids. They were so focused on the others that they didn't notice a bunch of vines sweeping down to pick up a knocked out Aylnivi and bring her into the trees.

Aylnivi opened her eyes to find she was sleeping on a mat made of vines up in the trees. She blinked a few times trying to get her vision to clear, she rubbed her eyes and that helped her vision come back.

"Oh you're up!" said a voice. Aylnivi looked up to see a girl sitting on a branch, her hair the same color as the trees behind her. Aylnivi blinked at the girl for a moment, the girl smiled at her.

"You're beautiful," the girl breathed.

She felt something brushing her cheek. She wanted to wipe it away but her body wouldn't move. The scent of wood surrounded her with a floral scent mixing every once in a while.

"You're the first one who actually wanted to be my child." She heard a voice accompanied by the sound of shuffling leaves. The leaves' sounds seemed to dance around her.

"What?"

"No other child has offered. The others received so many."

"I don't-"

"And so I have been waiting for you."

The shuffling stopped as the voice got closer, "The first one," she whispered. "I will do anything I can do to help you."

She felt a flower touch her forehead for a moment before pulling away.

"I'll learn how to be a parent and you just have to be you."

"I...okay...I can do that," she said.

"Time to wake up."

Kaknei blinked her eyes to see the sky around her as she lay in a wide circle of dead grass and dying trees. She frowned as she sat up, brushing her hands over the dead grass. When she did, it started to grow again and she smiled. Kaknei smiled at the now green grass.

"Did I..." she looked at her hand before looking up at the dying tree.

"I wonder if I can fix that too," she muttered to herself as she stood up. She reached out towards it, but before she could touch it, a vine wrapped around her arm and tugged her away. She looked down at the vine with a smile

"Oh do you want some too?" She petted it and the vine grew a little greener, looking healthier than before she touched it.

"Alright now then-" she turned back to the tree only for the vine to tug her arm again.

She frowned at the vine.

"What do you not want me to do?" another small tug on her arm.

"Is it because you're greedy?" This time the vine didn't move.

"Is it only that tree?" again no movement.

"Can I help with other things like the grass and flowers?" This time, she got a tug. She looked around her and there wasn't much that had died from what happened around her. Grass, trees, a bush or two. When she reached out for those the vine didn't do anything so she decided to bring it back.

When she had first helped the grass, she hadn't noticed anything but this time, when helping the bush, she felt a pull from her energy. She could also see a line coming from her neck to the bush. Once it was better, she touched her neck but didn't feel anything there.

She looked around at the trees then back at the bush before looking at the vine still around her arm.

"So the only thing I can't bring back are the trees?" another tug.

"Is it because it's bad...for me?" another tug.

Kaknei gave a small smile.

"Thanks for looking out for me mr. vine."

The vine suddenly squeezed her arm and started tugging it from side to side. It wasn't hard enough to hurt but Kaknei did frown, "Not Mr. vine?" she asked and the vine stopped its movement.

"Do I know you?"

She got another tug and looked up at the sky as she thought. She didn't remember much of her past life but it could be someone that recognized her.

She took too long thinking and the vine released her, dropping to the ground. She watched it for a while, before the bush she had just brought back started to shake as if there was a wind.

Her eyes went wide, "Are you...nature?"

The shaking got faster and she kneeled to get closer to it. She thought about her conversation with nature before whispering, "You're my parent...so you're looking out for me?" the shaking had stopped when she spoke but started up again once she finished.

Kaknei smiled, "So then you're sticking around. We'll figure this out together."

She pet the bush again, enjoying it, shaking against her hand.

The first thing Kaknei learned was that her mother could do as much as she could, a limit created by making sure life of the plant flowed naturally, if Kaknei had to guess. Because of that limitation, her mother was only able to interact with one plant at a time. She used the vine when she wanted to point or show Kaknei an arm motion when teaching her. Mother took control of a bush to answer questions, a slow shake for yes and a fast shake for no. Mother didn't ever take over trees because their movements were limited more than the others.

Kaknei spent the time in these experiments asking questions. If Kaknei was controlling something Mother couldn't take over, Kaknei could take control from Mother. It was probably caused by Kaknei putting all her attention on something while mother's was only partially.

Kaknei started to collect seeds from nearby plants. Placing them in her pocket to carry around with her wherever she went. She spent two weeks living in the woods with mother. Mother kept bringing food that she could eat and Kaknei was content but knew she couldn't just stay here alone.

Mother pointed her towards the closet town and Kaknei followed the shaking branches that led her. It was half a day before she first saw buildings. A vine grabbed her arm and she quickly looked at it. It let her arm go and then pet her on the head.

"Are you not coming in with me?" she whispered, the vine dropped to the ground and a bush next to her started to slowly shake.

"You are? But then why the head pat?" she tapped her foot before turning to look at the town. "Was it because you won't be able to communicate with me?"

Again the bush shook slowly.

"I'll be fine. I just want to take a look around."

Kaknei entered the town but didn't get far before a woman gasped.

Kaknei turned to her.

"The child," she whispered.

"Um...hi?" Kaknei asked, taking a step towards her. The woman fell to her knees and Kaknei moved over to check on her but the woman just grabbed Kaknei's hand and brought it to her head.

"I...are you okay?"

"You arrived, you arrived, you arrived," she kept repeating. People were starting to join in, copying her, falling to their knees around her. All saying similar things as the first woman. Kaknei tried to pull her hand away but the lady was holding on too tight. Kaknei didn't like all the attention. The people slowly surrounding her were making it hard for her to breathe. She was looking around, trying to find some way out. The noise from the muttering was just growing louder and louder other hands were reaching out to her and she was trying to shuffle away from the hands.

She reached into her pocket and pulled out a vine seed, throwing it onto the roof. She started to grow it but the woman pulled her hand down again, breaking her concentration. She turned to glare at the woman. She ground her teeth and pulled her hand free.

"Let me go," she shouted.

As she lifted her hand up from breaking it free, the vine she failed to grow wrapped around her arm pulling her onto the roof and away from the group.

Kaknei breathed heavily as the vine let go of her arm and moved to pet her head. The group moved to watch where she moved. All of them stayed on their knees, staring up at her.

"You have arrived. We waited so long," the first woman shouted up to her.

Kaknei took a few more breaths before speaking to them, "I don't know what you're talking about."

"The Child of Nature. We have been waiting for your arrival."

Kaknei frowned, "How did you even know I was her child?"

"The butterfly tattoo on your neck was the sign."

Kaknei rubbed her neck. She wondered if that was where the line connecting to any nature she controlled came from.

"You must come down. We want to pray to you."

"That's weird!"

Kaknei watched as some of them were frowning.

"You are our child."

"I am my mother's child, not yours."

People were starting to stand up but Kaknei held her ground, "You are the Child of Nature. This is Willedale Town of Nature. You are ours."

Kaknei glared at them, "Never! I have a mother!"

By now all that were kneeling before were now standing. The woman had pushed herself to the front of the group to shout at her.

"Come down now."

Kaknei sighed as she turned to the vine that was still petting her head, "It was a bad idea to come here." She turned the vine back into a seed and put it into her pocket. She glared once more at the group of people before turning away from them, sliding down the other side of the roof and landing on the ground.

She started running back to the forest not wanting to stay any longer in the town. She could hear anger behind her but grew some vines to block the path to where she lived. Once she got back to her clearing she started to stomp around muttering about the town that she only spent minutes in.

Mother grew flower after flower forcing the direction Kaknei was stomping, the twisting and turning eventually made Kaknei calm down to the point of having a small smile. Eventually she flopped to the ground staring at the town.

"What is wrong with them?" she felt a few flowers brush her face.

She sighed before turning onto her stomach to stare at a bush.

"Do you think I handled that wrong?"

The bush shook quickly back and forth.

"Should we go back there?" Again the bush shook quickly.

Kaknei sighed, "I suppose you're right." Kaknei smiled. "It looks like you'll have to deal with spending all the time with me."

Flowers burst up around her and she laughed.

The next week was peaceful between the two of them. They started to experiment with plants, mixing different kinds of flowers to create new ones. One day she heard noise nearby but ignored it thinking it was just an animal. When suddenly arms wrapped around her, she tried to fight them but they were much bigger than her, easily lifting her off her feet.

A vine tried to grab her attacker but another man grabbed it. A group of men walked around the clearing cutting anything in the area, Kaknei knew it wouldn't hurt Mother but she still felt sadness as the guy holding her started to walk back to town.

Once they got to the center of town, she was suddenly let go, falling into a pit. She looked around to see the pit was barren with walls made out of wood. She stood up to find that the pit was twice her height. People were standing at the edge of the pit staring down at her.

"What is this?"

"You are the Child of Nature, that means you are supposed to do what we say."

Kaknei crossed her arms, "And what are you planning to do to make me listen?"

The man crossed his arms, "You'll stay here until you learn to listen to us."

Kaknei shifted to sneak a seed out of her pocket. "Oh will I?"

The man nodded, "The pit was made just for you, nothing will grow there."

Kaknei kicked her foot to see under the layer of dirt was cement.

"So you all planned this?"

"Right so you'll stay here till you listen."

The group started to laugh and she shook her head. They started to leave, heading back to their homes, Kaknei smiled and started to grow the vine. By the time it had grown enough for her to get out of the pit, the people were all back into their homes.

She shook her head as she walked back to the forest, leaving the vine as evidence of how she got out. Once she made it back to the clearing she was sad to see so much damage. Mother and her worked hard to fix the plants that could be saved and pushed the ones that were dead to the outside of the clearing.

A week later Kaknei was talking with mother when suddenly a net landed over her and she was pulled back to town. The net was made of metal so the vines mother sent couldn't break it. Eventually she was dropped back into the pit, the rope that had attached the net was dropped in with her. Kaknei looked around at the new pit, she noticed it was a little taller and the floor was just cement.

"Did they think the dirt was why it grew?"

She noticed that the walls were again wood but more like trees nailed together rather than planks making it seem like a rush job.

She walked over to the wood with a smile. Mother and her had found out that part of her power meant growing dead plants. She had done some practice but this would just help her improve.

She touched the tree and watched as her magic connected to it. She started to grow branches out of it in a straight line up, evenly spaced apart.

She started to climb up the ladder until she was out of the pit. She looked down at the tree but decided to leave it as it was, it would give them another clue but it would also take more energy to put it back. She walked back to her clearing and sighed looking around "I think we're going to have to move. They know we live here and I doubt they are going to stop coming after me."

The bush next to her shook slowly.

Kaknei nodded her head "Right."

She didn't have much to collect, mostly her carvings of trees she had started to make. She started carving bits of tree into certain patterns so all she would have to do is grow its shape how she needed. This method took much less energy than dealing with full trees.

The two wandered around the forest until they found an abandoned house. The two started to fix it up at night and hang out at random locations so that when the townspeople came after her again they wouldn't find her new house.

After another week, the townspeople found her at the lake when she was washing her clothes. The next pit was the same height but the wood had been removed and a glass roof had been placed over it once she was in. The people avoided waking on it so she wondered if it wasn't very strong.

She waited till everyone had left again before ruffling through her pockets and pulling out the piece of wood she was looking for. It was one of her hollowed pieces but this one had a chunk cut out of it like an entrance and slots cut up the inside. She walked over to the wall and placed the piece onto the floor upright. She started to make it bigger, holding it till it was half the size of her body and could stand on its own. She stepped a bit away and started to grow it slowly watching as it eventually broke the glass. Once she was sure all the glass was done falling she ran over to it climbing up the notches.

Once outside she held an edge of the wood and rapidly shrank it knowing damage would only happen if it grew too fast. Once finished she went back to the lake to finish cleaning her clothes.

They had been doing this for months now. The town would capture her, she would break out, they would improve the pit and capture her again. A little game of back and forth that Kaknei was actually coming to enjoy. At some point though the reasoning of the town changed. They no longer just wanted to keep her captive, the last few versions seemed to want to kill her. All of them had a roof that was slowly coming towards her. She used the wood to get out most days.

She could tell Mother didn't like this new situation but there wasn't anything she could do about it. That was until a group of people came over to the island on a path of ice. She was watching from the trees as the group decided to rest. She was trying to get a better look when the last girl came crashing back into the clearing. Kaknei watched as she made a sheet of ice before falling to the floor. She waited till the mob followed the kids, everyone forgetting about the fainted girl. Kaknei just lifted her up with a group of vines letting her rest on a mat of them.

After only a few moments Aylnivi opened her eyes. She lightly touched the back of her head to find a bump flinching slightly from the pain.

"Oh, you're up!" said Kaknei leaning towards her. Aylnivi looked up to see her sitting on a branch, her hair the same color as the trees behind her.

Aylnivi blinked for a moment, and Kaknei smiled at her, "you're beautiful." she breathed.

"What?"

Kaknei leaned a little forward, she almost slipped but leaned back to stop herself from falling, "I've never seen someone so pretty. My name is Kaknei and yours?"

"I'm...Aylnivi..." she looked around her, "What happened?"

Kaknei sighed with a small smile, "Even your name is pretty."

She jumped off the branch and landed in front of Aylnivi.

"The townspeople who were chasing you. When they got here you fainted? They then noticed your friends so they left you alone to chase after them." She pointed in the direction behind Aylnivi.

"But I couldn't just leave you there so I scooped you up and brought you here," she said, pointing to herself.

Aylnivi frowned, "And where are the others?" standing up slowly stumbling slightly, Kaknei grabbed her arm to help her stand.

Kaknei shrugged, "Probably captured. The town has had a few months to get used to capturing people. Since they've been trying to do so to me for that long."

Aylnivi frowned at Kaknei, still holding her arm. Kaknei smiled and let it go, rocking back and forth on her feet.

"Well…thanks for the help but I need to go."

She wanted to walk off but then a vine grabbed her ankle to stop her.

Kaknei ran in front of her. "Where are you going?"

"To save the others?"

Kaknei blinked at her, "Do you even know where they are?"

"I can find them."

Kaknei shook her head and pointed to herself. "Let me help out. I know where they will be and how to get them out."

Aylnivi looked her over, "And why do you want to help?"

Kaknei smiled, "I can't leave a damsel in distress."

Aylnivi crossed her arms.

Kaknei sighed before pulling down the turtleneck she was wearing "I'm like you all."

"How did you know we were like you?"

She tapped the side of her eyes, "I can see the source of people's powers. Normal people have it all around them as if it just leaked from them. We have it coming from where our tattoos are." She covered her tattoo.

"To prove it." She pointed at Aylnivi's feet. "Yours is there. I could list off the others if you want."

Aylnivi sighed, "I wouldn't know where most of them were. I've only seen Vadixas's by chance."

She looked Kaknei over, who fluttered her eyes. "Alright, how are we going to save them?"

Kaknei clapped, "Don't worry. I got this."

The group didn't know what to do. Tesirew was trying to comfort Aphiqalena, who was curled up in the corner, muttering to herself. The others were trying to find a door that might have been hidden in the walls.

"Why don't you help us?" Kihakso snapped at Tesirew.

"I'm trying to help. Aphi needs me."

"And why is that?"

"For need to know only."

Tesirew snapped before turning back to Aphigalena. Kihakso glared at her but kept looking. They didn't know how long they had but they had already noticed the roof was very slowly coming down on them.

"If she could help we would maybe get out of this," Kihakso shouted at Tesirew.

"She can't. And you can't make her," Tesirew shouted back.

"Let's not fight, let's keep looking," Gizlae said, placing her hand on Kihakso's shoulder. He breathed through his teeth but said nothing. They looked for a while before a rumble suddenly filled the room.

Kihakso turned to Aphiqalena, "Is she actually helping?" but Aphiqalena looked the same as she did when she noticed what kind of room they were located in. He frowned only for cracks to appear on one of the walls. Then without warning, a tree broke through the wall and through the roof above them.

A section on it opened up to show it was hollow inside.

"Your rescue has arrived," said a girl popping her head out of the hole. She looked at the group in the room. "Can you get up on your own or do you need help?"

Tesirew looked at her carefully before raising her hand, "I need help with Aphiqalena." The girl nodded and vines came out of the hole to pick up both Aphiqalena and Tesirew. Tesirew sighed once they were out of the room looking up to see Aylnivi there. Before they could say anything, Kaknei then used the vines to pick everyone else up and bring them up. She then leaned against the wall of the tree with a sigh.

Vadixas looked her over, "You shouldn't use your powers for a bit. You're getting close to death."

Kaknei sighed, "Yeah I don't usually make daring rescues."

She smiled at Aylnivi, "But when a pretty girl asks you to do it, you have to go all out, right?"

"How long will this stay up with the roof coming down?" Tesirew asked, knowing Aphiqalena wouldn't be moving for a while.

Kaknei nodded slowly, "Yeah."

She patted the wall she was leaning against "I made this out of a pretty thick tree. Even if the part we're in is hollow, the top isn't and should hold up for a while."

She frowned, "We're going to have to leave it though, so I will have to make a replacement."

The group rested there for a few moments but Aphiqalena didn't seem to be improving any. She was the tallest of the group, so she was impossible to carry. Instead Kihakso and Ceaxtra decided to put her arm over their shoulders to get her out. Aylnivi started to take a step but Vadixas took her hand. Aylnivi looked over at her watching as she frowned while looking at her hip, Aylnivi gave her hand a squeeze making Vadixas look up at her. She gave her a small smile and Vadixas breathed a small breath out.

In the small amount of time, Kaknei had gained a little energy from their relaxing, so she was able to walk on her own, if slowly.

The group made their way up the tree that Kaknei had made. At the end of the tree was another one that was like a ladder. When Aphiqalena was brought into the light she blinked slowly and lifted her arm off of Ceaxtra and reached out. Tesirew moved over to her, giving Aphiqalena a hug.

"What's happened..." Aphiqalena muttered, moving more into the hug. Kihakso released her when it looked like she could stand on her own.

"We got rescued, we're fine."

She moved closer to Aphiqalena's ear, "No crushing," she whispered for only Aphiqalena to hear, who nodded.

The group started to climb up one by one, with Kihakso being last. Once everyone was out, Kaknei grabbed the edge of the tree and shrunk it down, putting it into her pocket.

They were slowly walking away from town when a vine wrapped around Kaknei's arm to pull her along.

Vadixas looked at it. "Hey, no you're already weak."

Kaknei looked at it with a small smile, "It's okay, I'll be fine."

Vadixas shook her head, "No you won't be. If you use any more magical energy you might die."

That only made the vine pull her along more frantically. She laughed and let her be pulled. The group followed until they hit a clearing with a river. The vine let her arm go to get her some water.

"You really shouldn't be using your magical energy," Vadixas whispered.

Kaknei shook her head, "I'm not." She accepted the cup from the vine "everyone meet Mother." the vine waved.

"Who?"

"The Element of Nature? She doesn't have a name for you all to call her though," Kaknei said with a frown.

"Wait, you actually interact with your...parent?" Ceaxtra demanded. That was something she wanted from the start

Kaknei's frown only grew, "What? You don't?"

"No. Wind refused to answer my questions!" Ceaxtra started to pace back and forth.

Kaknei turned back to the vine.

"Mother, could you answer her questions?" Kaknei asked.

The vine flopped and the bush to her other side shook slowly. "Would you like to ask something?" she asked Ceaxtra.

"No, I'm going to find Wind and ask her."

Kaknei blinked before laughing.

"Well we should be fine for now, the townspeople won't have another pit for a week. They decided to believe her and rested there for a while. Mother made flowers for all of them.

After a while though Kaknei, who had laid down at some point, sat up.

"Someone is coming this way, they've been stepping on grass for a bit."

Tesirew and Kihakso stood in front of the group, Tesirew more in front of Aphiqalena, their arms up in defense. When the person broke through the tree line they saw it was Awrosk.

Tesirew sighed, "Oh you came back. How was your town?" She moved too quickly as she went over to him and accidentally made eye contact with him. She groaned and held her head.

"Tesirew?" she asked quietly, moving closer to her.

Almost as soon as she held her head she moved back from him eyes wide.

"No."

Everyone looked between her and Awrosk.

Vadixas moved closer to Awrosk she opened her mouth to say something but Tesirew interrupted her, "Don't get close to him."

Aphiqalena looked at Tesirew before turning to glare at Awrosk.

Even as close as she was, Vadixas couldn't make out much of what Awrosk was muttering.

All she could hear was, "Because of you.... because of you..."

They watched as in his clenched fist a sword formed. He took a swing at Vadixas but Aphiqalena was waiting for it. She made a wall of earth rise up between the two. The water sword cut the wall but the earth moving forward to create the wall under her made Vadixas topple backwards out of harm's way.

"What are you doing?" shouted Kihakso.

Tesirew pulled on Aphiqalena's sleeve, "He won't stop."

Aphiqalena nodded before turning to the rest.

"We'll stop him, just go."

She then turned back to where Awrosk was still glaring at them.

"But-" Gizlae said.

Kihakso grabbed her arm and started to pull her away. Ceaxtra looked around before grabbing Vadixas and dragging her along since she hadn't moved while still staring at Awrosk. Aylnivi looked at Kaknei who was struggling to stand. She moved over and picked her up in a bridal carry before following the others, having longer time to gain her energy back.

Awrosk watched them go before turning to Aphiqalena and Tesirew. He put his hand on the remaining pile of earth to climb over it when his hand sunk into the pile. He glared at it and put his foot on the pile to better pull his hand out. He managed to get his hand out but in the process his leg sank until it was covered midway up his thigh. He tried to pull it out but it wasn't working.

Aphiqalena nodded before pulling Tesirews hand, "Let's go."

The two started to run, with Aphiqalena leading, when Tesirew looked back and gasped.

"Aphi!"

Aphiqalena looked back to see an arrow of water coming towards them. She turned and lifted an earth wall to block it. She put a few more between them and Awrosk before dragging Tesirew again following the others. It seems that as they were running either Kaknei or Mother took the lead since when Aphiqalena caught up to them the others were standing in the yard of an abandoned house.

Kaknei cuddled closer to Aylnivi, "Aren't you the perfect package? strong and beautiful."

Aylnivi frowned, "If you can joke you can walk," She said letting Kaknei go. But because of Kaknei's arm that was still around her neck though only her feet dropped to the ground.

"Don't drop her Aylnivi, she is still weak," Vadixas muttered, not looking up from the ground.

"Yeah I'm still weak," Kaknei said, holding on a little tighter, making it almost a hug.

"So am I," Aylnivi muttered moving to one side and placing Kaknei onto the ground slowly. Once she was supporting herself Aylnivi lifted Kaknei's arms above her head before going over to Vadixas, pulling her to sit down, holding her hand.

"Why would he do that? Why would he turn on us." Kihakso growled.

Everyone was silent before Ceaxtra spoke up.

"Maybe he didn't."

"He attacked us. How could he have not?"

"What if he was mind controlled?"

"What?"

"What if Chabnorl mind controlled him to attack us?"

Gizlae was nodding along to Ceaxtra's conclusion, "That does make sense."

"He wasn't," Tesirew whispered, but no one but Aphiqalena, who had her arm over her shoulder, heard her.

"If that's the case, we have to free him," said Gizlae as Vadixas looked up at them hopefully.

"So we just need to figure out how he did it," Ceaxtra said.

"That's not what happened," Tesirew said but none seemed to hear her too focused on Gizlae and Ceaxtra.

"Maybe we should go after him right away if we can stop him from attacking now he'll be much happier."

"No, we should go after what is mind controlling him. That way he'll go back to normal faster."

"He won't!" Tesirew shouted, drawing the group's attention.

"What do you mean he won't?" Vadixas asked sadly.

Tesirew curled more into Aphiqalena, "He isn't being mind controlled. There isn't anything to destroy to make him go back to normal."

"How can you be so sure?" Kihakso asked.

Tesirew shifted, trying to get closer to earth. "I saw it."

"On your last run?" Ceaxtra asked. "if you had seen so-"

Tesirew shook, "No I mean...our eyes met, so I saw it happen."

Kaknei looked around but seeing as everyone else looked as confused as she felt. She decided to raise her hand, "I don't understand what you're saying, could you start again."

When Tesirew said nothing Aphiqalena sighed and pulled her into a proper hug before looking at the group.

"You all know how we have a special power for our eyes."

She waited till they all nodded, she hadn't been sure but since both her and Tesirew had them then she could assume it was the same for them. "Well Tesirew's is that when she makes eye contact with someone all of their memories go into her head."

Aphiqalena waited a moment for all of them to absorb that information.

"It's why she wears her hat," Aphiqalena patted it lightly, patting Tesirew's head at the same time. "If she blocks at least one eye she doesn't get the memories."

She waited a moment again but this time Tesirew spoke up, "This time when I ran up to Awrosk the brim flipped up." She reached up and grabbed the brim, pulling it down a little farther. "Our eyes met. and I saw it."

"Saw it?" Vadixas whispered but since no one was saying anything she could easily be heard.

"I saw when he arrived back at his home to find everyone slaughtered. I saw the moment when he fell to his knees crying at the lake edge. I saw the moment Chabnorl started talking to him, convincing him that if we hadn't taken him from his home he could have protected it. I saw the moment he agreed to work with him to kill us."

Everyone was silent, trying to come to terms with what they just learned. Vadixas just stared at the ground as Aylnivi rubbed the back of her hand with her thumb. Kihakso kept crossing and uncrossing their arms like they didn't know what to do with themself. Gizlae moved over to them leaning against their side. Kaknei just watched them all having never met Awrosk.

It was Ceaxtra that broke the silence, "That we can work with."

Everyone looked up at her and she started to pace, "He hates us and wants us dead but we might be able to talk him out of that hatred."

She looked at Gizlae and Kihakso, "We saw that town. They didn't care for him, just what he was. We convinced Vadixas that her town was bad, so we just need to do the same for him."

"He's not going to let us just talk to him," Aphiqalena said, looking back the way they came.

"He won't but we can fight him. If we get a pair of his cuffs then he can't attack us and we can talk."

Gizlae frowned, "I don't like the thought of using his cuffs."

Ceaxtra frowned, "Well there isn't another way to weaken him."

Gizlae sighed but Tesirew spoke up.

"There is." Everyone looked back at her again.

"There is another method to weaken him but..." she took a breath. "But it might be permanent, unlike the cuffs."

"What do you mean?" Kaknei asked, she didn't even know what these cuffs they were talking about were.

Tesirew pulled away from Aphiqalena sitting up straight, "In the past there was a thief. This thief was a specialist mage. She could create gemstones that could steal someone's magic away."

"Like temporarily?" Ceaxtra asked.

Tesirew shook her head, "No. Once the gem absorbed your powers it became a gem of that power and you could use them like your own."

Gizlae gripped Kihakso's hand, "What if she makes more, could someone use them on us?"

Tesirew frowned, "She can't make anymore, she died and her magic was lost with her." Everyone took a breath of relief, "But her gems weren't."

"Did she have a gem that could weaken someone?" Ceaxtra asked.

Tesirew shook her head again, "No, when she died she had a few empty ones. We could get them and use them on him."

She bit her lip, "But like I said, it would be permanent. Even after her death the magic stayed in their gems."

Everyone was silent as they were so focused on the Awrosk issue that only Kaknei noticed a problem.

"I have a question."

Tesirew nodded for her to go ahead, "Are these gems somewhere easy to get to?"

"They're in a museum, I've seen them on one of my runs."

"Are they well known?"

Tesirew shrugged, "Not unless you went looking for them. They are very blatant about what they are."

"Then what is stopping Chabnorl from getting them and using them on us?"

"I..." Tesirew was silent for a moment. "I think he wants to save it for last...he hates them the most and would want the panic to build."

"It?" Ceaxtra asked.

"Termouron the City of Earth. The thief was a sacrifice and her belongings were put in the museum they have."

"A museum?"

Tesirew grimaced but nodded, "A place to show off what the failed sacrifices left behind. They like to claim it is a way to look into how they ended up there. I think they just like to show off their trophies."

"So, we should probably go there soon then," Kihakso said

Tesirew sat up straighter, "What!"

"It's important that we get those gems before him. He has a few towns left to attack so we should go right away."

Tesirew looked at Aphiqalena quickly, "No we can't go there."

"You've already been once."

"That was...I needed to but...but we can't go...Aphiqalena can't go."

"Why not?" Aphiqalena asked.

"You shouldn't, I don't want you to see-" she covered her mouth to stop her from saying any more.

"I'll be okay. I have you with me right," Aphiqalena said

"We need to go. We need those gems, if not to use on Awrosk to at least keep us all safe."

Kihakso took a step forward, Gizlae pulled them back.

"But it's so far and I don't know if they are even still there. I haven't been back in months."

"You could go there in a second," Ceaxtra pointed out.

Tesirew shook her head and started to shake.

"No! I can't go back. They...they..."

She shook her head and wiped her eyes. "I don't care how much we need them. I'm not going back there alone," she whispered, holding herself tight.

Aphiqalena pulled her into a hug, "And I won't let you." Glaring at the others to challenge her.

Kihakso sighed, "Then we need to go even if it is a failure."

The others nodded beside Tesirew.

"We camp her tonight then head out. You at least know the way, right?" he turned to Tesirew, and she nodded slowly.

"Then you'll lead."

They set up camp and went to bed.

The next day they left the island with Aylnivi once again, making a platform for them to cross. Once they got to the other side, Kaknei grew a vine quickly to check to make sure Mother could still interact with things. After that Tesirew informed them it would be a few days of travel. She quickly ran off to Gillabury to check up on everything there but nothing had changed.

On the second night when Ceaxtra was taking watch, Tesirew joined her. Ceaxtra looked over to her, "Can't sleep?"

Tesirew shook her head, "Haven't been doing as much running as I normally do."

"Do you want to do some running now?"

Tesirew shook her head, "No it would probably wake everyone up."

Instead her foot bounced.

"Could I ask you a question?"

"I don't know if I'll have the answer."

"Well, I wanted to know how you use your magic to fight?"

"To fight?"

"Yeah I've been trying to learn from everyone."

"I don't know if my style would work for you without a lot of work."

"What do you mean?"

Tesirew tapped her hat, "I always have to wear this since I don't want peoples memories. but having this on means that half my view is always blocked so in a battle it's hard to attack and not hit Aphi."

Ceaxtra nodded, "So, I use my magic to focus on the enemies to make sure I can dodge their movements."

"How do you do that?"

Tesirew held out her arm, "When we move our body there are electronic signals that I have memorized." She did a fake punch before lowering her arm, "So if I focus on a person I can feel them and follow what they are doing without actually seeing them."

She looked at Ceaxtra with a smile, "So, if you want fighting tips talk to Aphi. My job is just getting us out of the way."

"Are you always planning to wear the hat?"

Tesirew froze at the sudden question, "I only have to worry about it the first time I look someone in the eye. So I don't have to do it when it is just me and Aphi. I don't mind wearing it otherwise."

Ceaxtra frowned, "I don't mind if you don't want to wear it around me."

"But then I would see your memories."

"It's not like I remember them anyways," Ceaxtra said with a shrug.

Tesirew touched the brim lightly before she smiled and pulled it off straightening her messed up hair. After a moment she looked up to meet Ceaxtra in the eyes. She flinched after a moment but soon she started to relax again.

"Do you always flinch?" Ceaxtra asked.

Tesirew shook her head as she placed her hat on her lap, "No, only for us children of the elements because I see both your current life and your last one."

Ceaxtra's eyes went wide, "Can I ask you stuff about my past life?

Tesirew played with the brim of her hat, "Only slightly, while things might be important I think the reason we lost the memories in the first place is so we aren't burdened with things from back then."

Ceaxtra nodded thinking about what she wanted to ask when she remembered something. "Wait, if you're always careful with your hat then that time you slipped on the ice?"

Tesirew sighed, fiddling with the brim, "Vadixas kept saying that Aphi was different. Since I had Kihakso's memories at that point I knew I would be able to see what she does so I had to."

"For Aphiqalena?"

Tesirew nodded, "She's my older sister, I needed to make sure she was okay."

Ceaxtra nodded then her eyes went wide, "Wait did you say you have Kihakso's memories?"

Tesirew nodded, "When we first met you."

"You haven't mentioned it?"

Tesirew bit her lip, "I try not to mention it. People have secrets and I don't know if they would be okay with me knowing them."

"I see. Well I won't tell him."

Tesirew smiled at her.

The two spent the night talking to each other with Ceaxtra going to bed early since Tesirew still had energy to spare.

It took one more day before they arrived at the cave leading to Termouron. Since it was sunset the group decided to camp outside of it. That night Tesirew refused to sleep on her own, curling up next to Aphiqalena and still having a nightmare.

The next day the group gathered in front of the cave, everyone else was waiting as Tesirew shivered in place. Aphiqalena offered her arm and Tesirew grabbed hold, taking a breath before nodding and started to enter.

At first the cave had nothing, just lights to make it not dark but soon they started to see panels of glass ahead, Tesirew closed her eyes but they all kept moving forward. When they got to them, they could see what it was. A body placed into the center of a block of glass. Under it there was a name but it was worn with age and unreadable. The group looked forward to see more and more glass panels in front of them. They looked to Tesirew who had her eyes closed and Aphiqalena who was looking ahead.

They kept walking, doing their best to not look at them. No one could think of anything to say in the uncomfortable silence. Halfway down the hall they were surprised to see an empty square, like someone had removed the glass and body, the plaque under it read Rohgren. When they were getting close to the exit Aphiqalena slowed down to stare at one of the last ones left. It was a girl lying on her back with her tied hands reaching up to the sky.

"Aphi?" Tesirew said softly. She cracked an eye open to see where they had stopped. Aphiqalena moved a little closer and Tesirew did her best to not look at the body. She noticed a dent in the glass with a little blood running down from it. When she had first seen this it had been pristine, so even though she didn't know how it happened she could take a guess.

"I just...this one..." Aphiqalena touched the glass lightly, "this one seems...familiar."

Tesirew frowned, closing her eyes again, "Don't...don't worry about that."

The two stared at each other for a long moment.

"Can we continue?" Kihakso shouted while pointing at the exit, "We need to get to the museum before Chabnorl does. Remember?"

Aphiqalena looked back at the glassed body once more before nodding and following the others out of the tunnel, to take a look at Termouron for the first time.

The group moved along the main street heading in the way Tesirew pointed to them. Aphiqalena watched as Tesirew looked at each person before twice lifting her hat brim to look them in the eyes. Each time she groaned and on the second time Aphiqalena squeezed her hand.

"Are you okay?"

Tesirew nodded, "Yeah I just needed some information."

Aphiqalena frowned, "And you couldn't have asked?"

Tesirew glared "The less I talk to any of these people the better."

"How much longer till we get to the museum?" Ceaxtra asked.

"We should see the steps soon."

With one more left turn they could see the museum. It had a square in front of it and seemed to have a small amount of people coming out of it. As soon as they placed their foot on the first step the double doors burst open and Chabnorl was standing there with a smile.

The kids moved back while Tesirew moved in front of the group, "Run."

"What about you!" Aphiqalena shouted.

"I'll be fine just go."

With one last look at Chabnorl, they took off. She could hear their footsteps as they made it back the way they came.

Chabnorl chuckled, "Do you really think you could take me?" He held a small bag up for her to see, "I doubt it, now that I have this."

Tesirew took a step back but made sure to speak confidently.

"I want to make a deal."

"A deal?"

"I know you hate us but I know something you hate even more. I can give it to you."

He frowned, "There isn't much that I hate more than all of you."

"But there is one thing, and I can give you that if you let us leave." She looked at the bag he was holding, "That's all I want, for us to get away."

Chabnorl crossed his arms, "Alright what do you have to offer?"

"Wait here, I need to get it."

With that she was gone in a rumble of thunder. He heard it once again in town and took the steps down to wait for her return. Once he reached the bottom of the steps he heard another rumble and a second right in front of him. When Tesirew stopped in front of him and dumped an older woman at his feet.

"And who is this? How is this person someone I would hate more than you all?"

Tesirew pointed to the bag he had stolen from the museum, "The creator of those do you know her story?"

He waved to the museum behind him, "I know she was sacrificed."

Tesirew nodded, "She was, but she didn't think she would be."

"No one does," he muttered.

Tesirew shook her head, "She went into town with the same plan as she always had. She would go in and steal like she always did, and once she got caught she sat back and waited. Waited for her older sister to come and save her like she always did."

Chabnorl frowned, "And she didn't make it in time?"

Tesirew crossed her arms making sure to not look at the lady looking between the two of them, "Oh no, her sister got here early and was drawn into the town's philosophy. When she went to collect the thief instead of leading her out of town like always, the older sister led her to the hole." By Chabnorl's slight flinch she could tell she didn't need to mention what the hole was for.

"When they got there, her sister was the one who pushed her into it. And the one that she begged to save her as she was buried." His frown seemed to grow as she spoke.

"So here is what I am offering you." she waved to the lady that she had brought to him. "This is that older sister. The one who took all of her sister's hope and buried it along with her body."

Chabnorl was silent for a moment just glaring at the lady, "You're right, this is someone I hate more than you all." He looked up at Tesirew, "You can have this chance to escape. But next time I will kill you all."

Tesirew nodded, giving her another kick, without looking her in the eyes, before turning to head the way the others went. She took only one turn before her arm was grabbed by Kihakso. They pulled her along as if she hadn't been running that way.

"Was that all true?"

"Was what?"

"The stories about the two sisters?"

Tesirew was silent for a long moment, "It was the first memories I ever saw."

"So you waited this long to meet her again?"

Tesirew looked at them for a moment, "I've only met her this once."

Kihakso looked back at her, "Then who?"

But Tesirew was silent till they caught up to the others. When Tesirew saw Aphiqalena she quickly gave her a hug.

"You okay?" Aphiqalena whispered.

Tesirew let out a slow breath, "I am now."

Even if Chabnorl had let them go they didn't know if Awrosk was close enough to attack them. They rushed though the cave not wanting to think about what was happening to the town, but at the same time not caring. Once they were back to their camping place, they all felt they could relax if only slightly.

"Well that was a failure," Ceaxtra said with a sigh.

"Why was he here?" Kihakso muttered.

Tesirew shook her head. "I thought he would wait. Maybe he was informed about the gems? Like I said, the only reason you would know about them is if you were there before. The town treated them as if they were worthless."

"Well, what do we do?" Vadixas asked.

"Where should we go knowing that the two will be hunting us down?" Kaknei asked.

"We need to do something, Tesirew and I need to go back home eventually."

"We could still go after Awrosk, but it just might be harder," Aylnivi suggested.

"And what if he is with Chabnorl?" said Ceaxtra,

"Then we'll just know where his base is. I can wreck it again."

The group went back and forth talking about the pros and cons of if they should go after Awrosk.

"Even if we do go after him. How will we find him?" Vadixas asked in a quiet voice.

"Kihakso, where is Awrosk right now?" Gizlae asked them. She was staring them directly in their eyes. The others might have been looking at either of them but Kihakso couldn't tell, all they could focus on was her eyes full of understanding and knowing. And yet she'd asked them for one thing, one thing that they could not deny her no matter how hard they tried.

They pointed to their left, "He's that way."

Gizlae smiled but didn't look away.

"So we should probably start after him," Ceaxtra said, noticing that the normal leaders were just staring at each other.

"We'll figure out some way to knock him out," Aylnivi said mostly to Vadixas who nodded,

"Oh, right you can see us wherever we are when we're not in your sight," Vadixas said with a smile to Kihakso but they said nothing as Gizlae broke their eye contact first, moving over to kiss them on the forehead before getting ready for sleep.

That night Tesirew was taking watch since she had too much energy to sleep and because she would wake everyone up real quick.

Kihakso sits across from her, "Do you want me to take watch?"

She shook her head, "No I'm fine, shouldn't you be sleeping?"

"It's harder for me to sleep at night. With all the darkness around me, my energy constantly wants to be used."

Tesirew laughed, "Ah, that's how I feel all the time."

The two were silent for a moment just enjoying the crackle of firewood.

"The story you told to Chabnorl..." Kihakso began

Tesirew sighs looking at Aphiqalena for a moment before looking back at them "yes?"

"I'm sorry I eavesdropped on something you probably wanted to keep private."

"It's fine. Just don't mention it again. The story is done now, both players are probably dead."

They lapsed into silence again before once again Kihakso broke it.

"I wanted to tell you my pronouns are they/them."

Tesirew sat up straighter and just stared at them for a moment before looking at her hands. "Thank you for trusting me with that." They frowned at how she worded that "but...I looked in your eyes, on the day you all met Aphiqalena."

Kihakso let that sink in before actually realizing what she meant.

"So you knew this whole time?"

She nodded, "It meant talking to you was very awkward since I knew you didn't like he but hadn't trusted me enough with they yet. That's why I stuck to your name as much as possible." She gave him a weak smile "Sorry about that."

They watched her for a moment and she shifted under their gaze before sighing "You couldn't help what you learned by force. And I thank you for waiting till I was ready to tell you before mentioning it."

She gave them a bigger smile, "Everyone has secrets. I have to do my part if I learn them without them wanting me to."

"You two are close, will you be telling Aphiqalena the trust?" Kihakso asked.

Tesirew shook her head, "We do tell each other everything but Aphiqalena also understands that the secrets I gain through memories are not my own to share and won't ask about them."

"I see."

The two were silent again, Tesirew poking the fire every once in a while to entertain herself.

"You can tell her."

"Are you sure?"

Kihakso nodded, "I was planning to tell you two soon."

The Battle and The End

On the third day they were standing on the bridge that overlooked Chabnorl's base. Kihakso sighed before turning back to the group.

"So while we are here for Awrosk we should also go after the gems."

They turned to Tesirew.

"I know you don't want to but could you look in his eyes to see where he keeps them."

Tesirew shook her head, "I can't."

Kihakso frowned, "I know it is hard bu-"

"No, I've already looked him in the eyes, my power only works once."

Kihakso sighed, "Alright then we'll be checking everywhere while hoping not to run into Chabnorl."

"How are we going to stop Awrosk?" Gizlae asked.

Vadixas raised her hand, "Since we are trying to knock him out I can do it. I can always watch his magical energy levels to see when he is getting low."

"Will you be okay?" Aylnivi asked, watching her carefully.

"Well...I'm the only one who can." she said a little softer.

Kihakso sighed.

"Alright. We'll leave him to her." And with that they headed into the base. They were thinking they would have to sneak into the base until Awrosk found them. They weren't expecting to find him at the main entrance.

"So you did come," he said glaring at them."

"We aren't here to fight you," said Kihakso .

"Sure you aren't."

"You hate us but it wasn't our fault," Tesirew said, moving a little closer but Aphiqalena pulled her back.

"If I hadn't gone with you!" he shouted pointing at Gizlae, Kihakso moved in front of her. "I would have been in my town to protect it. None of them would have had to die."

"They weren't good for you anyways." Ceaxtra said with a shrug.

"Alpfeno cared!"

That made the three stop, they remembered him. He had been kind to them and an actual friend to Awrosk.

"I'm sorry he died."

"You aren't don't lie!"

"You aren't even looking," Tesirew said, knowing how his eye power worked.

He glared at her before forming his bow, "It doesn't matter. I promised to kill you all. I failed my promise to my town but I won't fail my promise to Chabnorl too." He shot at them but Vadixas blew a breath of fire to block it.

"Go" She pointed to a door on the side and the others nodded, running toward it. Awrosk shot at them but again Vadixas blew flames to stop it.

Once everyone made it through the exit Awrosk turned back to Vadixas.

"You can't stop me."

Vadixas glared back at him, "You care so much about keeping promises but forgot all about your promise to me."

Awrosk glared at her, dropping the bow knowing it would be useless "I kept my promise. I came back."

"If you meant like this I never would have wanted that promise."

~*~*~*~

The group moved down the hallway quickly, "Will they really be okay?" Gizlae asked, looking around at the group. Kihakso nodded their head but squeezed her hand a little tighter

"She should be, we just need to be fast."

They walked on for a little longer before Ceaxtra gasped, grabbing her head.

The others turned to her and she stood there staring ahead for a moment. She blinked rapidly before turning back the way they came.

"We need to go back."

"We can't we need to-" Kihakso said but Ceaxtra interrupted them.

"They are going to die. We need to stop it." She started to head back when a big hole covered the whole hall floor.

Chabnorl rose from the hole, he took a step forward with a smile.

"So two of you will die? Then why don't I increase that number?"

The group stepped back as he walked towards them. He looked over the group but focused mostly on Aphiqalena.

"I wonder how effective these will work," he said, holding up one of the gems in his gloved hand.

Aphiqalena turned to look at the others "Run I'll-"

Before she could finish what she was saying, Chabnorl ran up grabbing her arm, "I thought you were the self-sacrificing type." he muttered, placing the gem to her hand.

She tried to pull away but it wasn't working. Ceaxtra gasped again but this time it went by faster. She blinked rapidly, "We need to stop him."

Aphiqalena took a breath before pushing the earth up between them. He dodged back letting her go to avoid getting hit. Aphiqalena stumbled away and Tesirew moved over to Aphiqalena.

"Are you okay?" Aphiqalena was breathing heavily but nodded slowly.

Chabnorls sighing drew their attention, he was looking at the gem, "That one is finished." He turned to glare at the group "but I have a few more."

"We need to go," Kihakso said, running down the path pulling Gizlae along. Tesirew pulled Aphiqalena along while the others followed quickly behind. Ceaxtra pushed Chabnorl behind her to delay him from following them. They ran into a room and Ceaxtra closed the door behind them. They only had a moment to relax before a hole opened next to Aphiqalena.

~*~*~*~

Vadixas was struggling; this fight was the hardest she had ever been in. She didn't want to hurt Awrosk, she knew he was just misled and if she could just make him understand then everything would go back to how they were.

She kept dodging weapon after weapon that was thrown or swung at her. She used spells that used a small amount of energy but gave her room to maneuver, like her fire breath.

She was watching both of their energies, trying to keep hers above his and just outlast him if she could just get him to faint she could get him away from here.

She blew another breath causing him to jump back and pull out the bow. She took a slow breath; they were both about halfway through their energy, the bow was easy to dodge; it only had an arrow.

He shot one that went a little left and she didn't even need to move to dodge it. She watched him ready for the next attack when suddenly she was covered in water, before her head was submerged she took a deep breath.

~*~*~*~

Once again, Chabnorl rose from a hole in the ground, grabbing Aphiqalena's arm, "let's make sure you can't do that again." He said right before clasping the cuff on her arm. As soon as the cuff clicked her body crumbled to dirt.

"Aphi!" Tesirew shouted, reaching out where she used to be standing. Chabnorl was just staring at the pile of dirt now at his feet.

"You...you!" Ceaxtra's fists were shaking, she couldn't figure out what she wanted to say. Tesirew's mouth kept opening and closing, tears were starting to build in her eyes.

Everyone was just standing there not expecting this situation. Suddenly her voice came from the far wall.

"What just happened?"

Tesirew turned to see Aphiqalena standing there with wide eyes looking at her hands. Tesirew didn't care, she ran over to Aphiqalena, leaving two strikes of lightning one when she started running and one when she stopped. She jumped at her, making Aphiqalena cry out.

"What happened?" she pulled Aphiqalena close, Tesirew didn't let her answer.

"Never do that again. You can't leave me," she said crying into her shoulder.

"I...I..." Aphiqalena rubbed Tesirew's back looking between everyone.

Chabnorls surprise turned to anger when he saw that she was back. He looked at the cuffs then back up at her.

"How did you do that? You shouldn't have any power with them on."

"I...I didn't do anything."

He took a step towards her, "Sure you didn't."

Aphiqalena wanted to move but the grip Tesirew had didn't let her. "I didn't, the cuffs clicked and...and then..." She didn't know how to word what had happened, the feeling of losing connection and then the instant reconnection and what felt like her body coming together.

"You had to do something, these cut off your power to earth, you shouldn't be able to turn into dirt!"

"She didn't!" Tesirew shouted but not moving from her hug of Aphiqalena.

"She had to have done something! Your bodies don't just-"

She doesn't have a body!"

Tesirew turned to shout at him. She took a breath before realizing what she said and covering her mouth, she still had tears from the fear of losing Aphiqalena and she just shook in place. Aphiqalena pulled her back into a hug. Chabnorl took another step closer to them when suddenly Kaknei stepped between them. She held her hands out on either side of her. She then brought them together quickly, when she did a bunch of vines sprang out from the seeds she had thrown about the room, wrapping around Chabnorl. He struggled against the vines but they only held him tighter.

"What is wrong with you!" Kaknei shouted. Everyone looked at her, "Why do you hate us so much?"

He struggled for a moment before glaring at her, "Because you don't deserve it. Why did you all get picked when others didn't?"

"It's not our fault others weren't picked. Who got picked was the town's fault and those have already been destroyed. Isn't that enough?" she demanded glaring at him.

But it wasn't Chabnorl that answered her.

"It isn't!"

Kaknei blinked before turning to look at Gizlae.

"No, their destruction isn't enough. It would never be enough."

Chabnorl had wide eyes as he watched her.

"We suffered because of them. Why shouldn't they suffer for us? Why do they get to end their suffering quickly with death?"

"Gizlae..." Ceaxtra whispered.

~*~*~*~

She could see him standing there watching, no matter how she struggled she couldn't move. She knew this spell was draining his magic but she didn't know if she could hold her breath long enough to outlast him.

In a desperate attempt to use up more of his magic she brought her hands together in a circle and made a fireball, shooting it off as soon as it was strong enough.

She had thought he would dodge it but forgot it was smaller due to the compression, so it would be faster, when it exploded on him she gasped without thinking and started to choke.

~*~*~*~

"Do you even remember it?" Kaknei said, crossing her arms. "Even if you know how you died it doesn-"

"I remember!" Gizlae shouted as she glared at Kaknei "I don't know what you remember. But I remember the pain of what they did to me." Kihakso touched her shoulder but that didn't seem to help calm her down. "That pain is still here, I can remember how much they hurt me and I wanted them to hurt like I did." She touched the place on her chest where she thought the white void resided, glaring at the ground.

Everyone was silent, even Chabnorl, the only sound was Tesirew crying. Aphiqalena looked at her and rested her hand on top of her head.

"You aren't the only one." Everyone looked at her, "We all know Tesirew remembers our memories." Everyone just watched, "Which includes our past lives...including how they ended."

"She mentioned that when we talked one night," Ceaxtra said.

"She experiences the memories, so she knows what some of us have gone through." Aphiqalena glared at Chabnorl.

"I know you hate me. But you aren't the only one suffering because of those towns." Aphiqalena moved to pick up Tesirew who was holding her hat down on her head.

"No!" Kihakso shouted looking at the ground.

Gizlae moved closer to him

"Kihakso?" Gizlae whispered.

"The arrows, they're gone."

Aphiqalena stared at the two before glaring at Chabnorl. "Let's make a deal."

Chabnorl gave a cruel laugh, "And what do you have to offer?"

"You stole my property and I won't ask for them back."

"Your property?" he struggled against the vines but they still wouldn't budge.

"The gems." She gave him a smirk, "In my past life I was a famous thief. You want to keep my gems, you have to make a deal with me."

"And what deal do you want?"

"Stop hunting us. If you don't, I'll come back for my gems and use them on you." She didn't let him answer before turning and walking down the hall. They had failed and she didn't want to be here any longer than she needed to. The group followed her, leaving Chabnorl, who was still wrapped up in the vines.

Eventually they left the base, Aphiqalena didn't stop walking till she made it to the bridge. Tesirew had calmed down by then, "You can let me down now."

Aphiqalena set her down but then sat, the group decided to sit as well knowing they had some time because of Kaknei's vines.

"Why didn't the cuffs work for you?" Gizlae muttered.

Aphiqalena sighed, "I really don't know."

"They did,"

Everyone looked to Tesirew who is looking down at the ground, she fiddled with the brim of her hat before speaking again, "Aphi doesn't have an actual body."

"You mentioned that in the fight. What do you mean by that?" Kihakso asked.

Tesirew was again quiet for a long time before taking a big breath.

"You saw Aphi's body," she waved at Aphiqalena, "This...this isn't the real one. it's...it's a body made up of dirt."

"You need to explain more, this is not making sense," Ceaxtra muttered.

Tesirew sighed, "When we were going to Termouron do you remember that tunnel with all the bodies?" Tesirew looked at Aphiqalena who nodded. "And the one that Alfie stopped at...the one she was drawn to?" They all remember the girl reaching up her hands tied together searching for something it seemed.

"That was it. That was her real body."

"But she's here."

"I know...I think...this is something the element of Earth did when it couldn't find her actual body." Tesirew bit her lip, "So when the cuffs clicked around her wrist she lost connection to the Element of Earth and her magic energy that was being used to create this body was cut off."

"Her magical energy?" Kaknei asked.

Tesirew nodded, "Vadixas always said she was different, it's because her magical energy was always being partially used. So she was never at one hundred percent like the rest of us."

Day 13 Month 16 Year 1516
   I've...I've succeeded.
   I've killed two of them, two of the children that shouldn't exist.
   And yet...
   It hasn't gone down...
   The guilt...
   The pain....
   It's still the same...

~*~*~*~

   Ceaxtra looked at Gillabury, she had finally arrived again. She had wandered around a bit before deciding on living here. The group no longer having to watch out for Chabnorl decided they could split up and live how they wanted.
   Gillabury, she decided, was the best place for her to keep learning. Currently she was standing in front of the glassblower that Tesirew has shown to her.
   She planned to ask if they would teach her first and after that go from artisan to artisan and learn from everyone. When Tesirew heard she was planning to move here she promised to introduce Ceaxtra to a bunch of the artisans since she knew them all.
   Ceaxtra didn't know how long she would take to learn everything but she was excited for this new experience.
   Ceaxtra a nod to herself she grabbed the door handle and pulled it open walking inside.

Day 14 Month 16 Year 1516

I've been thinking about my last confrontation with them. I had them all in my grasp, I had one of them in my control, I had confirmation that two of them would die...

And yet I...

I let them go...

I hadn't known. Awrosk said he didn't remember his sacrifice. I had thought all of them were the same. That they got a second chance and forgot about their pain.

I thought they got to escape it unlike me...

~*~*~*~

Aylnivi sat on her throne contemplating what she wanted to do today. She couldn't go into town because they would just bug her about finally destroying Pitydden. But she had spent the last few days inside.

She was about to stand up when she heard the sound of breaking glass. She looked over to see Kaknei lowering herself down on a vine.

"Why are you here?" Aylnivi asked, following the vine up to see it had come through an upper window. It made sense, if Kaknei had come through the front door, the guards wouldn't have let her in.

"Not even a hi? it's been sssssoooo long since we last saw each other.

Aylnivi frowned at her, "It's been a few days."

Kaknei nodded, "It took me a while to find it."

"Find what?"

"The damsel in distress," she said with a smile, holding her hand out to Aylnivi.

"I can handle myself."

"But you're still locked up in a cage."

Aylnivi wanted to argue that but at the same time knew she couldn't.

"Why are you here?" she said instead.

Kaknei took a step closer to Aylnivi hand still out her smile only growing, "Well a damsel always needs a rescue."

"I can't just leave."

"Why not? What is keeping you here?"

"I'm the only thing keeping the two towns from fighting."

She looked at the ground then, before it had been her and Vadixas. She thought she had taught Vadixas enough to keep her safe.

She hadn't, she had failed.

Kaknei gave her a sad smile moving close enough to touch her hand lightly, "She wouldn't want you in a cage."

Aylnivi didn't look at her, "I failed her," she whispered.

Kaknei held her hand tighter "And you think punishing yourself with isolation will make up for it?"

Aylnivi stayed silent.

Kaknei watched her for a moment.

"Fine then," Aylnivi expected her to let go and step back but she just slipped her hand into a better position to grab Aylnivi's arm. "If you won't agree to a rescue then I'll just have to be a villain."

Aylnivi looked up to see that Kaknei was smiling brightly.

"Didn't think I would be a kidnapper but I bet Vadixas would want you to enjoy life rather than wallowing in sadness." Kaknei tried to pull her up but Aylnivi refused to move. her smile turned into a smirk.

"Playing hard to get huh?"

She didn't let go of her arm but turned to the vine, sending energy into it so that it would grow longer, slipping under Aylnivi and giving Kaknei a step before starting to raise them up to the roof.

Aylnivi frowned but didn't struggle.

"How long do you think you can drag me along?"

Kaknei pulled her a little closer so she could whisper something while looking Aylnivi in the eyes.

"Until I've won over your heart?"

Aylnivi couldn't look away from how determined her eyes were. It was the first time she thought Kaknei had looked at her like that. If she was truthful to herself, she wouldn't mind more of those looks. She was so distracted she hadn't even realized that the vine had let her go on top of the roof. She was the first one to break their staring contest to look around.

"So how are we getting out of her?"

Kaknei's smile returned, "This is my rescue/kidnap mission let me handle that."

Kaknei got to work shrinking the vine into a seed and moving to the edge of the roof reaching into her pockets for what she would need.

Aylnivi gave a small smile as she watched her work before looking out into the distance. Her eyes briefly scanned over Pitydden before they landed on the ground. It still hurt knowing she was gone, but Kaknei was right. She would live on and do everything she could so if they ever met up again she would have more to teach her.

Day 15 Month 16 Year 1516

    My last conversation with her...
    With the Child of Earth...
    She asked for a deal, their safety for my life.
    I could tell from her eyes it wasn't a threat for the sake of herself, or the other children, it was for the Child of Lightning...
    It was a threat for the sake of her younger sister...
    She would do anything for her sibling...I know it...
    I couldn't fault her for that... I've done worse for Rohgren myself...

~*~*~*~

    Aphiqalena sighed as she opened the door to their house. She knew tomorrow the kids would crowd and there would be tons of noise but today it was nice to come back to the silence.
    Tesirew followed her in, moving to the couch and immediately flopping on it. The two had broken off from the group first. Tesirew wanted a few days without her hat on and Aphiqalena wanted to digest all the information she had learned about herself.
    Aphiqalena moved to the kitchen to see if Rujthih had stocked their kitchen. They were a little early but there were still some snacks in the cabinets.
    She placed one on Tesirews head as she sat on a chair nearby. Tesirew turned her head, letting the snack fall, to look at Aphiqalena. "I'm sorry."
    "For what?"
    "For not telling you about the body thing," Tesirew muttered.
    Aphiqalena gave her a smile, "Well you always said there was stuff you couldn't tell me."
    "But this I should have."
    Aphiqalena moved to kneel next to her.
    "I forgive you so forgive yourself okay?"

Tesirew sighed but nodded, Aphiqalena stood up to pat her on the head, "We should go to bed, we'll be busy tomorrow."

Tesirew chuckled, "I wonder how soon the kids will know we're back."

Aphiqalena smiled, "Actually I wanted to hire you for a delivery."

Tesirew's eyes went wide as she looked up at Aphiqalena, "What should I deliver?"

"I have five keys to our root nest that need to go to some people." Aphiqalena said with a smile. Tesirew smiled back and practically bounced to bed.

Day 16 Month 16 Year 1516

    I hadn't thought I would agree with any of them...
    She had shouted what I was thinking...
    That they should suffer like I had...
    The pain the loss of my brother caused me...
    And she...
    I could hear it in how she shouted...
    Gizlae felt it too, whatever they had done to her she still felt it...

~*~*~*~

    "You look down," Gizlae said sitting next to Kihakso
    "Don't I always?"
    "Yes but you look more down than normal."
    Kihakso sighed, "It's all my fault."
    "What is?" Kihakso waved outwards but Gizlae understood what they meant.
    "You couldn't have stopped Awrosk, I don't think any of us could."
    "But if I had lied....Vadixas wouldn't have..."
    The two were silent for a moment
    "But I had asked."
    "That doesn't matter I should have-"
    Gizlae shook her head, "I should have let one of the others ask. But...I wanted to know so I asked."
    "Gizlae that doesn't-"
    "I know...."
    "Know what?"
    "I know you can't lie to me. I know you always tell me the truth."
    "Of course you do. I promised to."
    Gizlae shook her head again, "I know you can't, no matter how little the lie, that you can't tell me one."
    Kihakso was silent.

"I knew that, and yet I still asked. So their death isn't on you, it's on me."

"No, if I had lied..."

Gizlae sighed before putting her head on their shoulder, "Then we'll both hold the blame, equal parts. And work to make things right." Kihakso said nothing and Gizlae moved to look them in the eyes, "We'll make things right won't we?"

Kihakso started to look around and tap their finger on her hand for every arrow they counted. Gizlae waited, not wanting to disturb them. After they counted more than they were supposed to, the silence stretched on as the two sat up straight. She felt them count it again, and then a third time, and yet the number never changed. They looked over at her with wide eyes.

"It looks like we'll have a chance to."

Day 17 Month 16 Year 1516
   I don't know what I plan to do anymore.
   I still hate them, I still wish they were gone...
   They are still a reminder that I failed my brother.
   But they are also like me, suffering in their own way from their loss.
   And that deal...
   I have succeeded, but...would that be what Gizlae wanted?

~*~*~*~

   Two people sat on a dock staring at the sunset.
   They had woken up in an empty room with burn marks around the room. They were laying on the ground near each other, holding hands. The two sat up, looked at each other and recognized each other even if they looked different in the memory they shared.
   The two quickly left the location not trusting the building, they hoped to find the building in their memory but didn't know where to start. They just decided to just travel till they found it, hoping to find some connection to their lost past.
   One was a girl with hair that flowed from light blue to dark as it got longer and longer, it was midway down her back. She was playing with it as she swung her legs, her feet only slightly touching the cold water. She leaned against the boy with red hair that had yellow and orange highlights. In his other hand, he was flipping a dagger made of fire.
   The only memory they had was a secret conversation in a kitchen with a promise, whether the promise was kept didn't matter as they were together now. They didn't know anyone but they were together and that was enough.

Made in the USA
Columbia, SC
03 March 2023